The Roommate Remodel

A SWEET HOCKEY ROMCOM

GRACE WORTHINGTON

The Roommate Remodel by Grace Worthington

Copyright © 2024 by Grace Worthington

All rights reserved.

Published by Poets & Saints Publishing

ISBN: 979-8-9887709-2-3

Cover Design by Alt 19 Creative

This novel is a work of fiction. Characters are the product of the author's imagination or are used fictitiously.

Get a free romcom or bonus scenes at graceworthington.com

Romcom Novella

THE DATING HYPOTHESIS

What happens when you're forced to team up with the MOST infuriating man alive for a research experiment on dating?

You make sure you don't fall for him. Easy, right?
Not when it's the guy known as Dr. Romeo.

The Dating Hypothesis is a free prequel novella when you join Grace Worthington's newsletter at graceworthington.com.

ONE

Jaz

"Don't turn around now, but my brother's coming over," Mia says with a look that tells me she does not approve. I can already see the warning in her eyes: you will *absolutely* not dance with Brax MacPherson at my wedding.

"Who?" I ask, pretending I don't have a clue that Brax is headed this way even though I couldn't miss the charismatic hockey player if I tried. He's like an eclipse that I have to shield my eyes from—so untouchable, it's best not to take him in too long or else you'll scald your eyes.

Tonight, he's not dressed in his usual hockey uniform of bulky padding that hides his best features—the chiseled muscles of his arms and shoulders, narrowing to a V-shaped waistline. Instead, he's wearing a tuxedo that looks like it was stitched around every angle of his body. Well over six feet tall, incredibly fit with blazing hazel-green eyes and just the right amount of stubble peppering his jawline, it's no wonder all the women here are blatantly staring at him.

Did I mention I've got a soft spot for men in tuxes? The only problem is that his sister is the bride . . . and also my best friend. Conveniently off-limits. And devastatingly handsome.

My stomach rumbles, and I pluck a chicken satay from a

waiter walking by. I was too busy to eat anything before the wedding, and my stomach is angrily protesting now.

"My brother, the *commitment-phobe*." Mia leans closer to me. "Don't bother trying to impress him. Hockey will always be his first love."

The song changes to an upbeat Bruno Mars tune, and Mia's new husband, Jace, grabs her hand to pull her onto the dance floor.

"Stay strong," she calls over her shoulder. "And remember that your BFF knows best." She winks at me as Jace twirls her into his arms.

They make love look *so* easy.

Why is it so hard for me?

I glance over my shoulder to confirm that Mia's brother is still headed my way with his gaze laser-targeted on me, like I'm an enemy submarine he's here to destroy. I can't possibly hold up against those gleaming green eyes or that perfectly fitted tux.

So I do what any sane woman does who wants to avoid a conversation. I shove an entire peanut chicken kebab in my mouth.

With a full mouth, I spin around and realize what a terrible idea that was.

Brax is smirking at me, dangling another kebab in my face. "I noticed you liked the kebabs. Have you tried the steak?"

Well, *that* totally backfired. Not only is he being totally charming, he's not leaving until I take his offer of food. I wave my hands in a frantic *no thanks* signal, but he only stands there patiently and waits for me to finish.

I cover my mouth and swallow the appetizer, along with my embarrassment.

"*Like* isn't strong enough of a word for how I feel about these heavenly-tasting kebabs," I reply, taking his offer of food. "Don't judge. I didn't have time to eat before the wedding, with that marathon pre-wedding photography session."

Brax puts up his hands. "No judgment here. But I haven't

seen someone put down food like that in a long time. And I've seen some hockey players put down food."

This is not the kind of compliment that makes a girl feel better about having a hearty appetite. But at this point, I'm too hungry to care.

"I'm exceptional that way," I reply, biting into the steak kebab that's coated in a fragrant chimichurri sauce. I'm pretty sure I hear myself moan in pleasure when the flavors explode on my tongue. I point to the skewer. "That's like heaven on a stick."

Brax smirks and lifts an eyebrow, enjoying my reaction. "What's your verdict—steak or chicken?"

"When you're a hangry bridesmaid, the question is *not* steak or chicken. The question is how to avoid the rather pointed comments about catching the bouquet." I take another bite and notice Brax is looking at me, amused. "I'm sure you don't get those questions as a single man."

"About the bouquet? No," he says. "But I'll trade you the bouquet toss for the epic flinging of the garter. Especially since the bride is my sister."

I laugh. "Okay, you win. That is worse."

Brax glances over his shoulder and lowers his voice. "I have a plan to hide in a storage closet when the time comes. They can't force me to take part if I'm conveniently missing."

Is it possible that the hot and untouchable *"Big Mac"* MacPherson hates being singled out at weddings as much as I do?

"You're hiding during your sister's reception?"

"Only for that part," he says. "Care to join me?" His eyes have a mischievous glint in them, and I suddenly realize he's not kidding. He's inviting me into his devious escape plan.

With a stranger, I'd never consider it, but Brax is no stranger to me. He's Mia's brother. We've been working together tirelessly on this wedding for the last few days. How bad can it be?

I stop eating and tilt my head. "For how long? And will there be food in said closet?"

His lips curve into another amused grin. "*Both* chicken and steak."

The thought of hiding in a closet with Brax sounds like an answer to my wedding nightmare and exactly what Mia warned me *not* to do. My gaze flicks to Mia and Jace on the dance floor. As her groom sweeps her across the floor, Mia gives me a stern look and shakes her head.

I spin away and pretend I didn't see her. "I thought the chicken would deter you since you find my appetite so unattractive."

"You thought wrong," Brax says with that confidence that I'm sure makes most women weak. "About me finding it unattractive . . . or a deterrent."

I'll give him this. *He's smooth.* A lesson I learned the first time I met him at a Christmas festival last year when he flirted shamelessly with me.

When Mia got engaged, she told me Brax had agreed to be a groomsman at her wedding and had given him an invitation with a plus-one guest.

Since he's jaw-dropping gorgeous, I braced myself for his arrival with a bombshell model on his arm. So when he showed up alone, no plus-one in sight, the small flame I'd kept alive burned even brighter, despite his sister's warnings about falling for him.

During the last few days of wedding preparations, Brax has gone from flirtatious to full-on charming with his impeccable timing. No matter if I was decorating for the reception or arranging party favors, Brax would always appear as if by magic, offering his help.

"Hold still. You have sauce on your lips." He reaches for my mouth but stops before he touches me. "May I?"

I nod briskly, even though I can hear Mia's voice inwardly scolding me. *Bad idea, Jaz. Really bad idea.*

"Right"—he swipes his thumb over the corner of my lips gently—"here."

A shiver runs all the way down my body, even though he's saving me from the humiliation of having sauce on my face.

He licks his thumb and smirks. "Good sauce."

Right now, I just want to eat more kebabs so he can do that again. *And again and again.*

Has it been that long since a man has paid attention to me?

"Still hungry?" he asks, glancing at the appetizer table. "It looks like they just brought out more guacamole."

"I could eat that with a shovel," I say enthusiastically. Surely, this will frighten the poor man off.

Instead of looking at me like I'm insane, Brax's lips curve into the biggest smile. "My kind of woman."

As he walks away, my heart stutters in my chest. *My kind of woman? How could he say that?* Sports stars don't date regular girls like me. They go out with *Sports Illustrated* models. Or Taylor Swift.

The last thing I need is a crush on a guy sworn to lifelong bachelorhood. Not that I knew his intentions when I met him last year and was promptly bowled over by his disarming gaze and irresistible charm. It's Mia's fault, really. She roped me into assisting her with the Maplewood Mistletoe Festival, her Vermont hometown's claim to fame. Needing an escape from South Carolina, her invitation seemed like a Hallmark movie dream come true. A trip to a darling and ridiculously romantic Christmas festival? *Sign me up.*

After arriving in Maplewood exhausted from my early morning flight, I'd stopped by the most adorable coffee shop and ordered a large caramel latte with an extra shot of espresso.

When the barista set the drink on the pickup counter, I began chugging like my life depended on it. I didn't care if I scalded my tongue. I needed a jolt of caffeine to perk me up before I tackled a million mistletoe decorations.

Next thing I knew, a disgruntled businessman was in my face, angrily glancing from me to the cup in my hand. "You took my coffee," he stewed. "Can't you read?"

Everyone turned to stare at me. I suddenly wished an escape hatch would open in the floor and swallow me in one gulp.

I glanced at the cup and realized that instead of saying "Jaz," it said "Cal." *Not even close.* "I'm truly sorry," I apologized, my face heating. "I'll buy you a new one. And I can explain . . ."

He frowned. "I don't have time for a new one—or your flimsy excuses."

This guy was obviously having a bad day, and I had inadvertently gotten caught in the line of his snarky fire. Suddenly, this Hallmark town didn't seem so blissfully perfect, especially since I'd run into the town grinch.

"Is there something I could do?" I asked, even though I wanted to curl into a ball and put my face directly into this steaming cup of caffeinated goodness. I didn't have the energy to deal with grumpy Cal today.

He moved closer to me and snapped, "There's nothing you could do, dumb woman."

A flicker behind me caught my eye as a tall man stepped forward, dressed in a sharp wool coat, his eyes as hard as stone.

"What did you call her?" he asked in a commanding voice that made the businessman flinch. His brow pulled into an angry frown, his eyes narrowed, and a muscle in his jaw twitched.

"You know her?" Cal asked.

"Yes," the tall man snapped, wedging himself between me and the town grinch. "She's my girlfriend. And you won't speak to her that way *again.*"

I coughed, and coffee nearly spurted from my nose.

Cal's face turned the color of old paste. "I didn't know that."

The tall man gently placed a hand protectively on my shoulder, and the shock of his touch reverberated down my body. "You will apologize to her *now,*" he snarled in a menacing voice. "Or else you'll get to experience firsthand what I do to my opponents when I smash my fist into their faces."

Cal's wide eyes flicked to his curled fist. "Fine," he huffed before looking at me like I was a soggy piece of trash he was being forced to pick up at gunpoint. "I'm sorry," he grumbled before spitting out a forced, "Enjoy your drink," and rushing out of the shop.

The tall man dropped his hand from my shoulder, and put it out for me to shake instead. "Brax MacPherson. A pleasure to meet you."

His menacing tone had changed into something totally different. Something warm and kind, and his face reflected the same softness. It was such a startling transformation from the guy who'd just offered to smash in a stranger's face for me.

He cleared his throat. "Sorry for pretending you were my girl-friend without asking first."

I shook his hand, and the same jolt I'd felt before was now spreading through my arm, quickening my pulse. Instead of saying something, I kept shaking his hand until it became awkward. My brain felt sludgy, and the caffeine still hadn't hit my bloodstream yet. My face burned hot before I finally blurted, "No apology necessary."

"And you are?" he asked, finally dropping my hand.

The green pools of his eyes were striking in the winter light.

"Jazlyn Summers. My friends call me Jaz."

"Good to meet you, Jaz." He smiled, and my heart did a tiny, swooning flip.

Then he grabbed his coffee and turned to go.

"Wait . . . did you say your last name is MacPherson?" I asked as he was halfway out the door. "By any chance, are you related to Mia?"

He gave me a mischievous smirk before leaving. "See you at the mistletoe festival."

Turns out, I did see him again. Mia forced her twin brothers to help with the Christmas festival, which gave me every opportunity to watch the unreasonably handsome hockey player hang up mistletoe and wish I was under it with him. How bad could it be to indulge in a harmless little Christmas crush?

It couldn't last. I don't live in Vermont. He's a hockey player who traveled too much. Mia warned me he'd already sworn off committed relationships. When I said goodbye after Christmas, I never thought I'd see him again. He'd get traded to another team, most likely.

Until I showed up for the wedding preparations, and he magically appeared in a smoky charcoal suit, looking like he'd stepped off the cover of a billionaire romance novel.

Same green glint in his eyes. Same *knock 'em dead* smile. My heart was doomed.

Which is why I should escape out the back door of the wedding reception rather than hide in a storage closet.

I'm yanked back to reality by Brax, appearing with a stack of overflowing plates and a disarming grin. "Ready for our getaway?"

Energy bolts down my spine. He's loaded up with every appetizer from the buffet. "You brought enough for a zombie apocalypse."

"I'm exceptional that way," he says with a knowing smirk that makes my heart tumble. "And I don't cross a hangry bridesmaid."

He somehow balances three plates, like a circus act. "I saw a closet back here earlier," he says, leading me into a dark and empty hallway.

"You planned this from the beginning?" I ask, shocked.

Brax seems so cool and calm, like a silly wedding tradition would never affect him.

He looks over his shoulder at me. "Not a fan of garters, unless it's *my* bride's."

A ripple goes through my middle at the thought of Brax's hands slowly and deliberately peeling off a garter. Whoever ends up as his bride is going to be one lucky girl.

He nudges open a storage closet door with his shoulder, then backs up against it, still balancing three plates.

"After you," he says, flipping on a light to reveal a closet filled with shelves of toilet paper, parking cones, extra linens and, oddly enough, a leather-worn saddle draped across a sawhorse.

"Are you sure about this?" I look over my shoulder once more.

Hiding in a closet with Brax is definitely a bad idea. He's unfairly gorgeous. And I make notoriously bad choices when I'm hungry. But then again, when has that ever stopped me before?

He points toward the reception, where I can hear the "Chicken Dance" playing, my least favorite song of all time. "If you want to dance, be my guest. Or you can enjoy some chips and guacamole on this comfortable saddle."

His lips quirk into a crooked smile as he hitches his leg over the saddle and straddles the sawhorse. He looks like a ridiculously adorable cowboy, which is hardly fair.

I shake my head and steal his guac, settling on the floor instead. "It would be a shame to let this go to waste." I stretch my legs in front of me, arranging the silky pink bridesmaid gown over my crossed ankles and setting my beaded clutch to the side.

"Where do you think this came from?" Brax asks, plucking a random tiara off the top shelf. It's a weird thing to find in a storage closet. But then again, there's also a random saddle in here.

I shrug. "Maplewood High's prom? Mia mentioned the town uses this renovated barn theater for many events."

"The prom queen left her crown behind?" He looks at me, puzzled.

"Who knows what happened? It's a mystery. Like how we went missing from the reception."

"Well, it's yours now. *Finders, keepers.*" He holds it out to me, the fake diamonds glittering in the light. "It would look good on you."

"I don't want it," I say, pushing it back to him.

"Why not?" he asks, more seriously. "You look like a princess tonight."

There's a thousand reasons why I shouldn't. But the first one is that I can't play this game with Brax.

He kneels in front of me, so I can't look away from him. "In case you haven't noticed, every man out there is looking at you." Then he sets the crown on top of my head, sending goose bumps across my arms. He looks me over, satisfied. "You wear it better than any prom queen could."

My stomach does this weird flip as I glance away from his intense gaze, my cheeks heating.

Is he flirting with me? Because I think he's flirting with me, and I should walk out right now.

Just then, the emcee announces that the bouquet toss will happen in a few minutes. If I leave now, I'll have a bullseye on my forehead that says, *Hit me with your best shot.*

As if he reads my mind, Brax urges, "You don't want to go out there now."

Then he sits beside me on the floor and steals a chip, like we've settled into a comfortable relationship where we share food.

We spend the next half hour polishing off the appetizers as Brax asks me questions like we're in a speed dating round. I have all his attention now, and despite Mia's warning, he's not doing anything that sets off alarm bells.

"Favorite dessert?" he asks.

"Red velvet cupcakes with cream cheese icing."

"Steak or seafood?"

"Both."

"I should've guessed," he says, eyeing my mostly empty plate.

"Ice cream flavor?"

"Ben and Jerry's."

"I said *flavor.*"

"That is a flavor. *All of them.*"

He smiles at my answer. "Favorite color?"

"Pink." I shoot him a look. "Don't judge."

"Who said I'm judging?" His eyes flick over my gown. "You look stunning in that dress tonight." The compliment spreads like white-hot fire through my veins.

"Favorite Taylor Swift song?"

"'Lover,'" I say. "Closely followed by 'This Is Me Trying.'"

"Good choices," he says.

"You're a Swiftie?" I ask, surprised.

"That depends. With the *right* company, yes." He waits a beat, then asks, "Do you skate?"

"Depends what you mean by skating. I'd need someone to prop me up so I don't fall on my butt. But I've always dreamed of going on a skating date where they play romantic music and the snow is falling."

"I think you've watched too many Hallmark movies," he accuses with a grin.

"Shut up and let me have my sappy movies." I shove him with my shoulder. He barely budges.

"Single or dating someone?" he asks after a pause, then looks over at me.

"Single," I answer, avoiding his gaze. "But I could be persuaded to date. With the *right* company."

He smirks, then asks, "Do you dance?"

"That depends on the song. Taylor Swift is always a yes," I admit, finally gathering the hem of my gown, so I don't step on my dress when I stand. The music has started up again, which means the bouquet and garter tosses are done. "I should probably go," I murmur, feeling that small inward pull that tells me to stay.

Brax looks at me, crestfallen. "Already?"

"People will notice." More like *Mia will notice.*

"Well, I've enjoyed hiding in the closet with you, Jazlyn." He tilts his head, and I swear he looks a little disappointed that I'm leaving.

It's for the best. He doesn't want a relationship. And I'm a girl who's not looking for a short-term romance.

As if on cue, the DJ plays "Lover," and Brax's mouth curves into a grin. "One dance before you go?"

My eyes widen. "I can't."

"I seem to remember you saying Taylor Swift was *always* a yes."

I look around. "There's no room in this closet."

"Then dance with me in the hall." He levels those jade eyes at me, and my defenses fall like a house of cards.

He opens the door, and we step out into the hall, where the music is louder and the lights are almost nonexistent. He takes my clutch and puts it to the side.

Then he takes my hand and pulls me into his arms. I'm so nervous, I can't seem to find a rhythm, and he steps on my toes and apologizes.

"I'm a little rusty at this dancing thing," he admits with a laugh, breaking the tension.

"You're not the only one," I say.

It's not until he slides his hands across the small of my back that I relax, and we fall into a rhythm together, gently swaying. He pulls me close enough that I can smell his cologne, mixed with a subtle but spicy scent. It's not too overpowering, perfect and enticing, just like him. Then he rests his cheek against my hair, and I swear I hear him humming along.

I want to remember everything about this night now. The way he looked at me in the closet when he put the tiara on my head. The questions that made me feel like he was genuinely interested in me. The way he's holding me now, his hands sliding down my spine.

When the song stops, he doesn't pull away. He just looks at me, like he doesn't want to break this moment any more than I do.

My voice comes out as a ragged whisper. "I should really go." But instead of letting go, I don't move. It's like my brain and body are on two different time zones.

"Whatever you want," he says, as his eyes drop to my lips.

And I know exactly what I want. I want to kiss him. I want to remember this night with Brax. I want to burn it into my memory. *Even if it's a bad idea.*

I put my hands on his face, reach up, and put my mouth on his, gently, sweetly, letting all the warmth spread through my body.

To my surprise, he doesn't pull away. Instead, he kisses me longer, like a man who is drowning and I'm his air. Slowly, he cups the back of my neck and tilts my head to get a better angle, before reluctantly letting me go. With a surprised laugh, he says, "I'm sorry. I don't usually kiss women after the first dance."

"Well, I don't usually kiss groomsmen at weddings," I reply with a grin.

"Can I see you again?" he asks.

He wants to go out with me? The guy who's married to hockey? I nod, pushing back my worry about how I'll explain this to Mia.

"Except next time, I want to take you out for a proper date."

I don't even have to think about the answer. "Only if there's food involved."

"Oh, there will be food," he promises with a grin. "I prefer ridiculously expensive restaurants where I can spoil you."

"Jaz!" I hear Mia's voice calling me, and I'm torn between leaving Brax and finding the bride.

"I need to go." I try to pull away, but Brax sweeps me back into his arms one last time. When he does, the tiara slips, and I take it off and hand it to Brax to return to the closet.

"Give me your phone first," he asks.

"Why?" I say, fumbling for it in my clutch. Any time now, Mia is going to come barreling around the corner.

"I will contact you. This doesn't end tonight, Princess."

He takes my phone and enters his information without letting me see.

As Mia yells my name again, he hands me my phone. Then I run off, giving him a tiny wave over my shoulder, feeling like I'm leaving my heart behind with him.

———

Later that night, I get a text from "Best Kisser Ever."

I smile, finally understanding why Brax wanted to enter his own contact information.

The text is only two sentences long. But those two sentences make me happier than I've felt in a long time.

Brax: Today was the best day ever. Let's do it again soon.

For an entire week, I look for another message, but it doesn't come. As the days stretch into weeks, and the weeks into months, one thing becomes clear:

That's the last time I'll ever take a chance on Brax MacPherson.

TWO

Prax

NINE MONTHS LATER

I don't know what I expected when I stepped into my new hometown of Sully's Beach, but it wasn't this: a Carolina Crushers bumper sticker on the back of a dented, dusty truck with our team name crossed out. Over it, in black Sharpie, is written: Carolina LOSERS.

Ouch. So that's how people feel about my new team. It might not be directed at me, but it feels like a fist to the jaw just the same.

Now that my brother, Vale and I, have been moved to the Crushers, we get to share in the joys of getting picked on for having the worst record in the league. *Losers, indeed.*

I slam the door of my jeep, wincing as a twinge of pain shoots through my right shoulder. Felipe's hit during last season's final game was brutal, but I can't show any signs of weakness now that I'm starting training camp with a new team.

My last team might have had a better record, but the Crushers are the next stop on my way to the NHL. There's no way I'm staying with this team for more than a year. That would be career suicide. But for someone who wants to be a rising star in the AHL? It might not be the worst thing ever.

I rub my shoulder as I head inside the gourmet coffee shop

15

and bakery that looks like an answer to my rumbling stomach. Magnolia Brew Coffee Shop boasts worn pine flooring and exposed brick walls that give it a cozy feeling. The poured-concrete barista bar is located in the back, right next to a gleaming glass display case filled with decadent treats like carrot cake with cream cheese frosting and a luscious berry pie with a crumb topping. Hanging over the bar is a giant chalkboard sign, showing off a fancy handwritten menu.

Driving all night from Vermont to South Carolina is not for the faint of heart, nor those who run out of a steady stream of caffeine. My stomach growls as I look over the giant cinnamon rolls, bigger than my hand. Luckily, Vale and I have been tag-teaming it at the wheel, and the long drive has given us hours to talk about how we'll become a powerhouse duo this season. On our own, we're good, but together, we're unstoppable. Call it our twin power, but we're going to make this team better so we won't be called losers anymore.

Vale scrolls his phone while I stare at the fancy coffee drinks named after the area, like the Charleston Chai and the Low Country Latte.

"Heard from Lucian yet about where we're sleeping tonight?" Vale asks, looking up.

The team captain promised to help find us a temporary place to live before we started training. The Ice House where we practice is located just outside of Charleston, but rentals are nearly impossible to find in the city right now, so Lucian has been scouting the small town of Sully's Beach nearby since it's off-season for the tourists. "Said he found the perfect place yesterday. The only hitch is that we're not living alone. We're renting rooms at somebody's house."

Vale turns to me. "Living with strangers?"

He doesn't like this idea any more than I do. "Sisters who need some renters. They're fixing up the home."

He frowns. "For how long?"

"As long as it takes for an apartment to open up."

The girl behind the coffee bar gives me a soft smile, like she's more than happy to take my order *and* my phone number. This routinely happens, no matter what city we're in, and I've learned to avert my eyes and not give them even the tiniest hope. Another barista, named Scarlett, approaches and elbows the girl in disapproval. She frowns at her coworker while muttering, "Stop gawking and make coffee." Then she turns to me and offers an apologetic smile. "What will you two have today?"

After we place our order for two Americanos, a cinnamon roll and a slice of carrot cake, we wait on the other end of the bar while the barista grinds our beans. The scent is deep and nutty and reminds me of that coffee shop in Maplewood. I suddenly get a pang of homesickness.

"I wonder if either sister is single?" Vale raises an eyebrow, a playful smirk crossing his lips.

"Don't get your hopes up." I shake my head. "They're probably old enough to be our grandmothers." Vale already knows I've sworn off dating this season and that my reasons are justified. "The rental market is slim pickings around here. And I don't want to sleep in a hotel. We already do that too much on the road."

"Fair enough," Vale concedes. "As long as they're not overly strict."

"He said one sister was a hockey fan. That's in our favor."

Vale glances around at the locals, nursing their cups of coffee, shooting curious glances our way. Looks like this place is just as gossipy as Maplewood. That means it won't take long for people to find out we're here. If I have my way, there's only one person I'd like to keep in the dark. Which is why I'm planning on spending as much time as possible at the ice rink in Charleston.

"Do you think they'll care if we invite friends over?"

I glance at my brother. It doesn't take a genius to figure out that's code for *girls*. "Slow down, Casanova. We need to get settled first. Lucian said there will be house rules."

"Rules?" Vale asks, frowning. "Like what?"

I shrug. "Guess we'll find out." It's the difference between my twin and me. I'm a rule-maker. And he's the rule-breaker. We balance each other out.

Scarlett hands us our coffee cups and food and asks, "Where are you staying?"

"How'd you know we were new in town?" I ask, suddenly feeling the weight of everyone staring at us.

"Lucky guess," she says with a shrug. "Everyone knows everyone in Sully's Beach."

I nod and glance at my brother. "A place called *Rose & Thorn*. Ever heard of it?"

"Ah, Granny's old place. Very nice family." She glances at Vale's cake, which is nearly half gone. "Enjoy the sweets."

Vale smiles sheepishly. "Don't mind if I do."

I tip my cup to my lips too quickly and nearly burn my tongue on the first sip. Hockey has taught me to move fast before I think about the consequences. Problem is, that doesn't always work in life. *Or with people.*

"I knew we should have found our own place." Vale shakes his head skeptically as he takes his drink. "Letting Lucian set us up was a bad idea. He probably arranged for the worst place just to test us."

I wipe my mouth and hope the sting on my tongue doesn't last. "From what I've heard, Lucian's a good guy. What do we have to prove? It's no secret that the Crushers have one of the worst team records in the league. The question is *why*."

I roll my shoulder to stretch out the ache that's settled there.

Vale narrows his eyes. "Your shoulder hurting again?"

I shrug. "What doesn't hurt these days?"

"I thought you'd be over that injury by now." Vale frowns in concern.

"Me too," I chuckle, trying not to act worried. "I'll have the trainer tape me up for games. It'll be okay."

Vale tilts his head. "And if it isn't?"

I drag my hand through my hair. "Then I play through the pain." I walk out of the coffee shop ahead of him.

Vale tags at my heels. "Brax, you can't play in pain all season."

"Never stopped me before," I say, crawling into the driver's seat. "Hockey is a lot like dating. You take a chance even when you don't know how things will turn out."

A face flashes through my mind from last New Year's. Black waves falling across her shoulders, impossibly dark eyes. Her laugh was like a glass of champagne, bubbly and shimmering with light. *Man, I miss it.*

I took a chance on her back then, and look where it got me. Longing for something I can't have. Kind of like this shoulder pain. Some aches just don't go away.

Vale stares at me as I back out the jeep. "You don't think Coach will notice? Or the team?"

"I'm not planning on telling anyone. Which means you can't let it slip either. I'm not letting anyone baby me because I'm injured."

Vale stares at me for a second before muttering under his breath. "Next time I see Felipe on the ice, he is going to pay."

"You will *not*." I glare at him.

"The dude hates you," Vale reminds me, as if I don't already know. "He injured you in a game, and now you're still dealing with the fallout."

Vale only knows half of it. He's done way worse than body-checking me in a game. "We'll deal with Felipe the way we do everyone: by beating him on the ice. I won't see him until mid-season, anyway."

"You're seriously not going to let me tell the team?" Vale looks at me like I'm crazy.

"I don't need you or anyone else getting thrown out of a game. Leave Felipe to me." But even as I say it, I know Vale would have my back, no matter what. "We need to focus on other things. Like how to win over a new team who might not be thrilled we're here."

We drive through town and notice a string of quaint shops and restaurants boasting home-cooked food or *best breakfast in town*. Snaking through a charming neighborhood on the outskirts of town, I pull up to the address Lucian sent for the house. A wooden sign above the porch swing shows that we're at the right place: *Rose & Thorn*.

Vale nods toward the sign. "Who do you think the rose is and who is the thorn?"

"We're the thorn," I say, studying our new place. "Renters always are."

The house is a classic white farmhouse that's been built off the ground to avoid flooding during hurricanes. The wraparound porch is inviting, but from the looks of it, it's pretty old. The porch railing has some broken slats, and the paint is peeling in a few places, but it's got boatloads of character that you only find in old homes.

Vale lifts an eyebrow. "I hope these women know what they're in for."

"If they don't, they will soon," I mutter as I look over the white, two-story house with the wraparound porch and a *For Rent* sign on the door. "Lucian said two other guys from the team will move in later. He wants to make sure all four of us are settled in."

"Four?" Vale asks, arching an eyebrow.

"Two other newbies on the team. Call it forced bonding." I scan the windows for signs of life. The house looks well taken care of, but it's obviously not new. The wooden siding has been painted over several times, and the overgrown landscaping needs a good trim.

"Did you hear Scarlett call it 'Granny's old place'? I'm betting it's two spinsters," Vale remarks, scanning the place. "Maybe they'll be good cooks."

I roll my eyes. "It's not a bed-and-breakfast."

"There's got to be some sort of perk to living with the elderly. I don't know how I'll stand it if they're cooking and I'm not eating it." It's no secret that my brother likes food. With the energy he exerts on the ice, he can put down an entire turkey by himself. It's one of the things the MacPherson boys are known for: *nonstop food consumption.*

A shiny black sedan pulls up behind us, and a man with dirty-blond hair and a chiseled jaw steps out. If I didn't know Lucian Lowe already, I'd guess he was a fashion model. He's got the perfect face for it and a ripped body to match. "I take it you're the MacPherson twins?"

"How'd you guess?" Vale offers an identical smirk to mine.

"Are you Big Mac?" Lucian asks Vale, looking between us to see who claims the nickname. We're the same height and build, which means neither of us is bigger. But hockey names stick like gum on the bottom of a school desk. Once you get one, it's there forever.

"Nope, I'm Vale." They shake hands before my brother turns to me. "This is Big Mac."

"I prefer Brax MacPherson," I finish, shaking his hand.

He glances at Vale's long hair before looking back at me. "Never wear your hair the same or we won't keep you straight on the ice."

Vale drags his hands thorough his long brown hair, which has a tendency to fall over one eye. I keep mine short. "You'll notice our differences on and off the ice."

"Ready to see your new place?" Lucian asks, rubbing his hands together. "The ladies who own this place seem excited to meet you."

"Any chance they're over eighty?" Vale asks.

I jab my brother in the ribs.

Lucian frowns. "No, why?"

"No reason," he covers, giving me a quick side-eye.

We grab our bags and head up the steps to the oak front door. Even though the house shows signs of age, the craftsmanship is impeccable, with leaded glass windows and incredible wood-working details.

I'm so focused on the door, I hardly notice when it swings open and a woman pokes her head out.

"You're early!" she says with a nervous smile. Her dark straight hair is swept up into a high ponytail, and she's wearing a soft yellow silk headband. Her blue rubber cleaning gloves are a telltale sign she wasn't expecting us yet.

Lucian checks his watch. "The guys arrived in town an hour early." Lucian turns to me. "I hope you're just as quick on the ice."

"Guess we'll see," I say.

The young woman waves us inside, then realizes she's still wearing her gloves and hides them behind her back. "I'm Sloan." She peels off one glove to shake our hands and gives us a warm smile.

"I'm Brax, and this is Vale." She stares at me, like she's trying to place me.

"You ever watch hockey?" I ask. If she's an AHL hockey fan, then she's probably seen my name on the roster of my previous team, the Springfield Thunderbirds.

She points to a water bottle that's covered in the logo of my new team. "You can't live in South Carolina without being a Crushers fan." At least she didn't cross out the team name and replace it with LOSERS. This gives me a fleeting hope that there are at least dozens more fans like her. "My sister will be down in a minute." She glances at the curved staircase with the gorgeous newel post. "Make yourselves at home."

She leads us to the living room, where an antique damask couch sits in the center with two wingback chairs flanking the couch. A classic brick fireplace with a dark walnut mantel dominates the room like a relic from a bygone era, while a side buffet shows off an antique tea cup collection displayed on a lace doily. The place looks like it stepped out of a *Southern Living Magazine* from thirty years ago, even though Sloan appears around the same age as me. It's warm and inviting, even if it's old-fashioned.

As Sloan hurries off, Lucian checks his phone. "Will you

excuse me for a second? I need to return a call to Alexandra." Lucian heads to the front porch, leaving Vale and me alone.

Vale leans toward me. "Do you think that's the same Alex who's queen bee of the team?"

"Does it matter?" I ask, lifting a shoulder. Alexandra is the team owner, but I never let the boss intimidate me. It's too easy to play to impress them rather than play the way the team needs. I've learned there's a difference.

Vale circles the living room, checking out the beautiful crown molding. "I heard she runs the team like a dictator."

I shoot Vale a look to keep his voice down. "Dictator or not, she's our new boss."

"Sloan seems nice." Vale picks up a teacup from the buffet and studies it. We never had fine china growing up with a single mom, and Vale treats it like a curiosity from an antique shop.

I pluck the cup from his hand and gingerly set it back in the saucer. "Don't get any ideas about our new housemates. That only complicates things."

"Complicates, *how*?" He turns to me with a smile that tells me he knows *exactly* how.

"Remember how things turned out with Camille?" I arch an eyebrow. Before I even broke things off, she was cheating on me with Felipe. It's part of the reason he hates me so much. "We're here to play hockey. Not *fraternize* with the locals."

Sloan returns with a pitcher of orange juice and a plate of muffins. "I hope you're not allergic to nuts." She sets down the freshly baked banana muffins on the buffet. When Vale sees them, his eyes nearly pop out of his head.

"I'm not allergic to *anything*." Vale beelines toward the muffin plate. "Do you mind?" He's already reaching for the muffin plate before she answers.

She smiles. "Please do. We pride ourselves on our Southern hospitality. Lucian didn't mention where you're from."

"Vermont," I reply, noticing that Vale takes not one, but *two* muffins. I elbow him in the side, but he ignores me as he consumes half the muffin in one bite.

"Did you play for Springfield?" she asks with wide eyes.

I turn toward her. "You know the team?"

"Only from the website," she admits.

"Do you go to the local games?" I ask.

"Used to," she says, then looks at the floor. "I'm hoping my sister can snag some tickets this season."

Something crashes to the floor upstairs, and Sloan gives us an apologetic look. "I'll be right back."

She hurries upstairs while Vale takes the last bite of his muffin and closes his eyes like he's in banana muffin heaven.

I glance around the room looking for family pictures, but don't see any. Sloan isn't old enough for these antiques, but I'm guessing they belonged to somebody's grandma.

Vale picks up the teacup again. "Am I supposed to use this for the orange juice? I don't even know how to hold something so dainty." He awkwardly tries to curl his pinky in the air like an English gentleman, but he's no Mr. Darcy. His thick fingers don't fit in the ring, and he nearly drops the cup trying to force one in.

"Would you put that down before you break it?" I shake my head. "I'll look in the kitchen for two glasses." I head across the hall to a sunny yellow kitchen lined with cupboards from another era. The decor hasn't been updated in years, but the room has that grandmotherly smell of fresh bread and cinnamon still hanging in the air.

As I search through cupboards, I spot a pink apron hanging inside the pantry door. Curious, I push open the door wider and take the apron off the hook. A giant pair of red lips adorn the front with the words *Kiss the Cook*. Apparently, Granny likes *more than* just cooking.

Thinking this would be hilarious to show to Vale, I loop the apron around my neck and secure the ties behind my back. I look ridiculous, but it'll be worth it to see Vale's face before Sloan gets back.

Just as I wheel around, a woman walks into the kitchen, her eyes landing on my apron first.

I know that face.

"What are you . . .?" Her voice halts when her eyes reach my face. The horror in her gaze hits me like a thud in my chest, the weight of embarrassment nearly knocking me backward.

I know those eyes . . . *and that mouth.* The same lips that gave me a *melt-your-mouth-off* kiss in the back hall of Mia's wedding reception. The flush of heat on my neck is nearly instantaneous.

I forget the Pepto-pink apron I'm wearing and manage a strangled sound resembling a choking animal. "Jazlyn?"

For what's probably only a few seconds, she stares at me, like she's just seen the Ghost of Christmas Future announcing her imminent death. Except that ghost is *me*, dressed in an unfortunate *Kiss the Cook* apron with giant lips inconveniently placed at my belt line.

And she's not the one who's about to die. *I am.* From embarrassment.

THREE

Prax

"How did you get in here?" she asks in horror.

"I used the front door." I point to the entrance like it's not obvious. "Sloan let us in."

"You mean you're . . ." She gasps as the realization sinks in. "No. No. Noooooo," she moans, rubbing her forehead, like I'm a migraine she can't shake.

"What did you think I was here for?" *Does she really not know?* Based on her stunned expression, she had no clue.

"They told me it would only be Carolina Crushers players," she insists.

"I *am* a Carolina Crushers player."

She frowns and paces the kitchen. "This can't be happening. Lucian didn't give me names. And I didn't know you moved teams."

"Well, I didn't know you bought a house. I thought you lived in an apartment."

"That was before your sister got married. This house was my grandmother's, and I wanted it to stay in the family. My sister's had a rough go of it the last few months, so she moved in with me." She stops pacing and stares at me like I'm a stray cat she doesn't know what to do with.

I drag a hand through my hair. "Well, this is a *very* inconvenient surprise."

Where am I going to live now? There's no way I can stay here with her.

She covers her face with her hands. "Anyone but *you*."

I cross my arms over my chest and smirk. "That's not what women usually say when they see me."

She doesn't laugh, but the comment yanks her face back to mine. She narrows her eyes. The tension crackles in the air. "Oh, really? What do women *normally* say to you?" She doesn't ask it as a question, more like an accusation.

I smirk just to irritate her. "How I'm better looking up close."

Her eyes flick over my apron as she lifts an eyebrow. "I think you've looked better."

She has the upper hand here, but she's about to lose this game to one-up me. "As in, last time you saw me? I thought this apron might jar your memory."

She steps back, her eyes flaring. *Memory most definitely jarred.* That single event is permanently burned into my mind, making my skin erupt with heat.

She pokes me in the shoulder. "Just because we have a history doesn't mean it's going to be repeated." Right now, her stare is as icy as the hockey rink. "Personally, you look better with a bloody nose after a hockey fight." She crosses her arms, daring me to take another step.

"So violent, Jazzy," I tease in a bored voice. "It's intriguing, actually."

I'm trying to crack that cold exterior, make her smile just a little, but her face remains resolute, her arms folded. I can't accept the cold shoulder she's giving me now. A punch to the face stings less.

"I'm not the violent type," she replies. "Unless people ghost me and then show up at my doorstep uninvited."

"Oh, I *was* invited," I remind her. "You had a *For Rent* sign on your door. That's a public invitation if I ever saw one."

A muscle in her jaw clenches. "It doesn't apply to *you*."

"I didn't see a disclaimer at the bottom. And Lucian told me you needed renters. We're here as teammates, so if I leave, they all do." I smirk and fold my arms across my apron. "Face it, you need me."

She stops and glares at me, and I know I've hit the nail on the head.

"You are a . . ." She stops herself, but her fists roll into balls.

"I'm a *what*?" I narrow my eyes, daring her to say more. "I'd really like to hear you finish that statement. Your best friend's hot brother? A fabulous kisser?"

"You wish," she mutters. "Mia warned me not to get involved with you."

"You weren't the only one who got that warning, *Princess*," I shoot back.

Her eyes widen for a second. Apparently, she didn't expect Mia to have warned me not to date *her*.

But did I listen? *Absolutely* not. I couldn't rip my eyes away from her that night. And truth is, I like to play with danger.

We've both got stubbornness in spades. Which is why Mia was vehemently opposed to us dating.

She's like a match. I'm like the rough end of a matchbox. We'll either light something on fire or burn everything down.

She shakes her head. "Brax, this will *never* work."

"We don't have to like each other. We just have to live together. I can stand anything for a few weeks."

"But I can't live with *you*. We're arguing right now, and you haven't been here five minutes."

"I've been here fifteen," I correct.

She rolls her eyes. "See? We can't even agree on how long we've been arguing."

Who knew that arguing with a beautiful woman would feel like an exhilarating challenge? Like the more she pushes me away, the more I want to pull her close?

"You know what I think, Jazlyn?" I move closer to her,

shrinking the gap between us. "That you like arguing with me. Underneath, I drive you just a little bit crazy. In a good way."

"More like you drive me insane." She pushes me backward. "Go away, Brax."

"I don't think you mean that."

She shoots me a look that makes me worried she'd like to kick me in the crotch. "Oh, I really think I do."

"Then prove it."

She props a hand on her hip and frowns. "If I had a poison dart gun, I'd be aiming it at you right now. Then I'd chop your body into a thousand pieces and scatter it in the ocean as fish food."

I give her an infuriating grin. "I'll tell that to our children someday."

She huffs and turns away. "You're a thorn in my you-know-what."

"You're cute when you're frustrated," I say. It doesn't hurt that she's wearing a shirt-dress paired with boots that skim the hemline, showing off a tiny strip of light brown skin, which I'm trying to avoid looking at.

She glares at me. "See? This is why you can't live here. You make comments like that. There's too much history between us, Brax." Her eyes level on my face. "We both know that."

She's not referring to the kiss, although our chemistry is definitely a complicated problem. It's the way I handled things afterward.

Right now, it looks like she'd be thrilled to use my body as a punching bag.

I take another step toward her. "Maybe we can start over. Forget what happened."

"Forget?" She steps back, raises her eyebrows, and I realize the mistake I've made.

She thinks I mean forget the kiss. Forget *us*. When the truth is exactly the opposite: *I could never forget her.*

"So is that what happened?" she says in a voice that's most

definitely annoyed with me. "You forgot about me after your sister's wedding?"

I rub my hand over my jaw. "No, ma'am," I mumble, but there's no way to gloss over this problem. I messed up how I handled things. *Big-time.*

How can I explain that I had my reasons, even if she won't understand them? And that seeing her again sparks my attraction for her.

Instead, I fumble. "Hockey life isn't exactly conducive to maintaining long-distance relationships."

She gives me a hard stare—the kind full of pointy daggers she'd like to throw at my head. We both know this is a terrible excuse. Hockey might consume my life, but I wasn't too busy to call her. I just can't explain my reasons now. Especially when she's mad.

"Hockey *life*?" She nods in that deliberate way that women do when they're really ticked off. "Guess I'll use that as *my* excuse from now on."

Now I'm the one who's confused. "Are you coming to the games?"

"Absolutely." She gives me a smug half-grin, and there's a gleam in her eye that unsettles me. "I'm even planning on wearing a team jersey."

"Really?" I say skeptically, confused by this new game we're playing. "Whose?"

Lucian walks in from outside and catches me in the kitchen. "I see you've met Jaz."

I don't take my eyes off her. "Yes, we've met."

She turns to the team captain and says sweetly, "Lucian, thanks again for offering your jersey to wear to the first game."

"Any time." He smiles at her, totally unaware of our history.

She doesn't glance at me. Doesn't even blink a pretty little eyelash.

Just flashes him a smile as syrupy as sweet tea. "Anytime, huh? Might have to take you up on that."

The frustration rises to boiling inside my chest.
"Jaz," I growl like a warning.
She turns and shrugs casually. "What?"
She knows exactly what she's doing.
And it's totally working.
She might not ever give me another chance.
But no way will I let Jazlyn wear anyone's jersey but mine.

FOUR

Jaz

I swivel around and leave a stunned Brax in the kitchen, the heat of his stare burning me with every step.

As soon as I'm out of eyesight, I slip into the back hall and hide in the pantry closet, covering my mouth to muffle any sounds as I double over in laughter.

That was totally worth it. Brax's face looked like a steam engine about to careen off a bridge.

And he fully deserved it.

Nine months ago, Brax promised me he would call. Then the weeks stretched on without a single attempt. I texted him a few times.

Jaz: Thinking about that night we hid in the closet. I miss those kebabs. Think your sister ever found out?

Then I waited for the text bubble. Some sign of life. It never came.

Jaz: Just wondering if I have the right number? The "best kisser ever" put his phone number in my contacts. If you don't claim it now, the title reverts to someone else.

Surprisingly, no response. And then that ugly, gnawing feeling that I was being ignored *on purpose.* Steeling myself to write one last message, my thumb hovered over the send button for a few agonizing seconds.

Jaz: Brax, I'll take your silence as the only answer I need. Have a good life!

I didn't expect an answer after I sent it off into the universe, like a corked bottle thrown off the side of a ship. But a tiny part of me hoped he would say something. *Anything.*

Wherever Brax was at that moment, I'll never know. Was he in a hotel room in a strange city? Having drinks with another woman? A black smear of jealousy streaks through me.

Did he delete the message forever? Block my account? It's all so easy now: one quick *swipe,* and a person is gone *forever.*

At least rejection comes with a response, a definitive line drawn in the sand. But ignoring a person says something far more devastating.

You are forgettable.

What's more, I believed him when he promised to contact me. It's the oldest line in the book, and I stupidly fell for it.

So when he showed up dressed in *my* apron and pulled out his infuriating Mr. Flirty-Pants moves, all I could think about was how he had *ignored* me. Disregarded every word, all attempts at basic human contact. I simply didn't exist—or, more bluntly, I didn't matter enough to him.

Since Lucian so conveniently offered his jersey when we first met, it felt like karma. The perfect payback for a man who prides himself on getting what he wants.

Well, he won't have me.

Suddenly, the door swings open, and Sloan points at me with an exasperated look. "I knew you'd be hiding in here. Why were you rude to our guest?"

"Who said I was being rude?"

"Brax did," she says. "He mentioned you've met before under unusual circumstances."

"Unusual circumstances. *Ha!*" I exclaim, offended that our lip lock sounds like it belongs on a true crime podcast. "Did he tell you *why*?" I'm not about to let that man lure my sister over to the dark side. She needs to know the truth about Brax MacPherson, breaker of hearts and a big, fat liar pants.

Her eyes widen. "No, why?"

I grab her by the elbow and yank her inside the closet, slamming the door. We're squished together like clowns in a circus car.

"Why are we discussing this in *here*?" she asks, glancing at our cramped quarters.

We're surrounded by an array of sugared cereals, dried pasta, and canned tuna.

A pantry shelf pokes me on my hip, and I sidestep awkwardly. "I'm hiding from Brax, *obviously,*" I mutter, rolling my eyes.

She frowns. "What kind of history do you have with this guy?"

When I don't respond, she sets her hands on my shoulders and directs her gaze at me. "Jaz, tell me you didn't date him."

I bite my lip.

"You dated him?!" She shakes my shoulders on each syllable.

I pull away. "I didn't date him, okay?"

For a second, she looks relieved.

"But I did kiss him. At Mia's wedding. How do you like them pickles?"

Sloan's mouth falls. "You kissed your best friend's brother?"

I slowly nod, and she smacks me in the shoulder.

"Ow!" I flinch in pain and rub my shoulder. "What was that for?"

"I was being nice. I should've smacked you in the head."

"It wasn't my fault!" I protest.

"Oh, your lips just happened to land on Brax's mouth by accident?" She lifts an eyebrow.

"I thought you were supposed to be on my side!" I huff. "Just for the record, he's the one who deserves to be slapped."

"You insulted Brax MacPherson. One of the best players in the league *and* our new houseguest."

"Renter," I correct. "I would never invite him over as my guest."

She levels a look. "Be nice to him."

"I refuse."

She grabs my elbow, like she's going to drag me out of here. "You don't have a choice. We're stuck with him now. You already signed the papers and handed them over to Lucian before he arrived."

I yank my arm away. "But that's before I knew who he was!"

She points a finger in my face. "You can't back out now. We need the money or we can't pay the mortgage. You told me so yourself."

I push her finger away. "You don't know what he did to me."

"Is it really that terrible?"

I cross my arms. "Yes, it is."

"Let me guess," she says, tapping her chin. "He didn't text you back."

I frown. "Yeah, how did you know?"

My sister has the uncanny ability to guess things I'm hiding from her, which means it's next to impossible to keep secrets. What's worse, she's a straight-talker and never lets me off easy.

She shakes her head. "Jazlyn, that's just the way things are. When a guy doesn't respond, it's his way of letting you down easy."

"Easy?" I shoot back, not understanding how she could be so flippant about rejection.

Her voice softens. "I'm not saying it doesn't hurt, but it's not . . . *uncommon*."

I hate the way she says it, like my hurt is *not* uniquely terrible. Like I should just accept that ALL men do this, and it's the way things are.

Well, I *refuse* to accept it.

I close my eyes and massage my temples. "I wouldn't have kissed him if I thought it was a one-off."

"Maybe think before you pucker up next time."

I glower at her. "Your compassion amazes me."

I've tried to push that kiss out of mind so many times, but for the last nine months, it's tortured me nearly every day. Two people caught up in the moment, suddenly desperate for each other's touch, believing we could find the same love that Mia and Jace had.

Sloan crosses her arms. "Weddings usually make people feel absurdly high on love or incredibly lonely. Which was he?"

"No." I shake my head, her words pinching hard. It was more than a desperate, lonely grab at love. What we found was a deeper connection, something we both yearned for. "He *was* into me."

She doesn't respond, just tilts her head, waiting for the truth to sink in. Her words taint the memory of that kiss, like someone took paper hearts and splattered black paint on them. The desperation of that kiss wasn't because I was easy prey. It's because he wanted something more with me. Something *real*.

This wasn't a lonely guy groping me in the dark. It wasn't some bleary-eyed bar kiss.

It was a kiss to remember from a man who wanted to make sure I didn't feel alone that night. Every touch was tender, like an invitation. He made me feel beautiful and special.

But looking back at the memory through Sloan's eyes, I'm suddenly confused. The wedding and dancing and kissing all blur together, like a fuzzy photograph where the details are smudged out. Did he actually say how he felt? Or was I just the temporary bandage for his loneliness?

Yuck. The last thing I want is to be somebody's dirty bandage left on the floor.

Sloan looks at me, and her face softens. "Look, I've been to a few weddings where people hooked up because they wanted the same happiness as the bride and groom. They were just drunk on the *idea* of love. Not actually drunk, mind you. But the wedding makes anything seem possible. Even the fact that true love exists." She shrugs. "It happens."

"Not to me, it doesn't," I insist, my stomach sickening at the idea that I might have been drunk on love. I scrunch my eyes shut, trying to remember Brax's exact words. *Had he ever confessed that he wanted more than a fling?*

My sister looks at me sadly. "You thought he was into you because he's a flirt. Sports stars can be very persuasive. He probably hooks up with girls in every city."

I open my mouth to defend . . . *who,* exactly? A guy who probably never cared about me in the first place? Or myself, when I should've known better? I clamp my mouth shut and kick a dustpan out of the way.

No wonder Brax never responded. Sloan's right. It was his way of letting me down easy. *The stupid girl who still believed love was possible.*

Sloan shakes her head, just like when we were kids.

"Now what'll we do?" I ask.

"Suck it up, buttercup. Apologize to him before we lose these renters."

"I am *not* apologizing," I say firmly. Maybe he didn't fully deserve what just happened, but I refuse to humiliate myself by apologizing to him.

"Don't do it for him. Do it for *this house.* For the life you want to make here." She already knows that our money situation is dire. The endless house repairs and sizable mortgage have us strapped, especially since she can't work right now.

I know what this means to her. She's been cooped up in this house for four months since her car accident, unable to work and struggling with depression. Living with a bunch of live-wire hockey players would give her something to look forward to while she heals from her concussion. It's a win-win for everyone . . . *except* me.

Can I survive seeing Brax every day? The painfully honest

answer is: *I'm not sure.* And I'm still not satisfied with his reaction about why he ghosted me. It seemed so unlike him. But then again, maybe I don't know the *real* Brax MacPherson like I thought I did.

"Fine," I mutter, not happy with this arrangement at all. "But I will not grovel at his feet."

"Nobody said you had to." Then Sloan gives me a reassuring smile. "I can see why you kissed him. And he has a twin to match? Good heavens, that's too much!" She slips into Granny's southern drawl and fans herself with her hand.

I laugh and grab her arm. "Sloan, let my mistake be your lesson learned. Don't fall for a Mac brother."

I straighten my spine and head to the kitchen without her, ready to choke out an apology I don't want to give. I'm about to chug a cup of bitter humiliation and pretend it's not pee water.

When I get there, Brax is alone, looking out the kitchen window like he's lost in thought. For a moment, I'm swept away by this gentle giant in front of me. He's as dangerous as he is beautiful, like a tamed stallion who can only be admired at arm's length.

When I stop in the door, his head turns and the gentleness falls away, replaced by an intimidating coldness. He's probably already thinking up all the ways he can ruin me.

I twist Granny's opal ring on my finger as anxiety spirals inside me. "I came to . . ."

"Ask me to leave?" he finishes, rising to his feet. It's not harsh or demanding. More like he expected it. "Vale and I can find another place to live."

"That won't be necessary," I force out, the humiliation smothering my chest like a lead weight. I know Sloan is listening in the hall, and I hope Brax's brother can't hear or I'll be mortified. "I overreacted when I saw you earlier. I'm sorry." The word tastes like sawdust in my mouth. No matter what happened at that wedding, he should be the one apologizing for making promises he didn't keep.

"This is . . ." He narrows his gaze, like he's trying to figure out this sudden change of heart. "*Unexpected.*"

I don't dare reveal to him our financial struggles. He'll only pity me, and that's worse than a forced apology. Not only am I unlucky in love (and apparently very susceptible to handsome groomsmen), but also desperate to help my sister.

He steps toward me. "I'm the one who should be . . ."

"Don't," I say firmly, putting my hands up. I can't go there. "We'll only argue more."

The muscle in his jaw clenches again as something flashes in his eyes. Regret, maybe? Does he feel guilty for not calling . . . or guilty for kissing me?

I fold my arms across my chest and give him a look that makes it clear how things will be from now on.

Our kiss was a mistake. *He* was a mistake.

If I could, I'd erase the memory of that kiss with a bleach wipe for the brain. From the look on his face, he already has.

"I can show you your room," I suggest, trying to move on from the weight of his stare.

"Perfect. I'd like to shower after the long drive."

Another image I need to wipe from my mind. *Brax in nothing but a towel.*

Somehow Sloan ended up in the living room with Vale, happily chatting away about hockey stats and season predictions.

When she sees me, she waves me toward Brax's brother. "This is my sister, Jaz."

He squints like he's trying to place me. "I met you at Mia's wedding, right?"

"Yeah," I say, shaking his hand and giving him a nervous smile. More than anything, I hope he doesn't know about the kiss. I sneak a glance at Brax and notice he's staring at the floor, totally avoiding his brother. Apparently, I'm not the only one who's good at keeping secrets.

"Ready to settle in?" I ask and they both nod. I wave them toward the staircase in the main hall that leads to the second floor.

When we reach the top, I point out the four bedrooms set up in a square formation and the bathroom the players will share. "Since you're the first to arrive, you get first pick."

When Brax steps inside my favorite bedroom, the one that gets all the dappled sunshine from the giant oak tree, he pauses for a moment. The room is simply decorated, mostly because we couldn't afford more lavish decorations. I've learned from my friend Ella that great style can be uncomplicated, and I embraced that motto when I put the final touches on this room. A farm-house-style double bed takes up most of the space with a sturdy walnut dresser and small white end table with a reading light. Granny's old wooden chair, now painted a deep blue, sits in the corner. The pine floor is covered with a woven blue and cream rug. But the focal point of the room are the four enormous windows. While two of the windows make you feel like you're in the oak treetop with the birds, the other two overlook the back-yard, with the peach trees and Granny's rose garden.

"This is the one," Brax says as he sets his bag on the floor. Then he turns to me. "So you live downstairs?"

"My sister's room is next to mine in the back hall next to the kitchen. We share a bathroom down there, so you guys can have the one upstairs." I shift my weight from one foot to the other as his eyes flicker toward the floor. He probably wants me as far away as possible, so he doesn't have to see me. "Hope that won't be a problem?" I add, suddenly feeling anxious about this living situation.

"Of course not," Brax assures me. "We're both adults." Then he rubs the back of his neck. "Boundaries and all that."

"Right," I agree. "Boundaries."

If only I'd had more boundaries at that wedding.

A silence settles between us, and he sinks his hands in his pockets. The same hands that slipped across my waist when we slow danced, like they were made to fit there.

I force my thoughts away from that jarring thought and turn back to the stairs. "Well, I'll let you unpack."

"Hey, about what happened . . ." he begins.

I grip the railing, ready to close the door to this conversation. "It's water under the bridge, Brax. Let's just keep things professional from now on."

"Professional," he repeats quietly. "Got it."

As I disappear down the stairs, I try to ignore the sinking feeling in my chest. He didn't argue with my suggestion, which means he's totally okay pretending it never happened. Sloan was right.

But how can I *forget* the best kiss I've ever had? The sting of his rejection still lingers like the bruise on a soft peach. I can't fall for him again, not when he's already proven how easily he could disappear from my life.

"Boundaries," I remind myself. If we're going to make this work, I need all the boundaries I can get, even if that means building a mile-high fortress around my heart.

———

To my relief, I avoid Brax and Vale the rest of the day. After unpacking and getting a house key, they shower and leave to take care of some paperwork and don't return until after I'm in bed. Not that I'm sleeping. More like I'm staring at the ceiling, trying to forget that Brax is sleeping above me.

I know I'll get used to having Brax here, but for now, his presence stirs a soft prickly feeling inside me.

Tomorrow's going to be a full day. The other two hockey players are arriving, and then I need to head to the Crushers' office.

Oh, yeah. The other awkward thing I haven't told Brax yet. My new job with *his* team.

As the brand-new community relations manager, my job is to build support for the team through community outreach. Basically, *make people like the players*. Alexandra already informed me that the team is losing revenue from local advertisers pulling out.

And that community support is in the toilet. My job, then, is to show the players as real people with hearts, and not just tough guys punching each other on the ice.

But how can I even focus on my job when Brax is there? It's not like the office staff sees the athletes that much, but he should know before I run into him, like I did today.

As I stare at the ceiling, I list all the things that need to get done tomorrow. Alexandra's going to want to see my ideas right away. She's a type-A control freak. But I'll never get to sleep unless I can offload my ballooning to-do list somewhere.

My computer is on the desk in the living room, which is a short walk from the bedroom. With the house quiet, that means the boys are probably in bed after a long day.

Careful not to wake anyone, I crack open the door and check the hall. I tiptoe across the floor, passing the stairs before gathering my computer from the living room. As I'm heading back, I suddenly hear the patter of footsteps, then spot a shadow coming down the stairs. I freeze for a second, realizing that if I stay where I am, I'll get caught in my pajamas. Instead, I whip around the corner of the front entrance hall and plaster myself against the wall, holding my breath.

For a few seconds, there's no sound. Whoever it was must have left. I slowly let out my breath. As I round the corner, I slam into what feels like a solid wall, but smells like a soap that might have a description like *ocean breeze* with undertones of a spicy cologne.

"Jaz?" Brax's familiar voice isn't a comfort. It's like someone pulled the panic alarm in my brain. He fumbles for me in the dark, like he's trying to peel me off his shirt. When I try to step to the side, I trip on his foot in the dark and lose my balance. His hand sweeps around my arm before I fall, pulling me up against him at the last second.

The man has reflexes I don't even know about, probably honed from years of skating around on two thin blades.

He's also built like a tank. A cement wall would've been more comfortable to walk face-first into.

The feel of his hand on my skin only seems to highlight how much I like it there.

Bad girl! I inwardly scold, like I'm a puppy with a preference for leather shoes.

He sets me on my feet as if I'm the weight of a feather, right before the lights flick on.

"What are you doing up?" he asks, like this isn't my house. He lets me go, and a shiver runs across my body, reminding me I'm underdressed.

His gaze flicks over my pajama set as embarrassment pricks across my chest: a sparkly, pink-striped tank top over a matching pair of loose cotton shorts.

I fold my arms over my tank top. "I'd like to ask you the same thing."

He gives me an amused smirk. "Nice pajamas, Princess. It looks like a unicorn vomited on you." I can't tell if he approves of what he sees, but he's definitely not a fan of pink sparkles.

"It's none of your business what I wear to bed." I straighten my spine and pretend I've got the confidence of a Kardashian, even if I'm cursing myself for not wearing pajamas that resemble a potato sack.

He arches an eyebrow. "Who said I didn't approve?"

I sigh. "Brax, why are you down here?"

He holds up an empty plastic bag. "I need some ice."

"Isn't it kind of late for a drink?"

"Not to eat. After workouts. For recovery," he adds, glancing over his shoulder. "But then I heard something in the front hall."

"So you came around the corner to find out," I finish, replaying that delicious memory of walking face-first into his *ocean breeze* and the soft cotton of his shirt.

I motion him toward the kitchen and don't bother turning on the lights as I fill his bag with ice. "I can get you some ice packs to keep in the freezer. Just ask next time instead of sneaking around the house after dark." I zip the bag shut and hand it to him.

"I assumed you were sleeping."

"I wish." I slam the freezer door shut.

"Were we too loud?" Even in the dark, concern lines his face.

"It's not you." Which is only half true. Brax's surprise arrival has only heaped another layer onto my already teetering tower of blocks. "I'm starting a new job tomorrow, so there's first-day jitters and all that."

"Congratulations," he says with a grin. "What happened to your Etsy shop?"

I can't believe he remembers my side hustle—a custom fashion shop that specializes in unique sports apparel. When we were decorating for Mia's wedding, I showed him a few of the designs on my phone. He told me I had talent. I told him I wanted to design custom jerseys for the NHL.

"My business hasn't taken off the way I hoped, but I'm continuing to sell. It's just not enough income while Sloan's taking a leave of absence."

He tilts his head to the side, and the light from the hall highlights the sharp cut of his cheekbones. "Why is Sloan off work?"

I knew at some point we'd need to tell the guys. I was just hoping that Sloan could do it herself. "About four months ago, Sloan was in a car accident. She hit her head pretty hard and suffered a traumatic brain injury."

Brax's eyes widen. "I'm so sorry. Is she okay?"

"She still gets tired and has massive headaches that force her to stay in bed. Until she gets over those, she can't go back to her job coaching at the university. I'd just bought my grandmother's home. It was bad timing."

He shakes his head before dragging a hand through his hair. "I feel terrible that I didn't know."

"It's not your fault. I told your sister not to tell anyone. Sloan didn't really want me sharing it. She hates feeling like a charity case."

"I won't," he promises. "Is there something I can do? Do you need anything?" The lines between his brows deepen.

He's concerned about *us*? Earlier today, he only seemed interested in having a flirtatious face-off. It's easier to think of Brax as a heartless dirtbag. But seeing him as a guy who has an *actual* heart? I feel like someone just swept my feet out from under me.

I can't have these soft feelings for Brax while we're roommates. And I can't accept his help if it comes with strings attached. He's already got too many strings to my heart.

"It's nice of you to offer, but you're paying us rent, remember? Along with my new job, we'll be okay."

Maybe.

He looks at me. "I almost forgot to ask. Where are you working?"

I hesitate, suddenly wishing I didn't have to drop this bomb now. As much as I want to hide it, he's going to find out tomorrow. Maybe telling him now will help me get some sleep.

"I'm the community relations manager for this great team called the Carolina Crushers. Maybe you've heard of them?" I say, trying to lighten the mood.

He stares at me for a few agonizing beats. "You're working for the Crushers?"

I nod. "We're going to be seeing a lot of each other, Mac."

Brax scratches his head. "Wow. Wasn't prepared for that. Think you can handle it?"

"The job . . . or you?" I've been asking myself the same question ever since he arrived.

"Pick your poison."

I cross my arms. "If we don't kill each other first."

FIVE

Prax

I sneak down to the kitchen early in the morning, hoping I don't get caught by Jaz again. Her bedroom door is still closed, which gives me time to ice my shoulder. Since I wiped out the supply last night, I opt for a bag of peas instead.

Vale looks over the frozen vegetable I'm using as an ice pack. "Again?"

"I don't want Alex to think I'm not ready." From everything I've heard, Alexandra runs a tight ship. If she catches even the slightest hint of weakness, she'll make sure I find a new team.

"It doesn't matter what Alex thinks. If your shoulder doesn't heal, it's going to affect how you play."

I know he's right, but I'm too stubborn to admit it. For now, frozen peas will have to work.

"If Lucian is bringing over the other two roomies, I call dibs on the bathroom first." Vale grabs his muffin and heads toward the steps.

"How long are you going to be?" I call after him.

"This kind of beauty takes time." Vale sweeps his hair back like he's Rapunzel, and I roll my eyes.

"Just hurry, okay?" I grumble. The man loves his hair.

"There's another bathroom," he adds. "If you get desperate."

That man spends more time on his appearance than most girls I know.

After I scroll through hockey news on my phone, Vale still isn't out of the bathroom. With Lucian set to arrive any time, I grab my toiletry bag and head to the downstairs bathroom.

As I swing the door open, I'm immediately confronted by Jaz wrapped in a towel, razor in hand, and her bare leg propped on the sink.

"Get out of here!" she yells and levels a look at me like I'm some kind of perv.

I back away. "I didn't see anything! I mean, except for your . . ." I wave toward her bare legs.

"Don't you know how to knock?" She shoves me out of the room.

"Well, good morning to you too, Princess," I grumble. "Need I remind you someone failed to lock the door?"

She holds up the razor, which now looks like a dangerous tool aimed at me. "Need I remind you that same someone is holding a sharp object?"

I take a step back and put my hands up in surrender. "Sorry."

"First rule of the house: *Always* knock." Then she slams the door in my face.

Now that we got that out of the way.

In less than twenty-four hours, I've stumbled into not one, but *two* compromising situations with her. How many more accidental run-ins before she thinks I'm a total creep?

If this is what it means to live in the same house together, I don't know if I can take it. Not just running into her, but the thought of her *imagining* me as some slimeball who only wants to see her half-dressed.

I'd punch anyone who even thought of her the wrong way.

Yet, my mind is burned with that image. And I don't want to think of her only that way or have her look at me like she did just now.

Like she doesn't trust me.

Earning back her trust is first priority, but that will only work if I put some rules around our roommate situation. *And my feelings.*

Vale finally trots down the steps, his hair neatly combed. "Bathroom is all yours."

"Thanks to you, I walked in on Jaz in the bathroom."

His face snaps to mine in amusement. "Day two and you've already gotten on her last nerve? *That* takes talent."

"She threatened me with a razor blade."

Vale chuckles. "I wouldn't leave your door unlocked at night."

As I toss the peas back in the freezer, Lucian pulls up, and the two new players climb out.

The team captain greets us with a smile. "I trust your first night was okay?" I nod and my gaze flicks over to the jersey he's holding. The one promised to Jaz. A twinge of jealousy twists inside me.

Cool it. He's the team captain, trying to make her feel welcome. And the first game is two weeks away. She can pick any jersey she wants to wear, which I respect. But I still want her to pick mine.

"I'd like you to meet your new roommates." He motions to the taller one, with the chiseled jaw and the hair falling over one eye. "This is Leo."

The guy doesn't even crack a smile. Instead, he gives me a quick nod and grips my hand *hard*.

Save it for the ice, Mr. Ego. Even now, he looks ready to take me out.

"I'm Tate." The other guy, with the beard and dark eyes, steps forward. He immediately puts us at ease with a warm smile.

Tate's gaze flicks over my shoulder as Jaz enters, wearing a long black dress, her hair curled loosely around her shoulders.

She looks stunning, and it's obvious the other guys agree because they can't stop staring.

Do they think they even have a chance with her? Because they don't. She's way too good for them.

"This is Jaz," Lucian says. "She owns the house, along with her sister. Their rules are law around here, so give them respect."

She offers Lucian an appreciative smile.

"Is anyone hungry?" Sloan asks. "I can cook some bacon."

Vale raises his hand. "I'm always hungry."

"Why am I not surprised?" I mutter.

"What?" Vale shrugs. "Need to keep up my energy for our first day."

Sloan escapes to the kitchen to fry bacon while the boys gather around the enormous oak table in the dining room, passing muffins and coffee cups. The smell of bacon fills the house, while Jaz hangs back, nursing a cup of coffee and checking her phone.

"First things first," Lucian says, turning his chair around backwards so he can straddle it. "Let's talk house rules."

It's obvious why he's the team captain; he demands the attention of everyone here. "Jaz, do you want to be part of this conversation?"

She glances up from her phone. "You want to talk about house rules, now?" Based on the surprise on her face, she wasn't prepared for this.

"The sooner the better," Lucian says. "We need for this housing arrangement to work until some apartments open up."

Tate raises his hand. "I, for one, would appreciate knowing the rules."

Leo frowns at him, like he can't believe what he's hearing. "We're grown adults, Sheriff Tate. We'll get along just fine if we use common sense."

Tate glowers at Leo. "How do you know everyone has common sense?"

"Guys . . ." Lucian interrupts, shaking his head. "Let Jaz talk."

"We do need rules." Her eyes skate to me for a second before flicking away, like she's replaying the memory of me walking in on her. "But use your heads. Don't be idiots. What questions do you have?"

"Are you okay with us having friends over for a party?" Leo asks.

Lucian frowns. "Parties are out of the question. And you shouldn't be partying before a game anyway."

Leo huffs. "Seriously?"

Tate glances at Leo. "We just got here, and you already want to party?"

"I'm not planning anything," Leo argues. "She asked for questions."

"I'm glad he brought it up," I interrupt, folding my arms. "This is someone's home. We need to treat it with respect."

"Agreed." Lucian nods.

I like this guy already.

"What other rules do you think we should cover, boss?" Lucian asks.

"Places that are off-limits." She looks at me. "The downstairs bathroom is *only* for Sloan and me."

"It was an accident," I remind her, not wanting to turn this into an argument in front of the others.

Leo laughs. "Good way to make a first impression."

"He said it was an accident," Tate says in my defense.

From the kitchen, Sloan hands Jaz a generous plate of bacon.

As Tate and Vale reach for the bacon, she pulls it away at the last second. "Let's try to share, okay? Another house rule."

Lucian takes the plate instead and hands it to me.

"How can the guys help around the house?" Lucian asks. "I don't want you cleaning up after a bunch of grown men."

Leo frowns. "I thought we were here to play hockey?"

"This isn't a hotel." I give Leo the stink eye. "I recommend assigned duties, just like if we were living in an apartment."

If Sloan is still struggling to get out of bed some days, how would she be able to clean up after four guys? I don't want Jaz to shoulder the burden, especially since she's taking care of Sloan.

"If we were renting an apartment, I wouldn't clean up there either," Leo confesses with a shrug. "Just saying."

"Disgusting." Tate shakes his head, like he can't stomach the thought.

"As long as we live here, we're all responsible," I say.

Lucian nods in agreement. "If this is something you care about, Brax, would you mind making chore assignments with Jaz?"

"I can do it," Jaz interrupts. "Unless you have a problem with that?" She looks at me.

"Not at all." If she's testing me to see how quickly she can push me away, she's going to have to try a lot harder. I want her to know I'm on her side now. I fully respect that she's running the show here. "Your house. Your rules."

Something flicks behind her eyes. "The rules aren't difficult. We're all adults here." Jaz looks us over like we're a bunch of prepubescent boys. "And I'm *not* your mom."

"You certainly don't look like my mom," Leo says with a grin.

I kick him under the table. *Hard.*

"Ow! What was that for?" He glares at me.

"Being rude. Apologize now."

"I was complimenting her," he argues. "I'm not sorry for noticing a beautiful woman."

I lean across the table toward Leo and narrow my eyes. "That was *more* than noticing. Not to mention totally inappropriate."

Jaz clears her throat. "Guys."

"No one said no flirting is a rule," Leo reminds me.

"Maybe it should be," I grumble.

Leo leans across the table. "What about *her house, her rules*?"

"Guys!" she says, louder. "I'm standing right here. Stop talking about me like I can't hear you."

I lean back and cross my arms while Leo scowls at me. The guy has an ego the size of a Texas belt buckle.

"Let's get back to house rules," Lucian says, looking between Leo and me, noticing the tension between us.

I can already tell this housing arrangement is going to be . . . *interesting.*

"Our situation isn't ideal," I begin. "But living together is going to force us to learn to work with each other. We could use that to our advantage."

"How will that help?" Tate asks.

"We need to figure out each other's strengths and weaknesses. I can already see that we're pretty different." I glance around at everyone. "If we're going to play as a team, we need to figure out how to make things work."

Lucian stands. "I agree with Brax. Living together could be the best thing that's happened to this team."

Leo gives a doubtful laugh. "Or the worst."

"Then this will be your test." Lucian looks directly at Leo. "Can you adapt under pressure?"

My gaze slides over to Jaz. I've got a few people to convince that I'm on their side. And she's going to be the toughest one of all.

Lucian checks his watch. "This meeting is adjourned. We've got work to do, boys."

Everyone leaves the table while Jaz slips down the back hall.

I head toward her bedroom and make sure I knock first. When she appears in the door, to my disappointment, she's trying on Lucian's jersey.

"What do you think?" she asks, twirling around.

Jealousy stirs inside my chest when I see his name on her back. I'm not going to give her the satisfaction of making me jealous. Better for her to think I have no feelings than to see me react to her wearing the team captain's jersey.

"It looks . . ." I keep my emotions—and my face—in check. "Okay."

"*Just* okay?" she asks.

I'm trying so hard *not* to say the wrong thing, or let her know how much it bothers me that she's not wearing my jersey. But it's like she knows how to push my buttons. Every. Single. One of them.

She moves closer to me, and I can smell her perfume, sweet

and floral and delicious. "I want your honest opinion." She looks up at me with her doe eyes.

I lean against the doorframe and cross my arms. "Honestly? I think you'd look better in mine."

Her cheeks heat as her mouth opens. "I see you're breaking the rules already."

"And what rule is that?" I arch an eyebrow, still playing it cool while enjoying the flush across her cheeks. "No guests in the bedroom? You'll notice my feet have not crossed the line."

She glances at my toes, which are firmly on the other side of the doorway. "You know which one, Mac." She uses the nickname that only comes up when we banter. "I meant the no-flirting rule."

"I thought that wasn't a rule," I say with a smirk.

"It is now," she says with a flash of challenge in her eyes.

"Well, I wasn't flirting."

She looks at me doubtfully. "Then what was it?"

I hold her stare long enough for the air to crackle between us. "Only the truth. You were meant to wear my jersey."

SIX

The cold of the rink is a welcome relief after the tension of the meeting about house rules. Or maybe it's the churning in my gut from seeing Jazlyn in someone else's jersey. I didn't stay to see her reaction after I told her my jersey was meant for her.

I said what I said. If she's angry about it, then she'll probably wear Lucian's jersey just to spite me.

Since we're the first to arrive at the Ice House before the staff meeting, we circle the rink to get a feel for our new home. Vale skates next to me, unusually quiet after the tense meeting.

"What did you think about the new guys?" I ask, trying to get his take on things.

"I hope things are easier in practice. Tate's a breeze to have around. But Leo? He's a wild card. Makes me wonder how he'll be on the ice—and whether he'll be a thorn in our side."

I chuckle. "Thorny is right," I mutter. Even if I didn't have a history with Jaz, I'd find him annoying.

"What do you think of Jaz and Sloan?" Vale asks, keeping his eyes on the ice. I knew this question was coming.

"They seem . . ." I need to choose my words carefully. "*Nice.*"

"Nice, huh?" Vale glances at me with a smirk, then quickly

looks away. "I remember you and Jaz at the wedding. You seemed —how should I say this?—really *into* her."

"You think so?" I keep my eyes on the ice in front of me. It's not that I don't want my brother to know the truth. I'm just ashamed of what I allowed to happen.

Kissing an incredible woman is one thing. It's another thing to let her grab hold of my heart so completely, I'm still not over her.

Letting my feelings for Jaz snowball was stupid enough without my brother reminding me of that fact.

"I almost thought . . ." He stops on the ice and faces me, the question in his eyes.

"Thought what?" I glance away, feeling uncomfortable under his stare.

Vale hesitates. "There was something more between you two. When I brought up her name afterwards and asked you if you were going to pursue her, you almost seemed angry about it."

I rub my jaw. *Tread carefully*. "Can't a guy date around?"

"But you don't," he adds. "You haven't dated anyone since the wedding."

"I'm not interested." I grab my stick and keep my eye on the puck. "She's our sister's best friend. Mia made it clear she didn't want me near her."

I pass the puck to Vale, hoping I can distract him with some quick shots.

"That never stopped you before," Vale says with a smirk before whipping the puck back to me.

True. Mia is pretty vocal about who I should date, but that doesn't mean I always listen to her.

"It's still a bad idea. Jaz is our new roommate. She's also working for this hockey team as the community relations manager. You know what that means, right? *None* of us should date her." I shoot Vale a look that says this discussion is over. *We're over.*

Vale lifts an eyebrow. "Better tell Leo, then."

"Oh, I will, if Jaz doesn't shut him down first." I whip the puck toward Vale, who stops it easily. "I can't wait to see his face when it happens."

"Can I ask one more question?" He keeps the puck, knowing he has my attention now.

"No," I say, skating toward him and trying to steal the puck.

He blocks me with his stick. "Do you still have feelings for her?"

"I *can't* have feelings for her," I insist, still fighting for the puck.

"That wasn't the question." He grabs my practice jersey to hold me in place. "You're a terrible liar, Brax."

"I'm still not telling you." As I go for the puck, our sticks smack, and I finally grab Vale's arm to get him off me. "Lay off me."

"Are we holding hands now?" he asks with an aggravating smirk.

"You grabbed my jersey." From the outside, it looks like we're back in the peewee league, behaving like two immature boys. But we both know the truth. This isn't about hockey at all.

I stop fighting and skate backwards, putting distance between us. "I made a mistake with her, okay?"

He narrows his eyes. "What kind of mistake?"

"The stupid kind." A frustrated sigh escapes my lips. "I kissed her." Admitting it feels like I'm kicking myself all over again. "Then I let her go."

He shakes his head. "That *was* stupid."

"Thank you, Captain Obvious." I skate toward the bench, away from any more criticism. At least he's smart enough to not ask why.

"Don't tell the team," I add over my shoulder. "I don't need to give Leo any more ammunition."

"He's going to notice," Vale says, following me. "The tension between you two is like an electrical storm."

I sit on the bench, avoiding his gaze. "Then I'll stay away from her. Until we find a new place to live."

"And if we don't?" he asks, the question hanging between us. "It could be months before an apartment opens up. You can't keep exploding every time Leo lays on the charm."

"I know that," I grumble. "Doesn't mean I have to like it." I unlace my skate.

Vale sits next to me, gripping his stick and staring at the rink. "Do you think we belong here?"

"On the Crushers? Absolutely," I say. "I don't believe in accidents."

"So you don't think it's a coincidence that you and Jaz are roommates?"

"What are you getting at?" I ask, pulling off a skate.

Vale looks me in the eye. "If this wasn't an accident, this might be your chance."

"Are you talking about hockey or with her?" I ask.

"What do you think?" he replies.

"Pretty sure I ruined any shot I have with Jaz," I mutter.

When I look up, Jaz is standing on the opposite side of the rink, studying us. As soon as our eyes meet, she turns away, like she's been caught spying.

"You ready to face the Ice Queen?" Vale asks, referring to Alex, the team owner. With her reputation for *not* being the warm-and-fuzzy type, she's earned the nickname Ice Queen for good reason.

"Ready or not, this is what we signed up for," I say.

We change into our shoes and head to the large conference room in the office wing.

The room is bustling with players and staff when we arrive, and I give a quick wave to Coach Thompson across the room. As the oldest coach in the league, he's also one of the smartest. He knows hockey better than anyone here.

Vale and I are some of the more seasoned players, which

means we stand a chance at being top scorers this season. Not a bad way to earn some attention so we've got a shot at the NHL.

I quickly glance around for Jaz, but to my disappointment, she's not here yet. She's probably settling into her office and avoiding me as much as possible.

As Vale and I greet the rest of the team, Vale's elbow nudges my side. He nods toward the door, where Alexandra strides in with Jaz following on her heels.

Even though I saw her earlier, I'm still struck by her beauty. And I'm not the only one. Every guy in the room is looking at her.

Alex gives the team a tight smile, and everyone immediately hushes, like she's royalty. With her bleach-blonde bob and a form-fitting leopard-print dress, Alex exudes the air of someone with power and money.

According to a quick Google search I did before arriving, she used to co-own the team with her husband. After a bitter divorce, she took over control of the Carolina Crushers and is one of the few female owners of a hockey team—something she's immensely proud of.

But according to hockey fan chats, she's not afraid to play favorites. If you're not one of her darlings, she can make your life miserable, even keeping you from moving into the NHL. Nobody needs to explain how this game of hers works. If I'm going to survive on this team, I need to win her over.

As Alex parades to the front of the room, I glance over at Jaz, who is furiously typing on her computer. I know she feels the same pressure from Alex that I do, but there's more riding on her performance.

She'll work closer to Alexandra, which means she'll have to bend to her every whim. Plus, she's the breadwinner for her and Sloan now, shouldering the bills. This position isn't just a job; it's survival.

As I gaze at her across the room, she glances up suddenly, like she can feel the weight of my stare. My heart skips, and I give her a smile to acknowledge her. Her eyes widen before she looks back at her computer, like she's trying to pretend I don't exist.

"I'd like to start with good news," Alex begins, folding her hands. "It's a new season. Another chance for a winning record. A shot at becoming the best in the AHL."

Everyone from the team erupts in cheers, but Alex instantly smothers it by holding up her hand for silence.

"I won't sugarcoat this. Last year we had a losing record, and our community support has dwindled. We need to turn things around. That's why we've hired someone to take over as community relations manager. I want you all to meet Jaz Summers."

Everyone claps as Jaz slowly rises from her chair, nervously glancing around the room.

Alex touches her shoulder, stopping her from sitting. "Jaz, can you tell us what your plan is for community engagement?"

This woman does not mess around. A flicker of fear crosses Jaz's face. "Well, I just started today . . ."

Alex raises her eyebrows like she's not letting her off the hook. I want her to look my way, but she avoids me at all costs.

She clears her throat. "Community engagement begins with the simple act of giving back as a team. It means we'll be volunteering with local organizations and becoming more visible in the community. Only then will we be able to get our fans to see us differently."

"We don't have time to volunteer," a player named Rourke says from the back of the room "We're here to play hockey."

"Well, I haven't worked out the details yet, but studies show that when you volunteer in places like nursing homes and schools, community support skyrockets."

"We're going to hang out with old people?" Dawson asks, and everyone laughs.

"I don't know yet," Jaz replies.

"If it takes time away from practice, that means we'll lose more," Leo complains, his arms crossed.

A few guys nod in agreement.

"It won't interfere with practice," Jaz assures him, looking at Alex for help. But the owner lets her flounder, like she's enjoying seeing her squirm.

Already I don't like this woman because something about her seems . . . *off*. If she cared about the community supporting our team, wouldn't she be fighting for Jaz's ideas?

My eyes skirt over the team, who look as friendly as a pack of pit bulls. *This needs to stop now.*

I raise a hand to address the team. "If we're going to turn things around, we need to trust the people who are helping us. We should at least try Jaz's ideas before complaining about them."

I glance over at Jaz, who's staring at me with wide eyes.

"Then maybe *you* can be the first to volunteer," Leo suggests with a gleam in his eyes. "What would you like Brax to do first?"

He's just opened the door for Jaz to pick sides in front of the entire team. If she really wants to get me back for not calling her, this is the perfect opportunity. *Public humiliation.*

Leo goes on, "I'm not sure which Brax would like better. Kissing up to old ladies or cleaning up trash? Oh, wait. That's what I'm going to do with him when we meet up on the ice later today."

The guys burst out laughing.

I turn to Leo with a smug smile. "Where'd you learn to trash talk, Leo? Junior league?"

Vale snickers.

Alex looks a little too pleased about our banter, like she's enjoying the tension. "Okay, boys. Save your insults for the ice."

As Jaz takes her seat, I notice her relief. Her eyes flick to mine with a quick *thank you*.

After we plow through team introductions and reminders, Alex dismisses us for practice.

But I've got something else on my mind before I leave: Wishing Jaz good luck with her first day on the job.

As she hurries out the door, I call after her, "Hey, wait up." But it only seems to make her rush away even faster.

Finally, I catch her arm, and she turns. "You did a good job today," I say, out of breath from the chase, my fingers grasping on to the silky skin of her arm. "Considering you didn't really have time to prepare."

I'm trying to show her I'm not the bad guy here. I'm on her side.

She glances at my hand, like she feels the same electricity I do. "Thanks, Brax."

Standing this close to her, the gold flecks in her brown eyes shimmer, and I just stare, transfixed.

"Brax, is there something else?" she asks.

Touching her feels natural. But I can't let myself slip like this.

I drop my hand, shoving it into my pocket instead.

She looks over my shoulder nervously. "We still need to be careful or people might suspect . . ." She drops her voice as Tom, the Crushers' operations manager walks by, eyeing us as he passes. Jaz pastes on a stiff smile until he's out of earshot.

"Suspect what?" I ask. No one would guess we have history based on one comment.

She hugs her computer to her chest, like she's trying to shield herself from me. "I'm glad you want to help, but this is *my* job now. I need to handle things, even if that means failing sometimes."

I open my mouth, but the stubbornness in her gaze warns me not to interfere.

"I won't get involved," I finally agree. "But I'm not going to let the team talk to you like that."

"You have to," she says. "Even if they don't like me. Okay?"

This is not going to be easy—watching them put her through the fire because she's new. I let out a sigh. "Fine."

She arches an eyebrow and puts her hand out. "Shake on it."

I look at her hand. "Jazlyn," I groan. There's no way I'll let her fail while she works here. Not on my watch.

She grabs my hand anyway. "One more thing. No more calling me Jazlyn."

That's her special name and only a few get to use it. I claimed it as my own the night I kissed her.

She levels her gaze before saying, "From now on, I'm Jaz to you."

We'll see about that, Princess.

SEVEN

Jaz

As I watch Brax glide effortlessly across the ice, I attempt to concentrate on my to-do list. Now that I'm working for the Crushers, I'm going to have to get used to watching the *Brax Show* every single day. The way he commands the puck sends a shiver down my spine. *How can I focus on anything when he's here?*

If we were dating, this would be a delightful perk of the job. But since there's no chance of that happening, I feel like a starving woman salivating over a juicy steak. Not that I'm comparing Brax to a side of beef. But the man has way more assets than your average Joe, plus he smells yummy and makes me laugh. Pretty much the powerhouse trifecta of the ideal man.

While this might be the ideal opportunity to take mental notes of his assets, I'd rather not be stuck at the rink without an office. After today's meeting, Tom revealed that my new office was essentially a renovated storage closet which *no one* had bothered to clean out prior to my arrival.

With no place to go, I'm stuck at the rink with a laptop propped on my knees. And Brax being Brax, he skates by arching an eyebrow, like he's wondering why I'm here and whether I'm watching him.

You're so vain.

I duck my head and focus on my screen, which I maintain for less than a minute before Brax slams Leo into the wall in front of me.

As Brax hustles to the other end, he makes a sharp stop so that ice sprays from his blades. And in typical Brax style, he does it better than anyone else.

Showoff.

The other guys laugh and push him around like he's already found his place on the team. From here, I can see that he's fitting in just fine. Now if I can do the same.

"Earth to Jaz," Vale teases, stopping directly in front of me. His lips curl into a smile as he traces my gaze to his brother. "Working hard?"

My cheeks heat as my gaze snaps back to my computer. "It would help if I had an office."

He leans on his stick. "The view here isn't bad."

"I wouldn't know," I say, keeping my voice steady, my eyes glued on my screen. "I'm not watching."

"Oh, really?" Vale smirks. "It looked like you were staring at Brax like he's a life-sized chocolate statue."

I glance up from my computer. "For your information, I don't even like chocolate that much." Which is not entirely true, since I adore chocolate.

Who else noticed I was staring?

Right now, I can't get sidetracked by Brax. I need the team to like my ideas, or else I'll never be able to get them to participate in the community initiatives I'm planning.

"If you need any help, let me know," Vale says, looking back at the guys as they race across the ice, trying to prove who's fastest.

Maybe Vale would be a good sounding board for my ideas. I don't have a history with him the way I do with Brax, so my feelings won't get in the way. But he's also open to my ideas, unlike some of the other players.

"I could use your help with one thing, Vale." He turns to look at me. "What if I planned volunteer events that would help the guys bond?"

I see Brax look over at his brother, keeping an eye on us the whole time.

"What kind of bonding?"

"That's what I'm not sure about. We need our fans to see the other side of our players—the goofy, funny side. I'm thinking about having the team volunteer at various places where you could interact with the people. Maybe do something fun. I'd take pictures for our social accounts, and we'd do something to help the community. It's a win-win for everyone."

"Sounds good," he says with an easygoing smile that's so much like his brother's, I have to remind myself he's *not* Brax. "And I'm fully in support of volunteering in the community. Whatever you need, I'm happy to help."

"Thanks, Vale. I appreciate that," I say with a smile before he heads back to the ice. At least he's on my side.

Brax glances over at me once more, and I decide I've had enough of the *Brax Show*.

Snapping my laptop shut, I leave to check on the progress of my closet-office. To my relief, the space is empty. A small desk is pushed against the wall with the world's most uncomfortable-looking wooden chair. It might not be more than a dark cave to work in, hardly big enough for one person, but at least I won't have to watch Brax from here.

"Jaz?" I turn to see Brax standing in my door, filling the entire space with his massive frame. "Is this your new office?" He glances over my tiny room, which takes all of a second.

"Yes, welcome to my cozy hobbit hole. Won't be any team meetings in here."

He chuckles. "There are advantages to small spaces," he says with a curve of his lips as he steps inside and I have to back up to put space between us. "Reminds me of that closet we hid in during Mia's wedding reception. Remember?"

How could I forget? The memory makes me feel like I just crossed two sparking wires.

The room is so tiny, he could take two strides and crush me against the wall—a thought that makes my insides spiral.

You must not think of him crushing you like that, even if he is a Crusher.

That's when it hits me: I'm never going to *stop* thinking of him that way. I'm reminded of it everywhere I turn. It's even across the silky black athletic shirt he's wearing: *Carolina Crushers.*

I stare at the logo on his chest long enough that he rubs the back of his neck. "I take it that's a yes?"

My eyes snap to his, and I nod robotically. "Yeah, so many advantages." Like the fact that he's already standing so close that I can see his dark green eyes, the ones I'd like to swan dive into.

"I'll miss you at practice, though," he says. "It was fun having you watch today."

"Now I won't bother you."

I'm going to stay so far away from you, I might as well be in another state.

I cross my arms, trying to keep my limbs from bumping into him.

"You weren't bothering me." He frowns, almost offended I would even *think* that. "I want you to bother me."

Is this his version of a peace offering? *Or an invitation?*

He steps forward, closing the space between us. I can't even cross around him without touching him. He's too close, and I'm very aware that he has me cornered, so I can't get away.

He looks at me, and there's a softness in his eyes, a contrast to his very solid frame. "I just wondered what you were talking to Vale about."

"Nothing important." I dodge to the left to get around him, and he blocks me with reflexes that are lightning fast.

"If it wasn't important, why didn't you come to me?" He tilts his head, the question in his eyes. Doesn't he know the answers are too complicated?

"I . . ." I hesitate and dodge right, and he stops me. Our little game of dodge and weave is more than just physical. He wants to know why I didn't trust him enough to ask him first.

How can I explain that I needed to choose someone I'm not attracted to?

"I wanted his opinion on some ideas," I say, shrugging. "It wasn't personal."

He gives a slow nod. "I'm willing to do whatever it takes to turn this team around, too. That's how I roll."

"Anything?" I ask, testing him.

"Almost," he says, and I can see the warning in his eyes.

"How about dancing with some ladies at a retirement home?" I ask with a smile, knowing he'd hate it.

"You saw how I danced at the reception. I have two left feet."

I laugh, remembering how he stepped on my toes. I was so deliriously happy in his arms, I didn't even care. The memory spreads a fizzy feeling through my middle.

"I want this to work," he says in a low voice.

Does he mean he wants the team to work? *Or us?*

He's so close that his body is causing my heart to bump against my ribs like a drumbeat, and I'm afraid he can hear the thumping in my body, how agitated he makes me when he's this close.

"Don't worry, I won't compromise the agreement we made earlier," he says with a gaze so intense, it nearly causes me to want to take it back. "The one where we pretend not to have any history together."

My eyes drop to his lips. *So much history I can't forget.*

"I know the agreement," I mumble, if only to remind myself. *Keep my distance. Pretend there never was an "us."*

Why did I agree to this?

Oh, yeah. So we don't ruin our perfect arrangement.

Don't. Mess. It. Up.

He turns and brushes by me, his hand a gentle whisper across my arm. It wasn't an intentional touch, but it had the same effect. One touch sets off the fireworks in my body, making me want to rein him back and *repeat* some history.

But we both know why that would be a bad idea. He still hasn't given me an answer that satisfies my need to know *why*. What happened after our kiss that made him disappear? Until he answers me, that one question is the stumbling block to any future we might have together.

He disappears down the hall, leaving me to sink onto my rock-hard chair. At least we're on the same page when it comes to working together.

Now it's my job to stay away from him.

No problem, right?

The rest of the week, I map out plans for the year—including one idea that's absolutely insane but could be my best one yet. Even though I want to tell Brax first, I keep it a secret. I shouldn't treat him special, even though he's become a regular in my office, stopping by whenever he has a chance. He even left a chocolate truffle on my desk the other day with the note, *I heard you like chocolate.*

An obvious nod to my staring problem at practice.

As long as I'm working for Alex, I should get her approval for anything first. Not Brax. No matter how much he wants this team to succeed. I've worked hard to create this community re-engagement plan, but unless Alexandra signs off, I'll never convince the team to agree to it.

I look down the hall and notice that Alex's light is still on, even though it's past eight o'clock. If I can get her to approve my plan tonight, that means I can start setting up our community initiative tomorrow.

I knock on her door quietly and then peek inside.

Two men sit across from her, looking over a dozen papers spread across her desk. She glances up in surprise. "Jaz? What are you doing here so late?"

"Sorry to interrupt. Your light was on, so I thought . . ."

"Come in." She stands and walks toward me with her usual tight smile. "Henry and George, this is my new community relations manager. She might be helpful." She hesitates and looks me over, like she's picking out produce at the grocery store. "Specifically for our future plans."

I shake their hands and get the strange sense that they seem less than happy about me being there. "I should go."

"Have you told her yet?" George asks Alex.

"No. I was waiting until plans were more firmly in place." Alex rounds her desk and sinks into a large leather chair. Then she looks at me. "Can you keep a secret?"

I nod, knowing I don't really have another choice. I work for Alex, and if I want to keep my job, I need to do whatever she tells me.

Alex motions for me to sit in a nearby chair. "This isn't public news yet." She pushes her papers toward me.

One is an architectural rendering of an enormous building, with the words, "The Plex."

Alex taps the drawing. "This is going to be our new sports complex."

My mouth drops open. "You're building a new complex?" Alex might own the Ice House, but from what I've heard, the team hasn't met their budget the last two years because of low attendance and advertisers pulling their money. There's no way the team can afford a building project right now. "But how? I thought we weren't doing well."

"We aren't. That's why George and Henry are here. We're building a multi-sport complex that will bring in a lot more revenue than the ice complex. We'll be able to host basketball games, soccer, indoor football . . . you name it, we'll be able to host it." She turns to the two men in the room. "George is a local businessman who helps fund development projects in the city, and Henry is a councilman who will get the city on board."

"Oh." I nod, finally understanding. "So you'll use it in the off-season for other sports, but the hockey team will use it the rest of the time."

George and Henry give Alex a knowing glance.

"Well, not exactly." Alex looks away and adjusts her blonde bob behind one ear. "Hockey hasn't been very . . . how shall I put it? Lucrative. With another season of losses, we may have to decide what's best for everyone."

I frown and shake my head. "I don't understand."

Alex tightens her lips and gives me a smile that makes me feel stupid. "I'm saying the hockey team might not exist after this year. At least, not in this city."

"Wait, you're shutting it down?" I nearly fall off my seat. This is horrible news.

"I have the team's best interest in mind," Alex says in response to my shock. "But if they're not making money, then I need to do what's best for *my* interests as the owner."

It all sinks in so fast, I don't know what to say. To think that Alex could end it all so quickly. "You'd give up your team so you could make more money?" I blurt out.

"It might not make sense to you," Alex begins, folding her hands, her jeweled fingers glittering on the desk. "But when my husband and I divorced, he gave me the team and the Ice House as part of our settlement. He loves hockey, so I thought it was an enormous sacrifice for him. But after looking over the records, I realized I was a fool. For years, he's lost money on this team and facility. He didn't run things like a CEO. He gambled on luck and let everyone do their own thing. With no vision and no focus, he lost advertisers and our best players. Then he ran out of money. He just never told me."

If she can see the horror on my face, she doesn't show it. Alex isn't making this change out of love for the team. She's doing it because she wants to get rid of a team that's bleeding money.

"I'm sorry about what happened to you and your husband," I begin.

"It's done now," she says, her eyes hardening as she taps her fingernails on the desk. "But I have to fix his errors. And that means making hard decisions."

More like brutally unfair decisions. And where will that leave all the people she employs?

"But what if you could turn the team around?" I ask.

She sighs, like she's been over this before. "Community support is at its lowest in years, and so is our advertising income. That's why our last community relations manager quit. We're the worst in the league, and I don't see that changing anytime soon."

Ouch. I'm glad Brax isn't here.

"Then why did you bring in new players?"

"Public perception is complicated." She shrugs and takes a sip of her sparkling water. "I don't want to appear like I'm giving up. That will just cause the fans to think I bailed because of money."

Which is exactly what she's done. This is *all* about money. She just doesn't want it to appear that way. She never cared about saving the team.

"If the team shuts down, what will happen to everyone?"

She gives a little annoyed sigh, like she's done with my questions. "They'll find a new team. Or perhaps someone will buy the team and take it to a new city. Sometimes change requires a measure of sacrifice." She gives me a firm look. "From everyone."

If she shuts down the team, that means I'll be out of a job. Which means I have one year to turn things around and prove this team can make money. "When will this happen?"

"Nothing has been decided yet. If everything goes as planned, I won't announce it until the end of the season."

I glance at my laptop, where my community re-engagement plan waits for her approval. What does it even matter now if she's shutting down the team? It doesn't. Not unless she's willing to give the team a chance.

"I just need to know one thing. If the team *could* turn things around this year, would you reconsider?"

"You mean win? Or make money?"

"Both," I say, a little too confidently. I sound like Brax now. Maybe he has rubbed off on me in one good way.

She lets out a laugh of disbelief. "*If* that were even possible, then perhaps I would reconsider. But a winning season doesn't seem likely, even with the new players. They'll find another team, and Coach Thompson is retiring at the end of the season. As for you . . ." She looks over my pink-and-black dress in approval. "I think you'll do just fine."

The gentlemen chuckle, making my blood boil. How can they laugh when a team's future is at stake? If Brax knew this, he'd be furious.

She stands to face me, leveling her gaze. "I meant what I said about this news being top secret, or you might find yourself looking for another job. I can trust you not to say anything, right? Because if not, heads might roll." She gives me a smile so smug, I feel like I just stumbled into a mafia movie.

How is it possible I'm being blackmailed by my boss? And was that an outright threat?

I hesitate for a second, giving her a weak smile. "Of course."

I don't want to keep her secret, but I can't jeopardize my job either. Not only will I have to hide this from Sloan but also from Brax. I shudder to think how easily he can read me.

But I can't let him lose his position on the team or get sent down to the ECHL because of Alex.

The sweat on the back of my neck prickles as Alex nods at me to go. She doesn't really care about *why* I need this job. My sister's health and my grandmother's house are none of her concerns. Alex's words come roaring back in my head: *You'll do just fine.*

But it hardly means a thing if I can't save my sister and my home.

"Is that all?" I mumble, wanting to leave as quickly as possible.

Alex nods, and I beeline for the door.

As I'm about to slip away, Alex calls, "One more thing, Jaz. What is it you stopped by to tell me?"

I turn around to face her, remembering the plan I spent all day working on. It will hardly interest Alex now.

"Nothing," I mutter, returning her tight smile. "Nothing at all."

EIGHT

Jaz

When I walk into the conference room for a last-minute player meeting, I can tell something's up. The players are eyeing me skeptically, like they expect me to drop some bad news.

"What are we meeting for, boss?" Leo asks from the back, where he's leaning back in his chair.

"You'll find out soon enough," I reply with a grin as I connect my computer to the conference room's projector.

As I take my seat in the front, Brax steals the chair next to me. "You look like you've got a secret."

My stomach tilts, reminding me of Alex's secret news about shutting down the team. But Brax isn't a mind reader. There's no way he could know.

"Really?" I play dumb.

"You look happy," he notes.

Oh, good. Brax doesn't suspect bad news.

"I just came out of a meeting with Alex where she looked over my community re-engagement plan and approved it, which was a shocker." I stop myself, and Brax glances at me.

"Why is that surprising?"

"I just thought Alex would be worried about the cost. I held off telling her until this morning. When I explained the funds it could generate, she was all in."

"Smart," he says. "Do you have a plan to convince the guys?"

I glance around the room and realize that maybe Alex wasn't my biggest hurdle. These hockey players are.

"Dumb luck?" I say with a shrug.

I step to the front and decide that this is my one shot to convince the team of the value of giving back to the community. Unlike Alex, I'm not in it for the money. I want the team to become more than hockey players to the fans. I want them to see these guys' hearts.

"You might wonder why I called this meeting this morning. And the reason is that we're taking a trip this afternoon."

"A trip to where?" Tate asks, frowning.

"We're going to make somebody's day," I explain with a smile. "You might think that my job is about boring volunteer work." I glance around the room as a few of the guys nod.

"But really, community engagement is about showing our city that we care. That we're willing to help others. A team everyone looks up to."

"They'd look up to us more if we won," Leo grumbles from the back. A few guys chuckle.

"Winning helps, yes. But research shows that building a fandom is not just about winning games."

I turn on my slide presentation and flip to a line graph.

"This shows the rate of fan attendance for teams that don't volunteer in their communities. As you can see, it's flat. There's literally no attendance growth." I click to the next slide. "But when the teams participate in community initiatives, that's where the line shoots up dramatically. The more players volunteered, the more attendance grew. It didn't matter how much the teams won."

"But those statistics are from baseball teams," Tate says, studying the screen. "Not hockey."

"Yes, but the psychology of fandom is the same. Hockey fans

are some of the most avid ones out there. They love to see you play tough on the ice, but it wins them over when they recognize you *care*."

Leo raises his hand. "How are we going to fit this into our schedule? We're supposed to practice during the day."

"Most of the community events will be in the evening, and Coach Thompson has given me the green light for one afternoon event. That's today, which is why I needed to call this meeting."

A few guys are murmuring to each other. I'm sure they're not happy about this change of plans, but once they get there, I think they'll love it.

"What's our first assignment?" Lucian asks.

"An elementary school," I answer, flipping to a picture on the screen that shows Sully's Beach elementary school.

"Kids?" Dawson asks, his eyes widening. He's not the only one who looks scared.

I put my hands up. "Picture this: Big, tough hockey players, reading to wide-eyed children who hang on your every word. It's community relations *gold*."

"Sounds like babysitting," Vale says.

"The teachers will help in the classrooms. But they were thrilled with the idea. Did you know that a lot of kids don't have a male figure who reads to them? They'll idolize you. And it'll make us local heroes. Kids are easy to win over. And when children love a sport, they bring their whole families with them."

"But kids are . . . unpredictable." Brax's knee bounces under the table.

Leo smirks at him. "You scared, Brax?"

"No." He frowns at Leo.

I look around and see more than a few skeptical faces. "Trust me, it's PR magic."

"But how is this going to help with community support?" Tate asks. "It's not like these kids have money."

I shut off my computer slide show. "They may not, but their parents and grandparents might. And they are our target audience. We're going to hand out free ticket vouchers to the students and have you autograph something for the class. That might spur some attendance for our first few games. Plus, I've already lined up the newspaper to cover our visit, which will make you local heroes."

Leo raises his hand again. "Can I call in sick?"

"Not a chance, Leo," I say. "See you on the team bus this afternoon."

I dismiss the meeting, and the team shuffles to the locker room, leaving Lucian and Brax behind.

"Cool idea. I hope this works," Lucian says to me on the way out. Maybe he's trying to make me feel better about his teammates' less-than-enthusiastic reaction.

"Why wouldn't it?" I ask.

He shrugs. "Not to worry you, but Alex doesn't keep people on staff if their ideas aren't popular." He glances at Brax, who's hanging back. "I think the guys will come around . . . eventually."

I feel like he's giving me a warning about Alex, but it's not like I can work miracles. I need time and buy-in from the team, which starts with Lucian and Brax.

I turn to Brax. "I know you're not crazy about the school idea, but the kids are going to love it."

He nods unconvincingly. Something tells me he's hedging.

"Right. It's about the kids," he mutters.

"What?" I ask, tilting my head. Brax seems like the type of guy who'd be great with kids. I don't get it.

He shrugs. "I don't even know if I *like* kids," he admits with a sheepish look.

I laugh. "Then I can't wait to see you with a room full of kindergartners."

His face drains. "Wait, did you say . . . *kindergartners?*"

———

When we meet by the bus later, a palpable buzz of excitement fills the air. Everyone is waiting except Brax, who shows up late and looks as nervous as a middle schooler at his first dance.

We crowd onto the bus, and I sit in the front near Vale, while Brax takes a back seat.

"What's up with your brother?" I ask, glancing over my shoulder.

"Guys got a little rough on the ice today during practice. Took a hard slam to the wall. It doesn't help that he's nervous about this," Vale admits.

"Are you?"

Vale shrugs. "I may not know what to do with kids. But I don't let it bother me."

Unlike Vale, Brax likes to be in control. And this is something he can't control.

"But kindergartners are the least scary people in the world."

"You put him with five-year-olds?" Vale laughs. "No wonder he's scared. He has zero experience dealing with little people."

I glance back at Brax, and this time, he's holding his stomach.

"Does he always sit in the back?"

"He usually sits in the front because of motion sickness."

No wonder he looks a little green.

By the time we arrive at the school, Brax doesn't look well at all. As soon as we're off the bus, he hurries to the restroom. When he comes out, I've already paired up the guys and sent them off to their classrooms.

Brax still looks pale, but slightly better.

"Are you okay? You look—"

"I'm fine," he cuts me off. "I should know better than to sit in the back. Who's left to pair up with?" He glances over my shoulder at the list.

"No one except me," I comment. I point at an open door, where squeals of laughter spill into the hall. "Ready for this?"

Brax rubs the back of his neck. "I haven't read a children's book since I was a kid."

"Anyone can read Doctor Seuss, right?"

"Who?" he asks. "Is that an actual doctor?"

"Remember the Grinch?"

Brax squints. "I thought that was Jim Carrey?"

"Forget it. These kids will love you, no matter what. And you're going to be really awesome," I gush.

"Or really awkward." Brax shifts. "What if they don't like me? Or worse, what if they ask questions I can't answer?"

"Brax, when have you ever cared about being liked? As for questions, just be honest. Kids respect that."

"Respect from a five-year-old isn't high on my list, Jaz." He taps his thumb on his leg, a nervous habit of his I've noticed.

"Come on, think of it as a new play. You're good at adapting on the ice. Do it off the ice too." I touch his arm and try to ignore how strong it feels. Maybe it's a stupid move, given our past, but he needs a vote of confidence.

"Fine," he grumbles.

"Trust me, you might even enjoy it."

"Enjoying a firing squad of five-year-olds? Not possible. If I end up covered in glitter, you're on cleanup duty." A corner of his mouth twitches upward.

As Brax moves to the door of chaos incarnate, the scent of crayons, glue, and disinfectant fills the air. Tiny bodies dart around like pinballs, their shrill screams making it nearly impossible for us to catch the teacher's attention.

One kid stops in front of us with ketchup smeared across his shirt. "Who are you?" he asks Brax.

"I'm here to read a book. Where's your teacher?"

The boy points at a young woman who wears a slightly exasperated smile and has a short, messy bob with a streak of pink in it. She wears a white leather jacket over a Rolling Stones T-shirt and a pair of white Dr. Martens boots. On her lips is a bright red gloss. Definitely not your typical kindergarten teacher.

"That's Ms. Bennett." He runs over to his teacher and taps her on the shoulder.

Brax's eyes widen as he watches the nonstop energy. "These kids are in perpetual motion. It's like they were given a triple shot of espresso."

I laugh. "Haven't you been around kids before?"

"Not really. Vale and I were the youngest, and we didn't have any cousins close by. According to my mom, we were never still either. And there were *two* of us."

"Your poor mom." I shake my head. "They can't be a tougher crowd than the teams you play."

"At least my teammates don't bite."

I nearly snort-laugh as Ms. Bennett approaches us.

"Welcome to Little Monsters' University," she exclaims with all the enthusiasm I'd expect from someone who teaches energetic kindergartners.

I laugh. Brax gulps.

"I'm Janie Bennett." She puts out a hand to shake, and I notice a lovely floral tattoo next to her chunky leather bracelet.

"I'm Jaz, and this is Brax. He plays for the Crushers hockey team."

"Oh, really?" she gasps. "I'm not really a hockey fan, but this should be fun. Maybe I'll come to a game sometime."

I elbow Brax in the ribs, and he finally snaps out of his trance. A kid trips on the carpet and a violent wail erupts across the room. "Hockey games are kind of like kindergarten," Brax notes. "You never know when someone's going to get hurt."

"Sounds vaguely familiar," Ms. Bennett says with a smile. She claps her hands, and the room snaps to attention. "We have an exciting day, monsters! A *big* star for reading time."

Twenty-three pairs of eyes turn to Brax in admiration. Even the wailing child quiets down.

Brax clears his throat and frowns, like he's facing down an entire team on the ice.

I jab him with my elbow and whisper, "Say hello to them."

"Uh, hi?" He gives a small wave, which is met with a chorus of loud hellos and several blatant stares.

Ms. Bennett ushers the kids over to a large rug and places a chair in the middle for Brax.

"You need to stop looking so scary," I whisper.

"Believe me, I'm not trying," Brax mutters, totally oblivious to his intimidating scowl.

"Try smiling, at least?" I suggest.

Brax forces his lips into a strained smile. "Is this better?"

"Now you look like a creepy clown."

"Not helpful," he mutters between clenched teeth.

Ms. Bennett hands Brax a book called *The Knight Who Was Afraid of Dragons*, and I stifle a laugh because it sounds like Brax facing down kindergartners.

"Here goes nothing," Brax says under his breath, opening to the first page.

He's definitely nervous, and my stomach flip-flops as I fake a brave smile. *This is all my fault.* But I also know Brax has never backed down from a challenge on the ice before, and this will be no different.

I lean against a wall decorated with friendly monsters holding the alphabet.

Before Brax can begin, a girl in pigtails asks, "Are you a giant?"

"Uh, nope. Just tall," Brax answers, straight-faced.

"Can you fly?" a boy with freckles asks.

A corner of Brax's mouth tilts up. "Only across the ice when I'm going for a goal."

"You play hockey?" asks the same boy, his eyes widening.

"Yep," Brax answers. "For the Carolina Crushers."

"Are you famous?" a girl missing her front tooth asks.

"No," he says, shaking his head. "But I get to do what I love, and that's what matters."

"Have you ever fought a dragon?" the girl continues.

"Only on video games," he replies, and a few kids nod, as if this makes perfect sense.

The pigtailed girl raises her hand. "Is she your girlfriend?" She points across the room to me.

My cheeks heat as Brax hesitates. "We, uh, work together."

Another boy looks me over. "She plays hockey?"

"No, I'm terrible on the ice," I admit with a shrug.

"I didn't think you were on the team," the boy replies, then points at Brax. "He looks like he could crush you pretty easily."

My gaze flicks over to Brax, who has an amused smirk on his face.

"He probably could," I laugh.

As our eyes meet, something flickers across his face. Brax might be tough on the ice, but underneath, he's playful and kind, and I realize with a pang of disappointment that this is the guy I've missed. The one who brought me food at the reception, crowned me with a prom tiara, and danced with me in the hall.

"Read the book!" a girl pleads.

Brax breaks our staring contest and turns to the story. He flips to a brightly colored picture of a cat dressed in armor. "Once upon a time, in an enchanted forest, there was a cat named Sir Whiskers . . ."

His voice is shy and awkward, and it's such a contrast to the confident man who slams into opponents on the ice.

"Look!" A tiny finger points at the illustration. "He's like you!"

Brax turns the book to study the picture. "How so?"

"Because he's got big muscles!" the boy exclaims, and the class erupts in giggles.

"Does the knight fall in love with a princess?" the pigtailed girl asks very seriously.

"I don't know," Brax says. "I think he's more focused on fighting dragons than finding a wife."

"Like you?" she asks.

Brax smiles. "Something like that."

I bite back a laugh.

He's actually good with them.

Brax glances at the back of the room, where a boy in a wheelchair sits apart from the rest, clutching a well-loved stuffed kitten.

"Hey there, buddy," Brax says, setting the book aside and moving closer, kneeling down to his level.

"What's your name?"

"Ethan," the boy says.

"Well, Ethan, would you like to move closer so you can help me with the story?"

Ethan nods.

As Ms. Bennett clears a path toward the front, Brax pushes the wheelchair into place and then kneels by Ethan's side. "Can I borrow your cat? He can play the part of Sir Whiskers." Brax extends his hand in invitation, and the boy smiles, handing over the cat. "Now Kitty has a very important job." Brax places the cat on his lap, a makeshift prop in their unfolding tale. "He needs to watch for sneaky dragons."

"I know!" Ethan exclaims. "He could be a hockey-playing cat!"

The class giggles.

"Anything is possible in our story," Brax replies. "Who knows? He might even win over the princess." As he says it, his eyes flick to mine for a second before he turns back to the book.

A tiny hand clasps mine, yanking my gaze away from Brax.

I look down into a pair of wide eyes. "Yes, honey?"

"Is Mr. Brax a real hockey player?" the girl asks.

My gaze drifts to Brax. "What do you think?"

She taps her lips. "I think so. I bet the other hockey teams are scared of him."

I nod. "He's pretty brave on the ice."

Brax pauses in the story, and the girl loudly announces, "Your girlfriend thinks you're brave."

The kids snicker.

"Does she, now?" Brax's eyes dance.

"Yep, and my mom says women are never wrong!" the girl announces with glee.

Brax's lips curve into an amused grin as he stares at me. "Is that true?"

With his gaze directly on me, my body tingles again and the heat creeps up my neck. If I thought watching the *Brax Show* on ice was bad, this is even worse.

Observing Brax on the ice is something I can handle, but seeing him interact with kids is making me melt like chocolate left in a warm pocket.

"Maybe you should just finish the book," I suggest.

He gives me a quick flash of a grin.

For the rest of the class, Brax enchants the children with his story, answering more questions like a pro.

When he finally closes the book, the children break into applause. You'd never guess that this beast of a hockey player was nervous about facing a class of wiggly monsters.

He's a hero in their eyes. And a rock star to me.

None of this bodes well for my heart.

"Thank you, Mr. MacPherson, for coming today," Ms. Bennett says, beaming. "You were a big hit! Our little monsters would love to have you back any time!"

I raise my hand. "Can I take a few pictures of Brax with the kids—for publicity?"

"Be my guest," she says as the kids climb all over Brax, like he's a human jungle gym. He sets one kid on each shoulder and gives me a big grin.

"Say cheese!" I hold up my phone.

"Cheese!" the kids yell in unison.

As they scatter back to the tables, Brax hands Ethan his stuffed kitty. "Thanks for letting me borrow this today. Would you like a picture together to show your parents?"

Ethan's face spreads into an elated smile.

While Brax kneels next to Ethan and wraps his arms around the boy's shoulders, a funny feeling surges in my chest. It's more than attraction. It's something *deeper.*

This man is getting under my skin in the worst and best of ways.

I know Brax isn't doing this for the publicity. He doesn't care about that. He's doing this for Ethan.

What's more, I'm so proud of him, I can't hold back a stupid grin. I take at least a dozen pictures and promise to email them to Janie later.

"Mr. Brax, will you come back to read again?" Ethan asks, beaming at him.

"Of course," Brax says, returning a smile. Then he puts on his best Arnold Schwarzenegger voice and says, "I'll be back."

Ethan giggles.

I know he wouldn't make that promise unless he meant it. Even though I can't get enough of seeing Brax's softer side, I hate how gooey it makes me feel, like the soft center of a chocolate-covered caramel.

After waving goodbye and giving a dozen hugs, we finally head to the bus.

Brax leans close. "I'll be honest, I was a little doubtful about doing this. But seeing those kids—it was amazing."

"You're not just saying this to get extra brownie points, so you won't have to do our next community event?" I arch an eyebrow.

He laughs. "Not at all. I really enjoyed myself." He glances at me nervously. "Was I okay?"

I can't believe a professional hockey player needs reassurance *from me*.

"You were . . ." I leave him hanging for a beat. "Amazing."

He beams at me with a one-hundred-watt smile, and my heart feels like a water balloon about to burst.

He's handsome. *And* he's good with kids?

The perfect combination for making my heart stumble.

NINE

Brax

When I arrive home, the guys are gathered in the living room telling Sloan about their elementary school visit.

"They thought I was a superhero," Leo says. "One kid compared me to Ironman with skates."

Oh man, this is going to inflate Leo's head even more.

"You really fooled them." Tate smirks as Vale snorts.

"I am a big deal," Leo brags. "Even the teacher was into me. We might meet up after a game."

I grab a soda from the fridge and shoot Leo a look of disapproval. "Only you would hit on a teacher, *Ego.*"

"What's wrong with that, Brax?" Leo asks, propping his feet on the coffee table, making himself at home.

"Everything," I say, cracking open the lid. I roll my injured shoulder, which is still numb from the ice bath I just took.

Vale nods at me. "Looks like you survived without throwing up."

"Are you sure he didn't?" Leo jokes. "Did you cry for your mommy?"

"Shut up, Leo," I mumble, shoving him.

"Or wet your pants?" Leo snickers. I shove him harder this time, and Tate jumps between us, like he's the sheriff around here.

"He's pushing your buttons," Tate reminds me.

"Whatever," I mutter and leave the room.

As I head upstairs, Jaz follows me. "Brax, stop."

"I can't hang out with Leo tonight."

She stays a few steps away, letting me have my space. "Don't listen to Leo. You were great with the kids today."

"Thanks," I say.

Why is she being so nice? This is clearly a pity move to make me feel better. And it's not helping.

Jaz twists the ring on her finger nervously. "The guys mentioned heading out for wings. Apparently it's line-dancing night at Boots and Buckles."

I study her for a beat. She's changed into ripped jeans that show off her curves, a bright pink cropped sweater, and blue boots that make her just tall enough to kiss easily.

I can't tell if she's inviting me out of sympathy or trying to get my mind off Leo.

I rub the back of my neck. "You know I can't dance. And I don't need another reason for Leo to get on my last nerve."

"You didn't care what people thought at the wedding," she says, lifting an eyebrow.

I stop on the stairs and slowly turn to face her. Before we escaped to the storage closet that night, I was suckered into dancing with all the groomsmen. A move I still regret.

"That was different. It was a private wedding. I was with family. They've already seen how badly I dance."

"What about *our* dance?" Her eyes lock on me, and something shifts in my chest.

What kind of power does this woman have that she can turn my heart on a dime?

I shake my head. "Anyone can slow dance." Just thinking of that moment, the closeness of her skin, my hands skimming her bare shoulders—all things I shouldn't think about now.

"We don't have to dance," she says. "I doubt Tate will. Leo, on the other hand . . ."

"Leo *will* show off. It's Ego's second nature," I grumble.

She laughs, glancing over her shoulder to make sure Leo doesn't hear us. He's oblivious, still bragging about the kids who thought he was a superhero.

"I think you should join us," she says. "You guys need some bonding time. Even though you fit in at the rink, this is your chance to bond with them off the ice. Sloan and I are just tagging along for fun." She gives me a smile that feels like sunshine. Funny how one look from her cracks open my stony heart.

I should say no. I *need* to say no.

But the way she's staring at me with that curve on her rose-colored lips—I can't say no. With her, I'm a weak man.

She kicks at the floor, like she's holding back something. "Plus, I may have promised the guys I'd talk you into it."

"You said what?"

She bites her lip. "They asked me to convince you. They want you there, Brax. And I said you wouldn't bail on a team event."

I lift an eyebrow and point my finger at her. "You owe me for this."

"Fine. I *owe* you. But consider it your team duty. And I'd be disappointed if you didn't come."

———

When we arrive at Boots and Buckles for line-dancing night, the energy in the room is as boisterous as you'd expect from a crowd of people crazy about country music and buffalo chicken wings. There's random hollering from the line dancers, wailing steel guitars, and the stomp of boots as people scoot across the floor.

Worn wooden planks line the floor and saddles and wagon wheels decorate the walls. The servers wear leather aprons that look like chaps, along with fringy cowboy shirts, unbuttoned at the top. One end of the restaurant is open for dancing, and in the corner, a DJ plays every George Strait and Garth Brooks song from the last thirty years.

The scent of fried food and a zesty hot sauce lingers in the air. For the first time today, my stomach growls like a hangry toddler about to dissolve into a raging tantrum. The guys find a table in the back under a wagon wheel chandelier. When the drinks arrive in mugs shaped like cowboy boots, Jaz lifts her glass in celebration.

"Here's to a winning season," she says.

"Hear, hear," we say in unison.

We clink our glasses together, and I nearly spill my sweet tea when Leo socks my mug too hard. We order an entire chicken house of wings coated with the "Death by a Thousand Wings Sauce" and piles of fries smothered in cheese, which is probably the last thing I should eat while in training.

I'm going to pay for this later, but I'm too ravenous to care. When the wings are picked to the bone and our mouths flame from the heat, Leo glances at the dance floor and asks, "Who wants to work off that dinner with some line dancing?"

"I'm game," Tate says.

I stare at Tate in wonder. *Sheriff can dance?*

"Me too." Sloan scoots off her seat, following Tate. She shoots a look at Vale. "And you're not making fun of us in the peanut gallery."

Vale grins. "Who said I'd make fun? I'm coming with you." He throws his leather jacket on the table and joins them.

I turn to Jaz. "You want to go? I'll save your seat." She already knows how I feel about dancing, and I'm not in the mood to make a fool of myself.

"As much as I've eaten?" She pats her belly. "I should wait a few minutes."

I chuckle. "I'm glad Sloan is feeling well enough to dance."

Her eyes skirt to her sister, and she smiles. "Today was a good day for Sloan. I just wish every day was like that. She's still dealing with the migraines, dizziness and fatigue, but since you four moved in, it's like she has a new purpose. It's worth putting up with your stinky hockey gear to see her happy again."

She smiles, like a weight's been lifted from her shoulders. She wants her sister back to normal. We all do.

"And you?" I push my plate away.

She lifts a shoulder. "It doesn't matter what I think. I need to take care of Sloan and not lose the house. That's what Granny would want."

"But is that what *you* want? You never told me why you bought the house."

Jaz leans back in her seat and sighs as a twangy guitar wails across the room. "This house is my home. Granny raised us after our mom died, until my dad remarried. Dad wasn't interested in anything to do with Mom's past, and he thought Granny's house should've been sold long ago. He basically buried that part of his life with Mom. This is the only piece of family history we have from her side of the family. It's proof of the people I love. The things I don't want to forget."

I study Jaz as she tips her mug to her lips.

"Were you close to your stepmom?"

"Dad remarried a few years after Mom died. Then my stepmom raised us until we left for college. We were close until she and Dad divorced. Then she remarried and basically stopped all communication with us." She shakes her head, trying to push away the memory. "My whole family fell apart for a second time. I always thought family was forever, but here I am, in my thirties, essentially an orphan."

She gives me a sad smile, like she's trying to make light of the situation. But I see the hurt in her eyes. Just because you grow up doesn't mean you don't need your family.

I reach across the table and touch her arm. "You know my family would take you in. Mia always wanted a sister."

A corner of her mouth curves up. "That's what I was hoping for when I bought Granny's house—to hold on to a piece of my history. That's why I can't let it go, even if it's a renovation nightmare."

"You know I can help, right?" I offer.

She waves me off. "You're too busy."

"So are you. Who do you think helps my mom fix her house? Ever since Dad left, Vale and I have done most of the handyman work."

Jaz tilts her chin down and gives me a look. "I appreciate the offer, but I can't let you take on more work. Plus, I've found the sweetest retired man to help with remodeling for a very reasonable price. I'm hoping he can transform my downstairs and remodel my bedroom with some dreamy floor-to-ceiling bookshelves." She pulls out her phone and shows me some pictures she has saved of paint colors and her dream bedroom.

I lean my elbows on the table and study the navy bookshelves and built-in desk with gold accents alongside an incredible window seat. "I could do that for you. I like working on houses. Vale and I renovated my mom's kitchen this summer. It was her birthday gift from us. She bought the materials, and we provided the labor."

She gives me a quick glance, then shakes her head. "But you know things are going to change. Once you move or find a girlfriend, there goes your free time."

I frown. "I'm not looking for a girlfriend, if that's what you're trying to hint at."

"I wasn't trying to hint at anything," she says quickly. "Although I wonder why a guy like you doesn't have one. Look at you." She waves her hand toward my body.

"What?" I ask with a curious smile.

"That." She points at my shirt. "Especially when you wear shirts that show off your arms."

I glance down at my fitted T-shirt and smirk. "Ms. Summers, are you looking at my biceps?"

Her cheeks turn pink. "Just pointing out that when you're built like that, women notice."

"Some women notice. Doesn't mean I want them." I shrug. "I'm not dating because I'm not looking for just anyone."

She rubs her teeth over her lips like she's thinking about this. "Because of your hockey schedule?"

"That's part of it." It's hard when you compare everyone to her. "All I'm asking is that you let me help with the house. Stop being so stubborn. For Sloan's sake." I finish my sweet tea and wait for an answer.

Sloan is the trump card, the reason Jaz would sacrifice anything. No matter what's happened between us, this is the only way she'll let me help.

"You can help within reason," she says slowly. "But I still want to hire Joshua so it doesn't *all* fall on you. You've got games to win."

I smile. "Fair enough."

"And you have to dance tonight," she says, grabbing my hand and tugging me toward the dance floor.

I give her a look. "You know how I feel about dancing."

"Would you like me to ask Tate instead?" she asks sweetly. "How about Leo?"

"*Jaz.*" I say it like a warning, squeezing her hand harder. I don't want her dancing with Leo. Or anyone else.

"Don't think of it as dancing, Brax. Think of it as a competition. You're an athlete. Winning comes natural to you."

She still doesn't drop my hand, and it's incredibly distracting. The warmth of her palm, how soft her skin is. I'd dance with her just to have more of this.

She gives me a look of challenge. "Whoever lasts the longest wins."

I arch an eyebrow. "Are you daring me to stick it out longer than you?"

"Pretty much," she says, giving me that devil-may-care smile. "If you accept the challenge."

"What does the winner get?" I ask, not letting her hand go. It feels too good in mine.

She's walking backward toward the dance floor now, and I'm letting her string me along.

"Your choice of any chore," she says with a wicked smile. "But you have to beat me first, Mac."

"So this is why you're challenging me. You can't accept my offer of working on the house."

She raises her eyebrow. "I would feel better about letting you if I won."

"Just so you know, I don't give up easily, Princess." I level my gaze at her. "And my laundry really stinks."

"I know." Then she laughs, dropping my hand because we're on the edge of the dance floor and about to get crushed by some men in big boots.

I'm so going to lose this competition. Not because I can't outlast her. I've played hockey for years. I've learned to develop my endurance to Olympic levels.

But when it comes to her, *I'm willing to lose everything.*

As we step into a line, I focus on the moving bodies in front of me. Their feet are moving in patterns that make little sense to my brain, leaving me a step behind. Just about the time I get it, everyone turns to the left, and I'm still facing forward.

Jaz glances over at me. "To the left, Mac."

I turn just in time for the entire group to rotate back to the front again and I'm facing the wrong direction.

"Better keep up, or people are going to think you've been drinking," she says.

The group turns to the right, and one more time, I'm left behind. I mutter, "Maybe if I *did* drink, this wouldn't quite be so painful."

She smirks. "You'll catch on." She adds a fancy spin to one of the side moves.

"Showoff," I say with a smile.

A few rows over, Leo and Tate take notice of me on the dance floor, and I know I'm about to get roasted.

"Is that Big Mac on the dance floor?" Leo shrieks over the music.

I miss another turn, and he howls with laughter. "Nice one. Don't know your left from your right, do you?"

Jaz leans over to me. "Ignore him. You know it doesn't matter what they think."

I give Leo a look that's so fiery, if it were real, it would burn his eyebrows off. "Listen, if you don't shut it, you won't know *your* left from right."

The music ends, and Sloan begs the guys to stay for one more dance.

"Are you sure you're feeling okay, Sloan?" Jaz asks, looking concerned.

She has a right, given Sloan's condition, which can turn at the drop of a cowboy hat.

She tugs on Vale's arm. "Stop worrying, Jaz. Vale will catch me if I faint."

Jaz gives Vale a pointed look. "Watch out for my sister, okay?"

Vale gives her a thumbs up, and I pull Jaz back into line as the music kicks up again with a driving bass and fiddle. "Vale's as quick as me with his reflexes. Maybe quicker. Sloan's in good hands."

She seems relieved by this answer and hops back into the dance moves.

"I think you need to let go more than me," I say, glancing over at her. "You worry too much."

She shrugs. "And what do you propose I do?"

"You could start by letting people help you."

She gives me a side eye. "Says the man who wants to single-handedly turn this team around, while also fixing up my house."

"That's because I like to win," I say. "In more ways than one." I'm staying in time with the other dancers this time, and it finally feels good to cut loose.

"So do I. But you won't beat me tonight." Then she gives me a smile as hot as the Death by a Thousand Wings Sauce. I've totally forgotten Leo's taunts. Or even what I'm supposed to be doing. I'm totally caught off guard by that grin.

For the next hour we move across the floor, laughing at our missteps, bumping into each other, and very rarely nailing the routine.

Just when I think I've got the steps down, I step on her right foot, and she stumbles and falls into me. My hands grab for her waist, steadying her body, as our eyes catch. My palms fall along the curve of her waist, reminding me of the first time I danced with her. Touching her is like stumbling over a live wire.

As the crowd continues in perpetual motion, we're frozen in this moment, and I don't want to let go. My eyes drop to her mouth, and I remember what it's like to kiss her, how warm and soft her lips were against mine. In the background, a country singer croons about hopelessly falling in love. And I don't want to take my eyes off her.

That's when a body smacks into mine, knocking me into her.

Leo gives me his usual stupid smirk. "Oops. Did I hit you?"

I drop my hands and step back, quickly ending the moment.

Jaz's eyes flit around the room. "I need a drink." She hurries toward her abandoned boot mug and chugs her refill down like a woman dying in a desert.

Right now, my heart is bucking in my chest because that look between us took me right back to how things were before.

But since we're roomies now, the playing field has changed. What are we doing, pretending like we could be something again?

She returns to the dance floor, avoiding my gaze.

"Done yet?" I ask.

"And let you win? No way." Her mouth curves into a smile as she brushes past me. She has that look on her face—the determined one that says she won't back down. I'm tempted to kiss that look right off her pretty little mouth.

The song changes abruptly, switching to a ballad with a crying guitar and a deep bass voice crooning about lost love.

A few people wander off for a break as the rest pair up for slow dance heaven.

I freeze, suddenly unsure what to do.

She glances back at our table, like she's weighing her options. Slow dance with me. Or lose the dare.

Jaz's gaze lands on me with a question in her eyes. *Is this a bad idea?*

"I thought you said you're playing to win?" I say, trying to keep things light.

"Are you?" She tilts her head and studies me, like it's more than just a question of whether I'll dance with her.

I lift an eyebrow. "What do you think, Princess?"

I hold out my hand. It's an invitation. A take-it-or-leave-it offer.

Dance with me.

She hesitates before slipping her palm into mine. When she slides her body close, all the old feelings come back. The way she feels in my arms. Her incredible scent. How everything about this woman feels right.

We're inches apart now, our bodies nearly touching, but I still keep some space between us.

I want it to be her choice. Her move. After what I did to her, I'm not sure she'll ever accept me back. I'm no Prince Charming. I play the roughest sport around, one that encourages fighting to win.

What kind of man would I be to her?

I know I'd try to be the man she deserves.

Her dark eyes swirl in the light. Memories flood back—the night of the wedding reception, when we last danced slowly to Taylor Swift's "Lover" and it ended with a kiss.

The light touch of her breath brushes my neck, and her sweet floral scent clouds all logical thought.

Right now, she's everything that's right in my world.

As I close my eyes and rest my cheek against her hair, I wish I could stop time, bottle this, and pull it out every time I want her close to me.

But I know it's wishful thinking to believe it could ever happen again.

A future with me isn't the kind she deserves. I travel too much. I get moved around between teams. Life would be transient and unpredictable as a hockey wife. She deserves someone who could be there for her every day. Not just when the season is over.

I didn't call her back after the reception because I knew it was better this way. There are reasons she doesn't know about—things I kept from her to protect her.

But now I'm not so sure.

The song finally ends, and she glances up at me, uncertainty in her eyes, before her gaze falls to my lips.

I know that look. The same one I saw in her eyes the first time I kissed her.

But this time, I need to make a different choice. Even if it kills me inside.

I reluctantly step away from her. "You win," I whisper, before leaving the dance floor.

TEN

Jaz

I thought I knew what I was doing—that we could be roommates and work for the same team without getting involved romantically.

Then I made a rookie mistake. I let him hold me again. Everything in me collapsed like a house of straw.

He's not looking for a girlfriend. He made that clear when he ghosted me before.

But I hoped things could be different. When he walked away from me on the dance floor, I knew I'd be a fool to risk my heart again.

Despite his busy schedule, he's kept his promise to work on the house. And he wasn't lying when he said he was handy.

In the last week, he's fixed broken tile in the bathroom, a leaky showerhead, and a few loose boards in the front porch railing. But I can't rely on Brax forever. At some point, he's going to move out and move on, and I'll be stuck with the repairs myself.

Thank goodness Granny left a very detailed list of people who'd worked on this home over the years. Most of them are gone, but Joshua is one of the few who actually answered when I called.

Tate peeks behind the living room blind. "Jaz, Orville Reddenbacher is waiting outside for you."

I walk to the front hall while putting on my earrings. "His name is Joshua, and you're going to be seeing a lot of him. Please be nice." I shoot a look at Vale and Leo, who are both eating cereal. "And no growling!"

The old man who stands on the other side of my door has a weathered face beneath his John Deere cap. He wears a pair of worn overalls and carries a small metal box that I assume contains his tools. While most men his age are enjoying retirement, Joshua stays busy with his remodeling projects.

"Joshua, please come in," I say, waving him inside.

He gives me a warm smile as he steps into the foyer. When he looks around, his eyes get a faraway look in them. "I'd forgotten how beautiful this house is. Your granny always kept everything neat as a pin."

I tilt my head. "Well, I have four hockey players living here, so *neat* might be a different standard now." I scoot a pair of sneakers behind the door with my foot, trying to hide them from view. "As far as projects, I want to start on the first floor with fresh paint, tear down the wall between the kitchen and dining room and remodel my bedroom with bookshelves, a window seat and a built-in desk. I just don't know if I can afford it all."

Joshua gives me a grin. "Just like your granny. Always had plans bigger than her pocketbook. But she made this place something pretty over time, just like you will."

Brax comes down the steps, dressed in joggers and a sweatshirt, and takes a second glance at our guest.

I step toward him. "Brax, I want you to meet Joshua."

"It's a pleasure," Brax says, shaking his hand. "I'm so glad you can help Jaz."

Joshua grins. "I enjoy tinkering with my tools." Then he turns to me. "Can you show me your bedroom? I'd like to take measurements today."

I show Joshua to my room and he studies the space for a beat.

"You know, I think this wall would be perfect for the window seat." He points to a sunny window facing the bird feeders Granny always kept by the magnolia tree. "A built-in desk would be perfect on the other wall with the view of the rose garden."

I clap my hands together. "Oh, Joshua, now you're speaking my language. That would be so much better than the windowless closet I currently have at work."

Joshua looks at me, puzzled.

"Never mind." I shake my head, knowing there's zero chance Alex would ever let me work from home. But it will be perfect for my custom jersey side hustle. "Should I give you a down payment so you can get started?"

Joshua shakes his head. "Your grandmother was always trust-worthy, so I won't charge you until the room is complete."

His answer is a tremendous relief, considering my bank account can't afford another hit. But I'm determined to pay Joshua what he's worth, even if I'm not exactly sure how it's going to happen after Sloan's bills deplete most of our savings.

Brax stands in the doorway, looking in. "Bookshelves and a window seat, huh?"

"I know they're impractical," I argue. "But it's way more fun to start with a dream project instead of something boring."

Brax shoves his hands in his pockets. "I agree."

"You do?" I say, hiding my surprise. "I thought you might try to talk me out of them." Brax slumps against the doorframe, enjoying watching Joshua at work.

"If they make you happy, go for it," Brax says, before turning to leave.

A small grin spreads across Joshua's face. "He seems pleasant. Hope you don't mind me asking, but are you . . .?"

"Oh, no." I shake my head. "Definitely not."

Joshua stretches the measuring tape across the wall. "He just seemed unusually interested in your . . ." Then he looks over his shoulder at me. "Happiness."

"We're just friends," I answer too quickly. Why can't friends be interested in what makes the other person happy?

Joshua nods. "Of course. I don't know why I assumed anything more."

I leave Joshua to his measuring and head to the bathroom to finish getting ready for work. I let out a frustrated sigh as I pick up a gold necklace I left by the sink.

"You need me to do anything today?" Sloan asks, peeking her head around the door.

"Your job is to take it easy," I say as I sweep the gold chain around my neck. "Doctor's orders."

She looks me over. "What's the occasion? You're dressed casually today."

"Team-building exercises. We were supposed to go to a retirement home, but they had to cancel, so Coach planned a fun team-building event instead and asked me to be in charge."

"Have fun today," Sloan says, sitting on the edge of the tub and resting her elbows on her knees. "And I mean that. I'd give anything to be you."

The melancholy in her voice shakes me. I sink down next to her, wrapping one arm around her shoulders. "Someday it *will* be you. You'll get better, and you'll go back to being the best college figure skating coach in South Carolina."

She rests her head on my shoulder as I squeeze her tightly. "Love you, Jazzy."

"You too, sis." I grab my lip gloss and tuck it in my pocket before I notice Sloan looking at me funny.

"Is there something else?"

"I wasn't sure I should tell you," she says slowly. "I heard Vale talking with Brax the other night, and your name came up."

I slowly turn to her. "What about me?"

She bites her lip. "Brax admitted that not contacting you after the wedding was one of his biggest regrets."

I frown. "Are you sure you heard him right?"

She nods slowly. "I thought you should know. In case . . ." She stops, but I know what she's trying to say.

"He still feels that way?" I tuck a wisp behind my ear. "He made it clear there's not a chance." I turn away, hoping my face doesn't betray me. If there *was* a chance, I wouldn't give up so easily.

"Jaz, have you asked him about what happened?"

"I don't have to ask, because I already know the answer." I can't bring myself to talk about what happened the night we went line dancing when he just walked away from me. I thought I saw something in his eyes. But then he just left me standing there. *Was I the only one feeling that tension between us?*

"But he might feel differently now," she says. "You don't know what was happening in his life back then. He might have reasons for why he didn't call you after the wedding."

"Sloan . . ." I rub my forehead, wanting these feelings for Brax to go away. "I wish it were that easy, or that I could snap my fingers and make my problems magically disappear. But that's not the way life works. Brax becoming my accidental roommate has made my life more complicated. But it doesn't mean that things have changed between us. As soon as they move out, it will be easier."

She bites her lip. "That's the other thing. Tate told me there's still a shortage of rentals. It might be months before they move."

"Months?" I stare at her. That means there's no chance I'm getting away from Brax soon.

Every time I see him, it's like he's a black hole and I'm space junk. He's got a gravitational pull I can't resist. And the problem is, I'd gladly get sucked into his vortex and never come out again.

Which means I need to be more strict about rules around here.

No flirting. No dancing. And *definitely* no touching.

Because if he touches me again, I might not control what happens next.

Jaz

When the team piles off the bus for our team-building activity, Dawson glances at the woods behind me.

"Are we going hiking?" he says, crinkling his nose. It's obvious he's not excited about spending time in nature.

"Not hiking," I say, glancing at the treetops. "Something better."

"Unless there's a party back here, I can think of more fun things to do," Leo grumbles from behind me.

"No party, I'm afraid." I toss him a look over my shoulder. "Just fun in the wild. Do you enjoy throwing yourself off high places?"

"You're kidding," Leo drawls.

"Wait. Are we zip-lining?" Tate asks, his eyes widening. "Doesn't that go against our contract?"

"There's nothing in your contract, Sheriff," Vale says with a pleased grin. Vale's a natural risk taker, so he's all in for danger.

"Is anyone scared of heights?"

I glance around to see if anyone looks afraid. Even Brax looks pleased with the idea of strapping himself to a line and throwing himself off a platform.

That means I'm the only one who hates this idea. At least I can use my administrative duties as an excuse not to go.

I glance at my clipboard. "We're going to check in and then pair up. Coach Thompson asked me to draw names so you won't team up with people you already know."

For the next few minutes, I randomly select names from an envelope, writing each pair down as the group straps on helmets.

"Vale and Tate, Dawson and Lucian . . ." I finally reach the end. "And Brax is with . . ."

I feel inside the envelope. It's empty.

"Who is Big Mac with?" Vale asks, standing next to his twin.

"There are no names left." I scan the group, trying to figure out what to do about this inconvenient problem.

"Except you," Vale notes with a gleam in his eyes.

A rock settles in my gut. *There's no way I'm going with him.* "I thought I'd stay back in case Alex calls."

"Oh, no, you don't," Leo taunts, pulling me toward the helmets. "You're not getting out of this."

Tate agrees with a nod. "If I have to go, *you* have to go. It's only fair."

"Okay, Mr. Fairness Police," I huff, a jolt of worry snaking down my spine. I've never been on a zip line. The thought of plunging to my death has always been enough to scare me away.

"You don't have to pair up with me," I tell Brax, glancing down at my list, my cheeks burning like flaming torches. I don't want Brax to see me freak out up there. And he'd probably rather go with someone else.

"Do you have a partner?" he asks slowly.

"I can go by myself. It's okay. Really," I stammer.

"Why would you go by yourself?" he asks, frowning. "That's not safe."

"Why are you going all law and order on me?" I ask, irritated that the more I push him away, the more he clings to me like Velcro. "Are you turning into Tate now?"

"I'm more like Sheriff than Vale and Leo are. Rules are created for a reason," he concludes, putting his hands on his hips like he's playing good cop. "Is it a crime to be worried about you?"

He's right, and I hate it. The zip-line course agreed to stay open for us as long as we went in pairs. There are zip-line guides on the platforms, but they're mostly watching to make sure we follow the safety procedures.

I play with my pen, trying to think of a way out. "You don't want to go with me. I'll hold you back."

"You won't hold me back," he argues, moving closer to me. "I want to help you, but you have to let me first. Stop fighting me."

This guy is good. Every excuse I make, he volleys right back to me, like a never-ending game of ping-pong.

I tilt my chin up to meet his gaze. "Trust me, I *will* hold you back. Before this is over, you'll get frustrated and probably push me off the platform."

He smirks. "Nice try, Jazzy." Grabbing a helmet, he squashes it over my hair. "Strap your helmet on, partner. You're stuck with me."

Then he saunters off with the most aggravating grin.

That man is going to be the death of me.

As my shoes crunch on the gravel path, I wonder if there's still time to sprain my ankle, so I don't have to do this.

"You coming?" he asks, glancing over his shoulder, showing no mercy for me.

Brax is a few steps ahead of me, his massive strides forcing me to jog to keep up with him.

"Why are you walking so fast?" I pant, already out of breath. "It's not a race. And we're the last in line."

He shoots me a challenge over his shoulder. "Thought you could keep up."

Maybe it's better that he walks in front of me, then we don't have to talk to each other.

He scouts the first stop, a towering wooden structure with a platform that looks like walking the plank on a pirate ship.

"You ready to fly?" He flashes a boyish grin that sends my

heart cartwheeling. Maybe it's my nerves. Or because he's way too cocky about this. At this point, I can't tell the difference. I'm wound as tightly as a spring-loaded jack-in-the-box.

"Absolutely," I squeak as my heart thunders in my chest.

Brax looks at me a second longer. "I'll go first." He starts up the metal staircase that seems to touch the sky.

I swallow down the lump in my throat and force my feet forward, willing myself not to look down.

Brax races to the top with superhuman speed, not even bothering to use the rail. Then he glances down at me. "You planning on zip-lining next year?"

I scowl at him. "You can go without me," I utter as my hands sweat. "Just remember that I warned you."

"I'll wait," he says, looking over the top of the railing.

If I can't even climb to the platform without lead feet, how in the world am I going to hurl myself off of it?

Do people enjoy seeing their life flash before their eyes?

My stomach churns as I push the thought away. I won't let Brax see me afraid. I'll just force myself to step off the platform even if I throw up my lunch.

When I finally stumble to the top, out of breath and completely frazzled, Brax is lazily leaning against the railing, shoulders relaxed, like he's posing for a Patagonia magazine spread. To my aggravation, he's completely at home up here.

"The view from here is amazing," he says, glancing over the treetops. I force myself to tear my eyes away and look just beyond him. The land spreads out below us like a forest blanket, taking my breath away. The trees are a mixture of mossy greens, and small clumps of gold and red bushes punctuate the landscape. Even though I'm fighting a dizzying sense of vertigo as I peer over the edge, the view is stunning.

Suddenly, his hand lands on my arm, and I let out a strangled squeak. "What are you trying to do?" I shriek while shrinking away from him. "Push me over so I plunge toward my death?"

"No. Why would I do that?" he shoots back, holding up his

hands in innocence. "I was trying to help. You've gone all pale, and I thought you were scared. Are you okay?" His concern cuts through my mounting panic.

"Scared?" A shrill laugh escapes my lips. "I laugh in the face of danger, Brax MacPherson." My laugh turns into a cough, and I double over, feeling like I'm going to be sick. If I don't get myself under control, this is going to turn into a full-on panic attack.

I can't have Brax witness that.

"Right," Brax says, frowning at me. "Because you look about as comfortable as a cat in a bathtub." He arches an eyebrow.

"Fine." I straighten, trying to gain my composure, before I fold my arms defensively. "I haven't exactly been honest."

"About?" He waits for an answer.

I clear my throat. "Heights aren't my favorite thing. I'd rather strap myself to a railroad track."

"So you're saying . . ." He studies me carefully. "You've never been zip-lining before because of heights?"

I lift a shoulder in resignation. "Too afraid."

He frowns. "So you agreed to this event and weren't planning on going?"

"Maybe?" I squeak.

Brax gives me a look.

I shrug. "Okay, yes. I was always planning on bailing. I didn't want to let Coach Thompson or you guys down. After all, I'm the one who made you go to the elementary school. It only seemed fair. Except that I have this wee little problem." If I tell him, he'll only think less of me. Especially since he's the one who overcame his fear for me.

"Finish the sentence, Jaz. What is your wee little problem? Or is that a bathroom joke?"

"Not a bathroom joke. Although that would have been funnier." I kick at a leaf on the platform. It drops off the edge and floats to the ground, fluttering like paper. "This is embarrassing." I pull a wisp of hair behind my ear and start slowly. "I some-times . . . have these attacks. Heights seem to trigger it."

His forehead crinkles in concern. "Attacks? Like panic?"

I play with Granny's ring, then nod.

"Why didn't you tell me?" he asks, the lines deepening. "I could have left you behind."

"I tried, but you wouldn't let me. And I'm the one who made you read to elementary students. I felt like I had something to prove."

He reaches for my arm, and the warmth of his palm spreads through me. "You never have to prove anything with me," he says, his tone softer. "We can always head back."

"No," I cut him off. "I'm not backing out. The other guys expect me to finish. I just need a minute to . . ." I peer over the edge, and my stomach hollows out. "Acclimate."

Or lose my lunch. Could go either way.

"Take all the time you need," Brax reassures me, stepping back to give me space.

I take in a deep breath, the smell of composting leaves and rotting wood heavy in the air. The breeze hits the sweat prickling on my neck.

I need to do this. Not just for the team, but for myself. I have to prove that I fit in here too, the same way Brax has. Just like college sororities have rush weeks where recruits have to prove they're worthy, this one is mine.

"Okay," I murmur, my stomach still churning. "Let's do this before I chicken out."

I peer up at the steel cables disappearing into a canopy of green.

The zip-line guide steps toward us, and Brax holds up a hand. "I've got this." Then he turns toward me. "I'm going to take care of you up here. You know that, right?" He holds my gaze. "We will get through this *together*."

I glance over at him and give a weak nod.

"Ever heard the zip-line mantra?" Brax asks, tilting his head with a glint in his eyes.

"Don't die?" I offer.

"Close." He grins. *"Don't think. Just close your eyes . . . and jump."*

"That sounds like what people who jump off bridges say."

He chuckles. "This is safer. And I'm here to help you." He holds up a harness that looks like a complicated medieval torture device. "As long as you're attached to that wire, you're totally safe."

I give him a doubtful grimace. "Do the wires ever snap?"

"Humans are way too light." Brax holds the harness for me as I slip my legs through the loops, then he pulls the straps snug around my waist. His hand grazes my side, gentle but precise, and a strange fluttering brushes my stomach, like butterfly wings.

It's a welcome relief from the nausea I was feeling a minute ago.

"Let me check your helmet," he commands.

"I buckled it."

He arches an eyebrow. "It's crooked. Let me fix it."

I step closer to him and let him adjust it, even though it means he's near enough to brush his fingers against my jaw where the buckle is, then along the side of my face. His eyes are focused on the helmet as he tightens the strap, while I try to avoid staring at him. It's nearly impossible to keep my eyes off him, and they keep flicking back to his face, taking in the mossy green of his eyes, the scar above his eyebrow, the dark stubble of his jaw.

He gives a final tug to my helmet strap and his eyes meet mine. "Wouldn't want this pretty head to get hurt," he says with a smirk.

"Thanks," I squeak, feeling my heart do that weird bouncing in my chest whenever he's close. There are too many triggers up here. He's touching me, making sure I'm safe. Then he calls me *pretty*.

"Don't take another step," he commands, pointing at my feet. "Your shoe's untied."

"Rookie mistake," I say, trying to kneel. But my hands are shaking, and the harness is so tight, it's almost impossible.

"Let me," he offers, beating me to it.

"Brax, I can do it," I insist. Why is he being so nice?

"Don't argue with me, Princess." He kneels, then pats his knee for me to lift my foot onto his leg, and I dutifully obey. "When I said I was going to take care of you, I meant it."

This man who's a beast on the ice is tying my shoes. And he's doing it so carefully, like I'm his only concern in the world.

There goes my heart, right off the edge of this platform.

As he double-knots my shoe, he pats my foot before gingerly placing it on the ground like I'm Cinderella in a glass slipper.

"You look ready," he says with approval.

"One question, though." I tap my helmet. "Does this make my head look big?"

"I like big heads and I cannot lie," Brax deadpans.

I laugh, and it breaks the tension, making me feel a little braver about hurling myself off this platform. The rest of the group is so far ahead of us now, I can't even hear their hollers.

"Let's do this before I change my mind," I declare with a mix of terror and excitement.

He puts on his harness, tightening the straps. "Remember the mantra. Don't think. Just close your eyes . . ."

"And jump," I finish.

He hooks me to the wire before securing his own, and the zip-line guide gives us a thumbs up to proceed. "We'll go at the same time, so you won't feel so alone." He points to the double wire so we can zip-line in tandem, one of the unique features of this course.

"You want to witness the look of sheer terror on my face as I careen toward my death?" I say, only half teasing.

"Maybe I can take a picture of it and put it on the team social media account. Just like those roller-coaster pictures."

I smack his arm. "If you dare, I'll push you off this platform myself." I give him my dagger eyes.

"You're going to shove me off after helping you?"

"Maybe. But you're nice to have around. *Sometimes.*"

"Sometimes, huh?" He smirks.

"Don't get a big head about it, okay?"

He points at his helmet with a cheesy grin. "Already have."

I moan at his bad joke.

"Now, just hold still." He grabs my hand. A shiver runs through my body as his palm holds mine, like an unspoken promise that he won't let me fall. "I'll walk you to the edge."

Warmth surges through me at how patient he's being. He's not making fun of me the way the other guys might have.

"It's just like stepping off the curb," he explains. "Except, you know, with more flying."

"Curbs don't require participants to sign a safety waiver," I remind him, my heart racing with each step.

"First jump is always the hardest."

"Is that an official zip-line proverb?" I ask, my palms clammy.

"Trademark pending," he says, trying to keep the mood light.

I drop my hand and clutch the handle. Swallowing hard, I edge closer to the end of the platform, my heart thundering against my ribs. Then I make the mistake of looking down. The earth spins as my body wobbles, and I imagine falling to my death right here.

My chest tightens, like someone's wrapped me in steel cords. I gulp for air.

"Brax," I say in a strangled panic. "I can't breathe."

"Look at me," he commands gently.

I shake my head. "I can't." I squeeze my eyes shut. "I feel like I'm about to die." My breathing is shallow, like I'm being pressed under slabs of concrete.

"If you were about to die, you wouldn't be answering me," he reminds me.

True. But who says panic is ever logical?

"Jaz, look at me," he pleads again, more softly this time. "I promise you will not die."

"How do you know?" I say, my eyes squeezed shut, the fear threatening to overtake me.

"Because I won't let you," he says, softer still. "Reach for my hand."

I shake my head. "Too afraid to open my eyes."

"Then put your hand out, and I'll find it."

I obey, slowly wrenching one hand from the line, panic blasting through me like a wrecking ball.

I'm such a baby. But Brax doesn't say a word.

"Now, hold it out," Brax encourages.

I stretch my fingers wider, reaching into the void.

Fingers brush against mine, causing me to flinch.

"It's just me," he whispers, and I try again, stretching my fingers a little farther. His hand finds mine, and I tighten my fingers around it, like I'm drowning and he's a lifeboat.

If I'm squeezing hard enough to make nail imprints in his flesh, he doesn't respond. He just calmly says, "I'm going to hold your hand the whole way. I won't let go until we reach the other platform. And nothing will happen to you. I'll make sure of it."

My eyes are still closed, and I'm pretty sure I'm cutting off the circulation in his fingers. "Do you swear?"

"Only when I hit my thumb with a hammer," he answers.

I crack a smile. "You're infuriating."

"I solemnly *swear* to protect you with my life. Is that enough?" I don't have to look at him to know he's watching me, trying to use humor to get me to relax.

My heart slows, and the tightness of my chest recedes.

He uses our linked hands to push a stray wisp from my face, but he never lets go. "I promise, Jaz. Trust the gear. Trust me," he adds, softer still.

I exhale. "If we fall, we fall together."

"There's no one I'd rather fall with," he answers, a smirk in his tone.

"Are you saying you want us to die together?"

He chuckles. "Of course not. I'm saying that falling together is so much better than doing it alone."

I get the feeling that we're not talking about falling off the wire anymore. This is about something I'm not ready to discuss right now, even if I am taking my last breath.

"Remember the mantra." I can hear the smile in his voice that flows through me like a drug, relaxing every nerve in my body. "Don't think. Close your eyes . . ."

"And jump, I *know*. Let's get this over with," I urge.

"On the count of three," Brax instructs. "One, two . . ."

"Three." I rush the countdown and step off the platform before Brax.

For a second, his hand slips, and I plunge downward for a split second before the wire catches. But he's lightning fast, securing my fingers at the last second. My stomach leaps into my throat as the wind smacks my face, leaving me breathless.

"Look at you!" Brax sounds as exhilarated as I feel flying.

When I realize I haven't plummeted to my doom, my eyes flutter open. I watch as treetops fly past me. My heart hammers in my ears as I let out a whelp that sounds like a caged animal set free.

"Get ready for the landing," Brax calls as we approach the next platform. I brace for impact and land less than gracefully in a half stumble, half fall. But Brax has my hand the whole time, steadying me as my legs wobble.

He was right. He never let go.

He unclips our harnesses before scooping me into his arms. "You did it!" Brax wraps his arms around me, lifting me off the ground in a total-body hug that feels like he could smother me with one enthusiastic squeeze.

"Brax. Breath. Please!" I squeak.

"Oh, sorry," he says, putting me down gently. The giant of a man forgets his own strength. "Did you hit anything when you landed?"

"Feet are intact. Dignity . . . mostly so," I add, trying to steady my breathing. His hug knocked what little breath I had out of me. Not just because he's strong, but because it's *him*.

"*Mostly* is good enough for me." He gives me a wide grin.

"You surprised me. I didn't think I was going to get you off the platform, and then you stepped off before I counted to three."

I give him a playful smirk. "I was testing your reflexes."

"I bolted off that platform like you were a loose puck in overtime."

I wasn't trying to make him work so hard to keep his promise. But something about his confession makes me unreasonably happy.

"Thank you for keeping your promise," I say softly.

He holds my gaze. "Always."

His eyes stay locked on mine long enough that I look away first, glancing back at the chasm we've just crossed.

"Ready for the next one?" Brax's hand hovers near my back, almost touching me. Maybe he's afraid I'll do something stupid, like step off again before remembering to clip my harness on.

I nod. "You were right. The first one is the hardest," I admit with a satisfied grin as he clips me onto the next line.

The fear is still there, like a dull ache in my chest, but so is Brax. His confidence, his humor, his unwavering support.

He glances over, holding out his hand, a smile curving on one side of his lips. "This time, could you warn me if you're going to jump early?"

"Shut up and push me," I tease as I grab his hand again. We both step off together, my laugh catching on the wind as I soar through green canopies, the gentle hum of the line accompanying us.

I've let him see a part of me that nobody else gets access to— the fear I've stuffed down for so long. I've always held myself up as a survivor. I lost my mom young. When my parents divorced, I lost them again, in a different way. My dad chose to move away and cut off contact with Sloan and me. I suspect it's because we remind him too much of Mom, and that, in its own way, is painful. My stepmom chose her new family after remarrying.

Where does that leave me?

Like many things in life, the choices we make out of fear and hurt have repercussions that last for years.

Instead of facing their demons, they ran away for reasons I'll never understand.

But I'm not like them. I'm a survivor. And survivors face their fears.

Brax looks over at me and smiles.

My heart lands in my throat, and I'm almost choking on this happiness.

"You're practically flying." Brax's voice cuts through the rush of air.

"Or falling with style," I say, my voice steadier than my body as I land on the next platform. It's a sound I don't recognize, lighter, freer.

He puts his hand on my back, steadying my legs.

My heart bolts, not from fear, but from something much more potent. *Him.*

"Feeling braver?" he asks, trying to measure whether the panic attack is gone and he can let go of my hand.

But I like the feel of my hand in his, the security of feeling like if I fall, he'll catch me.

I want us both to fall, to do this together.

There's only one thing that keeps me stuck, like my feet are planted in wet concrete.

The fact that he's still holding back. Still keeping a part of himself from me. Especially since I revealed my fear to him.

Secrets are the one thing I can't tolerate. So why won't he tell me what's underneath his hesitation?

TWELVE

Jaz

We fly past the Carolina forests, the swampy marshes, the distant smell of salt sharp on my tongue. I unclip my harness and study the view. The forest below us ends abruptly, and the chasm ahead opens to a body of water.

"You okay with water?" Brax asks, his gaze tracing the cable that disappears into nothing across the lake, and a shiver runs down my spine.

"More time to enjoy the view," I say with fake confidence, my stomach squeezing. Even though Brax has patiently helped me through every zip line today, I feel like I have something to prove. I'm braver than the girl he witnessed on the first platform.

"It's the last one," he says quietly.

A note in his voice hints that he's not ready for it to be over.

I feel it, too. Things are different up here.

I know when my feet hit earth, everything will change.

Survivors gonna survive. That's what I've always done. I claw my way out of every dark hole.

"I think I'm ready to do this one by myself," I say, clipping myself to the line.

"Okay. Sure," Brax murmurs with disappointment in his voice. "Do you still want me to go at the same time?"

"Thanks, but I'm good," I say with more confidence than I feel.

Brax's jaw clenches. He's wrestling with stopping me, but he knows I'll just fight him on it.

"Be my guest," he finally replies. "I'll follow you."

The zip-line guide gives me a nod of approval before I take a steadying breath and push off, my palms slick as I grasp the harness. The forest blurs past in a dizzying kaleidoscope of green as I whiz along the cable. Then I'm over the water, like a human cannonball, feeling so alive, and simultaneously missing the feel of his hand in mine.

"It's for the best," I repeat to myself, the wind knocking my breath out of me.

Suddenly, I slow down, my body shuddering to a halt, suspended mid-air over the water like Tom Cruise in *Mission Impossible*.

I jerk myself forward, but it doesn't help. Below, the lake is a silver ribbon, indifferent to my predicament.

"Brax!" I call, waving with both arms to stop him before he races past me and I'm left dangling over the middle of the lake.

"Don't panic!" Brax calls from the platform. "Just hang tight! I'll be right there."

"Easy for you to say," I mutter, trying to suppress the mounting panic. I'm stuck with nothing to do but dangle and wait.

Brax lets loose across the line with practiced ease, which is both infuriating as it is reassuring.

"Typical," I mutter to myself. "My knight in shining armor has to rescue me. *Again*."

He slows to a stop next to me. "What are you doing hanging out here?" he asks with a grin.

"Haha," I say, not in the mood for humor. My plan to do this last zip line solo has been foiled. Not only have I messed up our last run; I've messed up Brax's too.

"Let's get you unstuck," Brax says, studying the line above.

"Please," I breathe, the panic slowly simmering beneath the surface. It's still in check, but that could change at a moment's notice.

"Can you reach the pulley?" he asks.

"Trying," I reply, stretching out my arm, my fingers grazing the cool metal.

"Push it forward gently," Brax instructs, his tone calm and steady.

"Like this?" I nudge the contraption forward, feeling it give slightly.

It's amazing how this man can problem-solve while dangling over a body of water, like a real-life MacGyver.

"Perfect. Now, pull back slowly." His hand is on my back, making me feel safer, even as the breeze whips against my body.

"Back slowly," I repeat, following his directions. I inch forward.

"See? You've got this," Brax encourages, then pauses. "You want to finish the rest yourself?"

Whatever hope I'd had of proving something to Brax—of doing this alone—has been erased now. If I get stuck again, what if he can't rescue me a second time?

"Do you mind going with me?" I ask. "In case I get stuck again?"

"Anytime, Jaz." He gives me that crooked smirk that makes me feel safe.

Then he reaches for my hand, and with one last tug, we cross the lake and reach the safety of the other side.

As I unclip for the last time, the rush of relief flows through me as Brax's touch lingers on my back.

I let out a breath, anchored by Brax's hand still guarding me.

"Hey," Brax says softly. "You just flew. How's that for a Thursday?"

"Flying is one way to put it." I turn to face him. The flecks of green in his eyes, like the forest treetops, are brighter and mixed with a hint of goldenrod.

"I thought for a minute you were going to have a panic attack over that lake, and I was going to have to pull you across."

I laugh. "I was afraid of that, but once you had me focus on what to do, it was like the panic faded. That's all I needed. Something to focus on." *Even if that something is you.*

He's the safety net I never knew I needed.

My one sure thing.

Right now the only thing I can focus on is him—the ripple of dark in his eyes, the way his hand lingers on the small of my back sending fizzy bubbles up the column of my spine. The world shrinks to just the two of us on that platform. The electric charge from standing so close is dancing along my nerves, igniting sparks wherever Brax's fingers graze my skin.

His eyes drop to my harness.

"Let's get you unhooked," he says, his hands moving to assist me with the gear. His fingers brush against my waist, sliding under the straps to release them. Every touch is deliberate, like he's afraid of touching me, of getting *too* close.

"Careful," I tease. "You're getting awfully handsy with my harness there."

"Professional hazard," Brax shoots back, his grin disarming. "You can file a complaint with the management later."

"I *am* the management."

Brax laughs, and it's so full of life, like a bucket of cold water dumped over my head on a sultry day. Then he peels off my helmet and the harness with so much tenderness I didn't know could exist in a man this strong.

He could break me if he wanted. Or he could catch me if I fell.

I have to accept either outcome. That's the risk of love.

"Ready to go?" he asks, still smiling at me.

I nod. While we move to the stairs, I can't shake the feeling that we're also stepping into something new. And maybe that's the biggest leap of all.

"Brax," I begin. He stops and waits for me as I reach the

bottom of the stairs and my feet finally touch the ground. "I can't thank you enough. For . . . everything." I gesture vaguely upwards, toward the lines we conquered.

"Hey, it was nothing," he replies, the corner of his mouth lifting in that endearing smile that makes tiny fireworks explode in my chest.

"Nothing?" I arch an eyebrow. "For someone who considers herself reasonably brave, dangling from a wire a hundred feet above certain death felt a lot like *something*."

"Okay," he says. "It was *something*. Best team-building event ever," he declares.

"Couldn't have done it without my partner in crime," I respond, playfully bumping his shoulder.

"Partners in crime, huh?" He tilts his head toward me. "Sounds like we make an unstoppable team." Something sparks in his eyes as he steps forward and wraps his arms around me, pulling me in for a hug.

My pulse skips, and this time, I know it's not from the zip-lining.

As I sink into his chest, a voice startles us from behind. "What are you doing?"

I wheel around just as Alex steps out from the shadows.

From the look on her face, she is *not* happy.

THIRTEEN

Jaz

"Alex!" I squeak, pushing Brax away hard enough that he *almost* loses his balance. Since he's built like a brick wall and is used to guys shoving him *hard*, he barely teeters.

"We were just finishing," I say breathlessly, which is more from her catching me hugging Brax than the actual zip-lining. "What are you doing here?"

"I wanted to give you some news." She crosses her arms and I get the distinct impression that she does not approve. "Everyone else is on the bus."

As Brax and I start toward the exit, Alex waves me over. "One moment, Jaz."

Brax stops to look at me, concern etched into his face, and I give him a faint smile, letting him know I'll be okay.

She waits until Brax is out of earshot and then turns to me. "I don't know what's going on between you two, but take my advice. Don't date a hockey player."

"We're not . . ." I begin, but she lifts a hand to cut me off.

"Whatever it is, it needs to stop. It's unprofessional. And you're both new. Not a good way to make an impression."

"There's nothing going on between us," I say, even though I

know that's not entirely true. Something was *definitely* happening on that zip line.

"Do you really want to date someone who's always gone? Getting hit on by other women? Is that what you want?" She lifts an eyebrow. "Now, let's get back to business. Your submitted proposal for the fundraiser is getting the green light. Tom approved it with some budget modifications. Personally, I think it's a great idea." Her lips curve into a tight smile, and I realize this is the first time she's given me a compliment.

"Really?" I hope my face doesn't look as flabbergasted as I feel. "Thanks, Alex."

"Why don't you tell the team and start making plans this week?" She wraps an arm around my shoulder as we walk back to the bus. "You're going to be a busy girl. No time for fun." She gives me a sidelong glance, like this is some kind of *mother knows best* lecture.

The busier I am, the less time I have to focus on anything else but my job. And that includes Brax.

———

For the rest of the week, Alex's words come true. I'm too busy to spend time with Brax because I'm swamped with work. That's not all bad. At least I'm not thinking about Brax as much as normal. Which is too much these days.

My phone buzzes with a text from Mia, who I've not heard from in months.

Mia: When were you going to tell me that my brothers are rooming at your place?
Jaz: I didn't know your brothers were even playing for the Crushers. I knew it would freak you out.
Mia: I am appropriately freaked out.
Jaz: Everything is under control. Promise.

Mia: *says the girl as her house goes up in flames.* You know this is a bad idea, right?

The knock at my door yanks me back to the present, and I swivel around to see a hulking silhouette fill the doorway of my office.

"Vale?" I squint, noticing his long hair swept away from his face.

"Are you busy?" he asks.

"Not too busy for you." I flip my phone over so he won't see his sister's text. Then I pat the extra wooden chair and invite him to sit.

He glances around. "They should really give you a bigger space. I can barely fit in here."

"One perk of being new." I shrug. "At least getting the closet under the stairs makes me feel like Harry Potter."

"Alex doesn't know what she's got in you. Have you seen the press we're getting about the elementary school visits? The local media is loving this."

I smile and can feel the blush hit my cheeks. It feels good to be complimented on my job, especially since Alex hasn't mentioned the media coverage. She's too caught up in her own plans with the new sports complex.

"So what's up?" I ask, leaning back in my chair. "Because I'm sure you didn't stop by just to tell me you're enjoying volunteering."

"Do I have to have a reason to visit you?" he asks with a playful smirk. "Can't I just pop in to have a pleasant chat?"

I narrow my eyes. "Yes, except you never have before."

He runs a hand through his hair. "Okay, fine. I want to talk about my brother."

Join the club.

"Brax?" I ask, as if I don't already know.

"Do I have another brother?"

"Not that I know of." I grab a pen and twirl it around my fingers. Apparently, a lot of people want to talk about Brax lately.

Vale rubs his hands together. "I'm sure you've noticed that he's not big on expressing himself."

"I thought he liked being a mystery," I note.

"I'm not sure he wants to be a mystery when it comes to *you*." Vale levels his gaze at me, and the gravity in his voice makes me fumble my pen.

"I can't guess what's in his head. If Brax wants to tell me something, then he should just say it."

"That's just his way. He plays by the rules when he's afraid." Vale leans forward, resting his elbows on his knees.

"Of me?" I shake my head with a laugh. "I don't believe it."

"He's afraid of disappointing you."

I frown. "If he's so worried about disappointing me, why didn't he contact me after the wedding? Let's start there."

Vale shakes his head. "You need to talk to Brax about that. It's not my place to say, other than he knows the mistake he made."

Of course Vale is not going to out his brother. It wouldn't be fair, even if I want answers.

Vale studies me. "All I can tell you is that I see the way he looks at you, and it's not like he looks at anyone else."

So much for having things under control.

I know Vale wouldn't lie to me. He knows Brax better than anyone. But if it's true, why wouldn't Brax tell me this himself?

"Well, he knows where I live," I say, turning back to my desk. It's not like he hasn't had an opportunity to explain.

"He needs to know you don't hate him. Because right now, he thinks you'd never forgive him."

How could he think that after we zip-lined together? If I hated him so much, I would've pushed him off the platform instead of letting him help me.

I face my computer, avoiding Vale. "I don't know why he would believe that."

"Because he notices everything. How you joke with the other

guys on the team instead of him. It's like you enjoy hanging out with everyone but him . . ."

That's the problem. *I enjoy him too much.*

I turn around to face him. "It's not that easy, Vale. We have a history. I made things clear that no one on the team should find out."

"Everyone on the team already suspects there's something between you two. Brax would never say this to you. He's trying to honor your wishes of keeping him at arm's length."

"Honor my wishes? Who said that's what I want?"

"It's not what you said, Jaz. It's the way you treat him. Like he needs to make up for whatever hurt he caused you in the past."

I wanted him to apologize for what he did, but not like this. I didn't intend for him to pay a never-ending debt.

"Does he know you're here, telling me this?"

Vale shakes his head. "I'd be in huge trouble if he found out. But I'm doing what he'd never do for himself." Vale stands. "Now it's up to you to decide what you want to do."

"Vale," I say, stopping him in the door. "Have you heard any of the players mention how Alex feels about players dating staff?"

He crinkles his eyes like he's trying to remember. "Lucian mentioned he dated one of the office administrators once. She didn't last long."

That's what I thought. Alex doesn't want any hookups on the team. Which means if anything were to happen between Brax and I—and that's a big *if*—we'd need to keep it a secret or else risk our positions. And I can't lose this job.

Vale looks over his shoulder, and his face shifts. "Hey, Brax."

Brax steps into the doorway alongside his twin, making me feel like I'm seeing double.

"Why are you here?" he asks Vale with a trace of suspicion.

"Can't your brother chat with me?" I tease, trying to cover up the reason for Vale's visit.

"Taking care of business," Vale says, slapping his brother's shoulder. "Or don't you trust your twin anymore?"

"I never said I don't trust you," Brax says. "But Jaz has important work to do, and she doesn't need you bothering her."

"Watching you two is entertaining," I say, leaning back in my chair and crossing my arms. "I'm not bothered at all. Vale, stop by anytime."

Before leaving, Vale gives Brax a smug smile, clearly irritating his brother.

Brax glances around my office, noting the new wall hangings and photographs I've added since he last stopped in. I figured if I'm going to be stuck in here, I should at least make it look like home.

"You really need to talk to Tom about moving offices."

"The notorious tightwad? He won't find me a new office unless I make the team piles of money." Which is a long shot, considering Alex's plan to shut down the team after this season, anyway.

"Maybe I can ask him," Brax suggests.

"Good luck with that," I mutter. "You can try, but don't be surprised if he laughs in your face."

"You don't know me. I can be very convincing when I want something." He looks at me intently, and I suddenly get the feeling that we're not talking about Tom anymore.

That weightless feeling in my stomach returns. The office suddenly feels like the walls are shrinking on us.

"Why are you here, Brax?" I tap my pen against my mouth.

"Do I have to have a reason to stop by?" he asks, innocently.

"That's exactly what your brother told me."

"It runs in the family," he quips. "I know I'm hard to tolerate."

"You are *more than* tolerable," I admit before I can stop myself. I remember what Vale told me about Brax keeping me at arm's length. "Who else would've been my partner for zip-lining?"

One side of his mouth tilts up. "That's why I'm here. I'm waving the white flag."

I shake my head. "What white flag?"

He shoves his hands into his pockets and shifts his weight. "No matter what's happened between us, I want to start over. If I hurt you, I'm sorry." I can see the hesitation on his face, how hard this is for him. "I'd like to make things up to you."

My stomach is in free fall before I find my voice. "You don't have to make anything up to me, Brax."

"I know. But I want to," he says, stepping toward me. "Go out with me for dinner tonight. Just you and me."

His gaze holds mine, making my stomach feel like it just bottomed out as the walls close in on us.

This isn't us being accidentally paired up on the zip line or dancing together at Boots and Buckles. Those moments weren't planned.

This is an intentional ask. Now it's up to me whether I accept it. I could shut him down now and stop this from going any further. *Remember Alex's warning about dating hockey players?*

But I also know what Vale told me. That Brax thinks I could never forgive him for the past. Even though I'm afraid, I want to move past what happened—as long as he knows I'm not handing over the key to my heart so easily this time. He's going to have to win me over.

"Okay," I say, narrowing my eyes. "If you're sure about this?"

Brax's shoulders dip and visible relief passes over his face. "Never more sure."

Is it possible that he's nervous about asking me out? The same guy who's a rock star on the ice?

I meet his gaze head-on. "Just so we're clear, there's one thing I want you to understand."

"Anything. Just tell me."

I cross my arms. "This time, I'm not kissing you."

FOURTEEN

Prax

"If that's what you want," I say, nodding. I keep my face cool, but my body prickles against that part of the agreement. Given that I really screwed things up before, she's not giving me a second chance. Unless I can change her mind, then it's *hands off* until she trusts me. "I'll go one further. I won't touch you."

She blinks. "I didn't say that. Not that I think we should touch," she stammers. "It's only that . . . I don't kiss just anyone."

"That's good, because I'm not *just* anyone." I smirk.

She shakes her head. "Too many falls on the ice have messed with your head."

"If I remember right, you're the one who doesn't skate very well."

"Which is why you won't get me on the ice."

I arch an eyebrow. "Is that a challenge?"

"No. And you asked me to dinner. Not skating. Now go, before Alex catches us." Her eyes shoot over my shoulder into the hallway, like she expects Alex to walk in at any second.

"Why would I care what Alex thinks?"

Jaz waves me into her office, then shuts the door behind me, leaving little personal space between us.

"She hinted she doesn't like staff dating players," Jaz admits. "Even if it is just dinner."

I frown. "I don't remember HR saying anything about that."

"Me neither. I think it's something she doesn't approve of personally, but it's not official policy. But I don't want to get on her bad side. So maybe we keep this date a secret?"

"Whatever you think is best." The last thing Jaz needs is problems with the boss.

She twists the ring on her finger. "It's not like it means anything."

It might not mean anything to her, but it does to me. And my job is to convince her it still means something. I just have to win her trust back.

"I won't say anything to the guys either," I assure her. "But it's going to be hard to sneak out with no one knowing." Especially Vale. He always knows when something's up. It's like we have this twin telepathy that doesn't allow us to keep secrets. Great for the ice. Terrible for love.

She thinks it over. "But what if the guys notice we're both gone?"

"Then we explain why they need to keep their mouths shut. Leo included."

After I slammed him into the wall in practice today, he'd only be too happy to run to Alex and tattletale. Most of the guys are decent, but Leo's the wild card, always determined to play favorites.

"I'll meet you somewhere after work," I suggest. "Then we'll figure out how to come home at separate times."

It seems like a good plan for now, but it won't work long term. Vale already knows how I feel about Jaz, and it's likely the other guys suspect something. Eventually, we'll have to come clean, but until I'm forced to, we have to keep things secret.

———

I check my phone for what feels like the fortieth time. Jaz is still not here. The longer I wait, the more I'm wondering if something went wrong.

I shoot her a text asking if she's okay. Then I stare at my phone, willing that little text bubble to appear, the one that proves she isn't ghosting me like I did her. I deserve her silence now, even if I did it to protect her. To my relief, the text bubble appears.

Jaz: Alex stopped in my office before I left and dumped a pile of work on me. Rain check?

Alex strikes again. It's like that woman is trying to keep us apart. I clench my teeth and let out a slow hiss. It's not fair that Alex unloaded work on Jaz last minute, but I can hardly ask her to risk her position for me.

Brax: You still need to eat.
Jaz: I'm fine. I have a granola bar in my desk drawer.

I glance at the menu. There's no way I'm letting her eat a granola bar when we were planning on filet mignon.

Brax: Don't eat that. Just stay where you are.

I don't know what Jaz would choose, but then I remember something from a long time ago. So I order two filets, a sweet-and-spicy Thai shrimp dish, creamy pasta with grilled salmon, and more sides than we could possibly eat, just to give her options. I don't even care what the bill is. I will not let her go hungry because of Alex.

Then I head back to the Ice House offices with four bags that smell like heaven.

If she can't go out on a date with me, then I will bring the date to her.

Since LeRoy, our facility manager, gave me an extra key so I could use the hot tub and ice bath after hours, it's coming in conveniently handy for sneaking in.

When I step into the administrative wing, every office is dark except for the light streaming from Jaz's open door. That's just like her, leaving her door open so any criminal could walk in.

I knock and then lean against the doorframe, holding up the bags. "Your delivery is here."

She swivels around in her chair, and her eyes widen as she glances at the bags. "You brought me dinner?"

"Didn't I say you will not eat that shabby excuse for a dinner?" I nod at the granola bar that's sitting on her desk.

"With Alex so kindly assigning me all this work, this might be breakfast."

"Not if I have anything to say about it." I arch an eyebrow and set all four bags on her desk.

She opens one and sniffs. "Mmm. Steak."

I open another sack. "And seafood. You like both."

She stares at me for a beat. "How did you . . .?"

"From the wedding. I asked if you liked steak or seafood."

"And I said both," she repeats, marveling at the options in front of her. "Thank you."

I push the food toward her. "Help yourself. It's really not safe for you to be working here alone. Especially with your door wide open."

She waves me away. "I'm perfectly fine. LeRoy locks all the doors at night."

"Yeah, but he also hands out keys behind Alex's back. Anyone could walk in here."

"LeRoy gave you a key?" she asks. "I was wondering how you got in."

"I have a reason to be here after hours. For my shoulder."

She frowns. "The other guys use the hot tub and ice bath after practice. Why don't you?"

I busy myself by getting out the food. It's a convenient excuse, so I don't have to look at her. "Too crowded after practice," I mutter, which is true, but not the real reason.

"Wait." She studies me, then touches my arm. "Are you trying to keep this injury from the other guys?"

I glance away, even though her touch is sending sparks through my body. She's too quick to figure things out, and I'm a terrible liar.

"It's a hockey thing. If Coach thinks I'm injured, he won't play me like the others. You know Leo would rub it in my face." I try to hide the niggling worry in my stomach. She won't understand that it could put future contracts in jeopardy. Especially if I'm trying to move up to the NHL.

"But if you tell Leo and the rest of the team, then you don't have to hide things. Wouldn't that be easier?"

"Easier, yes. But also risky." Like this dating thing.

"You never told me what happened," she says, taking a fork and stabbing it into a shrimp before popping it into her mouth. She closes her eyes as she chews. "By the way, this is delicious."

"My pleasure," I say, watching her savor the food. "To answer your question, I got slammed into the wall by a player who had it in for me. I got a shot past him that he felt deserved a penalty. The referees sided with me. So he slammed me into the wall and then started throwing punches, which earned *him* the penalty box. My face was a bloody mess afterward, but my shoulder took the brunt of his anger."

She winces like she's imagining the play-by-play. "That's awful, Brax."

I shrug as I pull up a chair to Jaz's desk. "It's part of the sport. I'm used to guys playing rough. That's what you sign up for. But Felipe has an anger problem. It wasn't until Vale pulled him off me that I realized how bad the injury was." I don't tell her the rest of the story. Felipe has continued to threaten me ever since, sending me text messages and threatening those around me. It's one thing to take it out on the ice; it's another to bully people outside of the game.

"Why are you keeping it secret from your team?" she asks, frowning.

I shake my head. "Not their problem."

"What about when you face him in your next game?"

"I'll handle it. I can't risk them getting involved."

She stares at me. "It seems like this would be important for them to know."

What she doesn't understand is that if I bring it up, it uncovers more ugly things, including the reason I had to end things with her.

I cut into a steak, avoiding her gaze. "Trust me. I'll be fine." I push the second steak toward her. "You've got to try this."

She digs into the steak as my eyes swing over to her computer screen, where her cursor blinks on the words *Fashion Show on Ice.*

I nod toward the screen. "Are you planning something for the local college figure skaters?"

"Um, no," she says slowly, glancing from her screen to me. "A fundraiser for the hockey team."

I snort-laugh. "Yeah, right. Good one. I *almost* believed you."

"No, really, it is," she says, setting down her fork.

I'm still not buying it. "I'd love to see Tate or Vale trying to model. That would be hilarious."

It's not until her face falls that I realize my mistake.

"I'm telling the truth, Brax. This is the secret project I've been planning."

She's not joking. "*This* is your secret project?"

"What did you think I was working on?"

"I thought we were doing volunteer work. When you said fundraiser, I thought you meant something like raising money for a charity. I didn't think it would involve us putting on a . . ." I can't even say the words.

"Fashion show," she finishes for me.

I try not to cringe. "Alex approves of this?"

"She was ecstatic about it. That's why she stopped by the zip line. It will raise money for the team *and* a charity. It's a win-win for everyone."

"People like to see us punch each other. Why not just sell tickets to that?"

"This is for people with money. The business owners who buy advertising space."

I point my fork at her to make my point. "Yeah, they secretly like the fights just as much as everyone else."

"I can't do anything risky that would jeopardize your career. Plus, we need something a little more elegant, like an evening of fashion, a silent auction, and hors d'oeuvres. When we rope them in with your fabulous smiles and winning personalities, we get them to commit to a donation or advertising. They're the ones with the influence in the community. This could change everything."

Everything in me bristles against this idea. I never signed up to model clothes. That's the last thing you'd ever catch me doing. Plus, the team can't be doing that badly, or Alex wouldn't have ended up with it in her divorce settlement.

"I'm here to play hockey, not prance around in evening wear."

"First off, you'll be wearing some of my custom jerseys that we're auctioning off for the event. Alex loved the idea of creating custom Crushers merchandise. Second, you'll be on skates. There will be no prancing."

I lift an eyebrow. "Promise?"

"Promise." She pats my leg for reassurance, and I wish she'd just keep it there. "I don't want you to be models. I want you to be yourselves. That's what makes it work. We need to show our fans you're more than just athletes. Since we're giving a portion to charity, it'll show that we're not in it for the money. Remember the kid in the wheelchair? We're giving the money to a charity that supports kids like Ethan. You can't tell me you don't care about helping him."

"Of course I care," I say. "But there are other ways to do it without turning this team into a joke."

"Who says this is a joke?" Jaz counters. "This is another way to give back to the community. It means the world for kids like Ethan."

Why does Jaz have to have such a big heart? And how does she so easily twist my arm and get me to agree to her schemes? No other woman could care so much.

I sigh. "Fine. I'll think about it. But only for Ethan's sake."

She crosses her arms. "I need you on board. If I can't get you to agree, I won't get the rest of the team on my side tomorrow."

"*This* is what you're presenting tomorrow?"

She cuts into a grilled asparagus spear. "It wasn't supposed to happen for several more weeks, but Alex had a last-minute trip out of town and couldn't run tomorrow's meeting. She told me this was my chance to sell the idea to the team. I have to get everyone on board, otherwise . . ." She freezes mid-bite.

"Otherwise, what?" I ask.

"Nothing. Forget I said anything."

It's obvious she's hiding something. I bump her shoulder playfully. "From the look on your face, there's something."

Her eyes drop to her plate as she pushes around her food. "Don't tell anyone, but the team is in financial trouble. If I say anything more, I could lose my job."

I put my fork down and stare at her. "With Alex's money behind this team, we shouldn't be in financial distress."

"According to her, we are. She's looking at all the options." She clamps her mouth shut, but there's no way I'm letting this conversation end.

I frown. "You won't tell me what all the options are?"

"Nope. Just trust me on this." She takes a bite of her roll. "Can I ask a favor? Can you please get the team to agree to this?"

I shake my head. "Some players won't be comfortable with the idea."

"Like you?" She looks at me. "Brax, what do I need to do to get you on board?" She looks at me with her big doe eyes, and I know I'm going to crumble.

I sigh. "What does it involve?"

"Modeling some custom jerseys. Possibly an opening number."

"You never said I had to dance . . ."

"I'm thinking of putting together a very simple synchronized skating routine on ice. There might be some choreography involved, but I promise to make you look good. Which won't be hard when you look like Thor's brother." Her eyes graze over me before returning to my face. "There's a reason that all the team social media posts featuring you get a crazy amount of comments."

She knows I don't care about social media or people stroking my ego. "Get Vale to do it. We're basically the same person."

"Not true. You are *not* your brother." She gives me such a pointed look that my heart stutters in my chest. "So, how can I get you to agree? I'm willing to compromise."

I hesitate, picking at my food before blurting out, "Then forgive me for what happened. And give me another chance." It comes out before I even realize what I'm doing.

She blinks, then shakes her head. "I'm not mad anymore, if that's what you're asking."

"That's not what I asked."

I can see the mask slip over her face. The distance she's putting between us. Whatever closeness I felt before is now a million miles away. Our little desk date was going so well until now. *Why did I have to bring up the past?* The thing I promised not to do until I earn back her trust.

She looks at her plate. "I forgive you. I just want to know why." Then she glances up at me slowly. "Was it another woman?"

I can't believe she'd even question that. "No," I snap. "There's been no one else. Not since you." *And that's because I can't get over you.*

Her eyes stay pinned on me as an uncomfortable silence settles between us.

"Anything else you want to know while you're interrogating me?" I ask.

She plays with her fork, rolling it between her fingers. "So you weren't looking for a girlfriend, just a date for the night?"

"Before the wedding, I'd already decided on not dating for awhile. But then you showed up. Despite my sister's warning, I couldn't turn away. I had every intention of contacting you afterward."

"But then you didn't. Was the kiss that forgettable?"

"*Jaz,*" I say firmly. "It was the best kiss I've ever had."

She blinks like she doesn't believe me. "Did you forget about me?"

I shake my head and put down my fork. "I just admitted it was the best kiss ever. How could I forget *that*?"

That's like forgetting how to skate. How to hit the puck. How to play the game I've practiced almost every day since I could stay upright on the ice. *I could never forget her.*

"There's a difference between forgetting a person and a kiss, Brax."

The hurt in her eyes makes my stomach clench. I can't believe I did this to her.

"That's what I meant," I explain. "I never forgot *you.*"

I can tell by her look that she doesn't believe me.

"You told me how much it hurt to not have your family around anymore, how you needed someone reliable. Someone who would be there for you," I remind her. "All I could think was how I'm a hockey player who travels for a living. I thought the distance would be too hard."

Her eyes narrow. "Long-distance dating isn't impossible."

"But that's not what you want, right? A long-distance relationship with someone who's always on the road? I know it sounds easy, but take it from me. It's *anything* but easy."

"Oh, right. Because you've had loads of women over the years," she says with a trace of sarcasm.

"Where did you get that information?"

"Nobody," she says, then glances away. "I assumed."

"Well, you assumed wrong. In the last five years, I've only dated two girls. So I'm actually pretty rusty at this dating thing."

"You don't seem rusty," she says, giving me a quick look. "You certainly haven't lost your charm."

"Is that a compliment?" I shoot a glance at her.

"Don't get a big ego, Mac," she warns.

"After the last breakup with another girl, I swore I was going to stay single. Remember Felipe, the guy who injured my shoulder? He's dating her now. That's why I wasn't looking for a date at the wedding."

Her mouth drops. "She started dating him after you?"

"Not exactly. They started dating while we were still together. It's part of the reason he has it out for me. She cheated on me with him. He's hated me ever since."

"But you didn't do anything," she says, defending me.

"Tell me about it. But he doesn't care. The fact I dated his girlfriend once is the reason he hates my guts. He told me once it's his goal to give me a career-ending injury."

That's only half of it. He also threatened to target anyone I cared about by making up lies about me and using them to hurt the people I love. He's ruthless, and until he finally leaves me alone, I refuse to get Jaz involved. That's why I didn't contact her after the wedding.

Her brow crinkles in concern. "Don't tell me you have to play this monster again."

"In about a month."

She shakes her head. "Tell Coach Thompson your history with this goon. Sit out a game."

"If I run away from him, he wins. I won't allow that to happen."

She stares at me like I've lost my mind. "But your shoulder still hasn't healed. What's going to happen if he pulls the same stunt?"

"I've got a plan, and Vale's got my back."

"And the rest of the team?"

"They don't need to know," I repeat.

"Then I'm telling them. Because I'm not letting you go out there on the ice and lose your career because of some jerk."

"You will not," I say firmly. "This doesn't involve you."

She crosses her arms. "You don't get to decide that."

"This is my problem, Jaz. Not yours. Even if that means using this as my bargaining chip with you."

She frowns. "What do you mean?"

"I'll talk the guys into doing your fashion show. Just let me handle Felipe, okay?"

She turns to me, her eyes racked with worry. "Okay, but all bets are off if I think your way isn't working."

"It *will* work." It has to. If not, I'll deal with it on the ice. It's the way I've always dealt with things.

"I don't want to see you get hurt." She reaches over and brushes my arm, and that touch spreads through me like warm honey.

"Me? Hurt?" I stand, putting some distance between us. "I'm more worried about you. You're working late. Not eating. Staying after hours alone. Anyone could hide out in this place."

A corner of her mouth rises. "Like you?"

I lift an eyebrow. "I'm not dangerous."

"I might disagree," she says, rising from her chair.

"The only place I want to intimidate people is on the ice." I level my gaze so she knows I'm not playing around. "With you, I'm a total pushover."

For a moment, our eyes lock, our bodies only inches apart. Those impossibly deep brown eyes make me feel like someone's sucked the oxygen from her office.

In a past life, I might have taken advantage of that look. But I made a promise to her. It takes all my willpower to step away from her, but I do it.

"See you at home?" she asks, before turning to the mess on

the desk and organizing it. "Maybe we could find a movie to watch, if you're game?"

"Is it going to be a cheesy romance?" I'm not about to tell her I'd watch the cheesiest romance on the planet if she asked me to. If Leo requested the same, I'd probably slam his head into the wall.

She looks up from packing the leftovers. "You could use a few cheesy romances in your life to balance all the testosterone in this place."

"For your information, I'm the most balanced guy on this team. Yesterday, Sloan made me eat a vegetarian stir-fry with tofu, and Tate is sharing his boring philosophy books with me. Not to mention the elementary school visits you're making us do."

She props a hand on her hip. "You're a softie when you get around those kids. Just admit it." Her lips curve up on one side, and I'm reminded how being with her feels natural, like a comfortable sweatshirt just pulled from a warm dryer.

I point at her. "It's all your fault I'm turning into a marshmallow. I'd have never stepped foot in a school if it wasn't for you. Then those kids went and won over my heart with their cherub-cheeked smiles. But you already knew that, right?"

She shrugs. "If it worked on Leo, I knew it would work on any crude Viking."

"Well, this Viking is willing to settle for a cheesy romance movie as long as ice cream is involved in tonight's . . ."

What exactly is this? It was supposed to be our first official date. But with the rest of the guys around, we'll hardly be alone.

"I'd bet money Leo and Vale already have dibs on the big TV," she says, packing up her laptop.

"Then I'll make them move." I'm not about to call it an evening. I'll kick them out. Promise them my firstborn. Whatever it takes.

"What will you say if they ask *why*?" She lifts her eyebrows, a subtle reminder that this is not supposed to be public knowledge.

"I'll tell them we're hanging out *without* them. Then I'll give them a look that will shut them up for good."

"Are we just hanging out?" she asks.

Not in my book. "It's our long-overdue date, and they're not invited. If we turn on a chick flick, that will scare them away."

She shakes her head, even though she's smiling. "I think you underestimate your teammates. I suspect they're sappy romantics underneath their caveman grunts."

"Yeah, right. You haven't heard them in the locker room. Their idea of a good time is seeing if they can burp the 'Star-Spangled Banner.'"

"You'd be surprised what meeting the right woman can do."

"I wish they would. They're around the house too much, acting like sad sacks. Every one of them needs a woman to keep them from turning into a bunch of Neanderthals."

"Too late," she says, reaching for the food sacks at the same time I do. Our arms brush, and we both pull back and look at each other.

Her lips curve up on one side. "When I get a new office, we won't be crammed in here like sardines."

"There are advantages to small spaces," I say, smirking. "Bumping into you is one of the perks."

She presses her laptop bag against her body, her eyes fixed on me.

"You've got that look on your face," I say, nodding at her.

"What look?" she asks, blinking.

"The one that says you're not sure about something. Did I offend you?" I know that this is part of the challenge. Getting her to open up to me a little at a time.

"Of course not," she says, shifting her feet. "Honestly? This dating thing scares me a little, especially since I know Alex is opposed to it. Not to mention how the team will react or your sister. If you remember right, things didn't actually end well for us last time."

"Last time," I clarify. "We weren't actually dating. That was my first mistake. I'm going to do things the right way this time and woo you like a proper gentleman."

"Well, Mr. Darcy, I'm going to be a lot more careful about making hasty decisions. Jane Austen got some things right when it came to romance."

I step toward her. "When you're ready, I'll be waiting," I say with a grin, brushing my knuckles down her cheeks lightly.

"Then you might wait a while," she says, jutting her chin out just to show me she's not caving now.

Challenge accepted.

"Waiting for what?" a voice behind us says.

I wheel around and my jaw nearly falls to the floor.

Leo stands in the door with a grin that tells me he's heard everything.

FIFTEEN

Jaz

I don't know how long Leo's been standing there, but from the way Brax's body tenses, he's not happy. Leo looks as smug as a fox who's just raided a chicken house.

"What are you doing here so late?" Brax says coolly as he steps in front of me. I elbow him in the side, shooting him a look to let him know he doesn't need to protect me. As much as I appreciate Brax's muscles, there's no need to use them now. Save it for the rink.

"I was about to ask you the same thing," Leo says with a smirky little grin to infuriate Brax. "I forgot something in the locker room. Then I saw lights on and wondered who was here. Late-night rendezvous?" He wiggles his eyebrows.

"No," Brax growls as he takes an intimidating step toward Leo. I grab Brax's arm to reel him back.

Leo throws up his hands. "Kidding, man."

"I had to work late," I explain to Leo while keeping my hand locked on Brax so he doesn't do something stupid.

Leo grins. "Alone in a dark office, after hours? Pretty suspicious, if you ask me."

"I didn't ask you," Brax growls.

Leo glances over to the desk, where the carryout bags sit. "What's with the food?"

"I brought her dinner," Brax offers without explanation. It's obvious he's trying to get Leo to leave.

"How romantic," Leo replies, peeking inside a bag.

"Like you'd know," Brax mutters.

"I know what women like." Leo smirks at Brax. "*Me.*"

Brax chuckles in disbelief. "You wish."

Leo shrugs blandly. "At least I'm honest with the women I date. I don't promise to contact them afterward if I'm not planning to."

"How did you . . .?" Brax asks, before clamping his mouth shut. It's a low blow, and Leo knows it.

"We're living in the same house," Leo says. "*Nothing* is private."

Brax steps toward Leo. "I didn't ask you to eavesdrop on my private conversation."

"Listen, word gets around," Leo defends. "Especially on this team."

"By listening in on people's conversations? *Nice.* That will build team trust." Brax turns away from Leo and scrapes a hand over his hair.

"You're the one who needs to learn about trust," Leo argues, giving Brax an accusatory look. "I'm not a tattletale. I don't care who you date." Leo puts a hand on the doorway, a look of warning on his face. "But you can't keep it from Alex forever."

———

I don't ride with Brax on the way home. After our unexpected visit from Leo, we agree that it's less suspicious if we arrive home in different cars. While Brax stops at the grocery store to pick up ice cream, I arrive home to what seems to be total chaos. The stereo is blaring a song with a heavy bass beat that rattles my rib cage, pizza boxes litter the kitchen counters, and Lucian is throwing a football in the living room. I enter just as the ball sails over Granny's teacup collection, making my heart do a double somersault in my chest.

"Hey, Jaz," Lucian says, totally oblivious to the mass destruction of china he almost caused.

"What is going on?" I gasp, dropping my bag on the floor.

"Football," Dawson answers cheerfully as Tate catches the ball next. He tosses it to Vale, who then pretends to rush the ball between the couch and the coffee table before Dawson full-body tackles him onto the floor.

"Time out!" I lift my hands as all the guys stop and turn toward me. "How did my living room become a football field?"

"It's game night," Dawson answers, climbing off the floor like this is a perfectly reasonable excuse.

Granny would be rolling in her grave if she knew. So much for a quiet date night with Brax.

"Hey, Jazzy!" Sloan enters the room, beaming. Her cheeks have more color, a sign she's feeling better. "Just in time. The party's starting."

"I think the party already has. Did you know these clowns were playing football in Granny's living room?"

"Yeah!" she says brightly before she looks at my face and her smile drops. "Was I supposed to tell them no?"

Even though Sloan's my sister, she doesn't always feel the same weight of responsibility as I do about the house.

"I can't afford to fix anything that's broken," I murmur as Dawson crashes into an end table and knocks a stack of books off of it.

"Whoops." He glances at the mess on the floor, then shrugs. "Don't worry. They're only Tate's. You could run over these with a front loader and they wouldn't break."

I stride over to the mess and pick up the books. "What will it be next time? Lamps? Glass? Somebody's tooth?"

"That'd be cool," Dawson says, nodding.

"No, it would not! This is not a frat house!" I shout.

Dawson's eyes widen at my outburst.

Sloan grabs my arm and reels me back. "Calm down. They won't hurt anything. It's about time we had some fun around here. You know Granny loved a good party."

"Not *this* type of party. Rowdy boys and flying footballs were not Granny's thing."

Suddenly, the front door flies open and Rourke, Jaxon, and Logan barrel through the door. I don't even know who's upstairs. Half the team might be destroying my house, for all I know.

"The party can finally begin!" Leo says, holding up a large container of cheese balls that will probably be crushed into the rugs later.

Leo tears open the can and challenges Dawson to catch as many as he can in his mouth like a free-throw shooting contest.

Sloan's mouth stretches into a wide smile. "I think Granny would be proud of us."

I gape at her. "Throwing cheese balls in the living room?"

"No, letting these guys in. This is the most fun I've had in ages." The joy on Sloan's face is unmistakable. For months she's been down, a shadow of her former self since the accident. As much as I want her well, I don't want my house obliterated.

Someone turns the music up, and Vale and Dawson start a horrible rendition of a conga line across the floor, pulling Sloan in with them. Vale grabs her waist and forces her into the train.

"C'mon, Coach," he says, using the nickname only her skaters call her.

Sloan looks back at me with a shrug and lets Vale sweep her away to the rhythm, looking happier than I've seen her in years. Over the pumping Latin beat, her laughter spills across the house. It's a sound I'd forgotten since the accident, something that makes my heart squeeze.

Seeing her so content, how could I ruin her happiness for my own?

She glances over her shoulder at Vale and tosses him a smile. I can't see her falling for Vale in any conventional sort of way.

But him falling for her? How could he *not* when she's this beautiful?

The door slams behind me, and I turn to see Brax frozen in the hall, his eyes bulging, the raucous scene unfolding before him.

He carries a wildflower bouquet in one hand and four Ben & Jerry's tubs in the other.

"How much ice cream did you think I was going to eat?" I say, looking over his haul. When he saw me at the reception, I was only half-joking about my love for food. Apparently, he knows my love language well.

"What's going on?" he shouts to the guys, still shell-shocked.

Dawson glances at Brax's flowers. "Awww, you didn't have to bring me flowers."

"I didn't," Brax growls, whipping the flowers away.

"You're not pretty enough," Lucian says, smacking Dawson in the arm. "And your socks reek."

Lucian is the darling on the team, the one person who probably is pretty enough, given his perfect features and dark blond hair. He dresses like a men's cologne model, and Sloan and I have secretly agreed that if anyone could get an endorsement for men's beauty products, it's him.

"Who's it for, Romeo?" Lucian asks with a sly grin.

My face grows hot as I turn away, letting Brax take this one.

"For the ladies," he stammers.

Sloan drops out from her conga line, grinning like a fool.

"Why thank you, Brax," she says, eyeing the flowers, then elbows me in the ribs.

I take the flowers from him. "They're so pretty. Just like Lucian." I tweak Lucian's chin before turning toward the kitchen in search of a vase. Spying one in the back of a high cupboard, I reach up on my tiptoes and skim the edge with my fingertips.

"You need help?" Brax asks, just as the vase tips and slips out of my hand.

Brax catches it before it crashes to the floor.

"Good catch," I murmur in wonder.

Considering Brax is super talented, you'd never know it. He never brags about his shots or all the times he's scored the winning goal. Even though he dominates on the ice, he's remarkably humble in person.

I turn to him slowly, realizing this might be my only opportunity to tell him. "Listen, I'm sorry about the movie."

The music changes to a southern rock number with a growly singer.

Brax tilts his head. "Why are you apologizing? I'm still planning on a movie after I shut this party down."

I glance toward the living room, where the guys are trying out a viral TikTok dance while Dawson records it on his phone. Half the guys can't dance but believe they can, and their bumbling bodies make it even more hilarious. When the song ends, Beyonce's "All the Single Ladies" begins, and a male chorus of bad falsettos join in.

Brax covers his ears. "It's like someone is scrubbing sandpaper across my eardrums."

"How will we watch a movie with *that*?" I nod toward Dawson who's now pretending to ride a horse and whoop around the living room as Leo attempts a Shakira-like hip swivel that he clearly can't do.

Brax looks at me for a beat, grabs my hand and growls, "Follow me."

During the chaos, we sneak upstairs to Brax's room, and he opens the door like a gentleman and nods. "After you."

I haven't been inside his room since he moved in. It's impeccably clean, his dresser top is completely empty, and it smells like an expensive cologne that makes my head spin.

"Wow. This room looks fabulous." I glance at the bed, which is made with a military precision. A steel-gray comforter is tucked with sharp hospital corners. White pillows are stacked perfectly. I'm afraid to even sit on it for fear of messing it up. It's not like he planned this to impress me.

He picks up a hoodie that's folded neatly on a plain wooden chair. "I didn't know anyone would see my room tonight."

He's apologizing for one sweatshirt out of place? If he saw my room, he'd be horrified to find a dresser full of scattered makeup, along with the three outfit changes left crumpled on the floor this morning.

Guess we're never watching movies in my bedroom.

"You can stretch out there." Brax nods at his perfect bed. "I'll sit here."

He waves toward a wooden chair in the corner.

I cross my arms. "For two hours? That's not comfortable. And don't even try to argue that it is."

I walk toward the bed and pat the cover, inviting him to join me. "I trust you enough to sit next to me."

I just don't trust my heart.

He blinks for a second before he realizes I'm not letting him off the hook, then climbs onto the bed.

"What are you waiting for?" he asks.

"I don't want to mess it up. I've never seen such a neat bed. It should be on the cover of a home and garden magazine."

"The guys give me flack about it," he admits. "Leo tries to jump on it whenever I'm not looking just to irritate me."

I stay at the side of the bed, still unsure whether this is a good idea. My bed is a happy place where I can laze around in pajamas and eat cookie butter from the tub while I escape in a messy pile of soft blankets. But Brax clearly has different standards.

He grabs my hand. "You can mess up my bed any day, Princess." Then he pulls me onto the comforter, sending butterflies floating through my body.

I sink into the pillows, the feather kind that feels like a cloud. He hands me a neatly folded throw that's made of the most sublime material I've ever touched, so soft I want to pet it like an exotic animal.

"You pick out soft throws?" I ask, open-mouthed. "What kind of tough hockey player are you?"

"One with a preference for things I like to touch," he murmurs, tucking a wisp of hair behind my ear with such tenderness, I'm not sure he's even the same man I've seen smashing guys in practice.

Even though my body is tingling, I rub the blanket against my cheek. "What is this made from? Magical unicorn tail knitted by fairies?"

He smirks. "No idea. How about we just call it magical Not Fur?" He spreads the throw over me so that no part of me is cold while keeping some space between us.

"Now that you're warm and comfortable, do you mind if I pick the movie for you?" he asks.

I look at him skeptically. "Nothing that will give me nightmares for the next week."

"So Hallmark meets Nora Ephron?" he asks with a lifted brow.

I blink. "I can't believe you even know who Nora Ephron is."

"I'm exceptional that way," he says with a knowing grin, reminding me of our wedding reception conversation.

When he picks my favorite rom-com, *When Harry Met Sally,* and opens a tub of Cherry Garcia ice cream, I can only think, *This is what love must feel like. All my favorite things that make my heart happy.*

I sink into the blanket and pillows in a state of ice cream bliss until my eyelids are so heavy I can barely keep them open.

It's not until I hear the door creak open and I wake up that I realize the movie is almost over and I've fallen asleep under the Not Fur blanket of silky softness.

Vale peeks his head around the door with Tate and Leo just behind. They almost stumble into each other like the Three Stooges when they realize Brax isn't alone.

Vale looks between us with a mischievous glint. "What are you two watching?"

"Nothing. Now get out of here," Brax instructs, throwing a pillow at them to get them to leave.

Vale tosses it back lightning fast, almost nailing me in the head. Luckily, Brax blocks it with his hand, keeping it from smacking me in the face.

I swear this guy has superhuman reflexes.

I prop myself on an elbow, suddenly aware of how my body has shifted during my nap. I'm curled toward him, my head nestled inside the curve of his muscular arm. At some point, I must have rolled closer to him. But the last hour is a hazy blur of soft blanket, the allure of Brax's yummy scent, and the black hole of his super-magnetic galaxy.

Brax is sitting comfortably, the same way he was when the movie started, except now his arm is propped up behind my head, cradling me protectively.

We're not exactly cuddling. But we've certainly lost the distance we started with at the beginning of the movie.

Leo arches an eyebrow. "First dinner, now a movie in your room?"

"What dinner?" Vale asks, looking glum. "Did I miss food?"

"Never mind," Brax says. "This was the only quiet place since your party took over the living room."

Leo shrugs. "Convenient excuse to get a woman in bed."

Brax stands, and the fire shooting from his eyes looks like it might sear Leo's eyebrows off.

Leo rotates behind Vale for protection. "Can't you take a joke, man?"

"Not when the joke involves *her*," Brax growls.

Tate looks from the movie to us. "Isn't this like a date-night movie?"

"Look at the company," Vale points out. "Lucky dude. Maybe I should see if Sloan wants to watch a movie." He spins around to find my sister.

Brax puts his hand out. "This isn't a double date!" Based on the way Brax has his jaw set, he's annoyed.

"Can we watch too?" Tate asks. "Or will that ruin your date?"

"Absolutely not," he says, sitting on the bed. "Can't we watch a movie without you assuming we're on a date?" Brax's words cut through the room like the sharp edge of a skate.

"You're watching a kissing movie," Tate explains, like a lawyer making a case. "And you had your arm around her." \

"Not anymore." Like it makes a difference. I can feel the heat radiating off his body beside me. The places where he's almost touching me.

"Looks totally platonic to me," Leo says sarcastically.

If we're going to keep this dating thing hidden, we're totally failing.

"What about the rules?" Tate asks, crossing his arms. Tate would remember the rules even though I'm the one who said *No girls in the bedroom*. That's before I even considered that something would happen with Brax.

I thought he despised me back then.

Brax crawls off the bed to face off with Tate. "Sheriff, she's the owner. *She* makes the rules."

Then Brax rounds the bed, forcing Tate to back up. "There's also a rule about no parties, and that was broken tonight. Do you want to tell the guys downstairs to leave?"

Tate backs into Leo, who stumbles into Vale.

"Not really," Tate says weakly.

Brax keeps walking them backward until they're out in the hallway, then he stretches his arms across the doorframe, looking like he could snap it in two. "In that case, I'll pretend *that* isn't happening if you leave us alone. See how this works?"

Leo chuckles under his breath. "Brax, you do a terrible job of hiding your intentions."

"My intentions are not up for discussion," Brax growls.

"Then how about the upcoming fashion show we don't know about?" Leo asks. "Is that up for discussion?"

"Fashion what?" Vale's head snaps toward Brax.

Brax turns to me with a questioning glance.

"I didn't tell him." I turn to Leo. "How did you . . ."

"I saw it on your computer screen earlier," Leo says. "Guess everyone around here has secrets, huh?"

"It's not a secret," I say defensively. "I was planning on telling everyone at tomorrow's meeting."

"So what else are you hiding?" Tate asks.

Leo steps toward me, but Brax keeps the way securely blocked.

"You're pretty tight with Ice Queen Alex," Leo says. "I bet she tells you everything."

The way he looks at me makes me wonder what he suspects.

"Even if she did tell me everything, I wouldn't tell you." I nudge Brax out of the way and slam the door in Leo's face.

Then I turn to Brax like nothing happened and brush my hands off. "Now, where were we?"

Brax stares at me in shock. "Look at you, telling off Leo for once." He pats me on the shoulder. "I'm proud of you."

My stomach twists uncomfortably. If he knew I was hiding Alex's secret, he wouldn't be proud. He'd be mad. Furious, even.

But I can't tell him before I try to save the team. If I did, Alex would fire me.

Everything I'm doing is for Sloan and for him. And I need time to make it work, even if time is the one thing I don't have.

SIXTEEN

I've always been excited about being on the ice. *Until now.* The thought of modeling clothes while people gawk at me—or worse, laugh at me—sounds as inviting as getting my head slammed into the ice.

Personally, slamming my head sounds better.

After today's meeting, I can tell most of the guys feel the same about the fashion show, even if they are modeling Jaz's custom designed jerseys. They're shooting me disgusted looks. Whispering behind my back.

The only people who seem remotely excited are Leo, Dawson, and Vale. Leo likes the attention, while Dawson and Vale are doing this for me. Vale knows my loyalty to Jaz. This is his way of being a team player and staking his flag for Team Jaz.

As I sit on a bench along the rink, Jaz rushes in, her hair pulled back in a ponytail, her white joggers and pink sweatshirt a stark contrast to our black practice jerseys. She waves us to the middle of the rink, while everyone around me grumbles.

Her eyes dart around, taking in the reluctant group. "Coach said I have twenty minutes to teach our opening number for the fashion show."

"We're dancing?" Rourke asks from the back. Rourke is grumpy about everything, especially things he never agreed to in his contract. "I thought we were just showing off clothes."

"It's not really a dance. More like synchronized skating," she says. "Part of the entertainment is letting the fans see another side of you. The fun side."

"I can show them another side," Vale jokes and then turns around and shakes his hips Leo's way.

Leo smacks his backside, and Vale turns around and socks Leo in the arm. Before I can stop them, the guys almost end up in a wrestling match on the ice. Dawson howls with laughter, while Rourke pumps his fist, yelling, "Punch him!"

"Stop. NOW!" I bellow as Lucian and Tate step in and pull Vale and Leo apart. "You guys are acting like a bunch of peewee players." I press my finger into each of their chests. "There will be absolutely. No. Fighting."

"Well, I'm not dancing like *that*," Tate says, crossing his arms. "My hips don't even shake that direction."

"Nothing in this routine involves shaking that," Jaz says. "Think of it more like the opening of a show where they see you and your Crushers merchandise for the first time. Something to warm up the audience. They're going to be bidding on the new line of Crushers clothes to raise charity funds as well as buying advertising space for the rest of the season. We need them to like you!"

The thought of this team in designer duds, gliding—and likely tripping—over the slick ice makes me wonder if we'll become the city's laughingstock instead of filling them with pride. If I wasn't so crazy about Jaz, I'd probably refuse to do it too.

But right now, whatever Jaz wants, Jaz gets. If she asked me to wear a tutu and dance like a fairy ballerina I'd do it, even if I hated myself every second.

You know you're a man in love when you're willing to sacrifice your pride for someone even if it involves total humiliation.

"What if we *can't* stay together for the routine?" Tate asks, looking around the group. Tate was noticeably quiet during this morning's meeting, and now I know why. He doesn't want to do this any more than I do.

Jaz walks toward him. "You don't have to be good. You just have to learn to move to the music. Kind of like hockey."

Tate raises his hand. "Correction! This is nothing like hockey."

"You're right," Jaz says, thinking over her words carefully. "But it's also not dancing. It's synchronized skating. With lights and music. All of you can skate. Just add a few jazz hands and a final pose!"

The guys groan.

Jaz props her hands on her hips, not ready to give up yet. "Here's the thing. I want to showcase your personalities. So find your mojo. Your good vibrations. And let loose, okay?"

"My mojo is punching people," Rourke says.

A few guys snicker.

"We won't be punching people," Jaz says, shaking her head.

She turns on the music, and the guys hang back to watch.

"Try to do what I'm doing. We won't be adding the skating yet, just the body movements." She steps to the beat, instructing us to follow along.

Some guys move right instead of left and bump into the guy next to them.

If we can't figure out this simple move, we'll look like idiots in front of the entire city.

Even though I'm confident during games, I've never felt so inept in my life. It's like my feet won't go the right direction.

When I look around, I notice about half of the guys are just like me. Two left feet.

Jaz glances over her shoulder at us and calls out the motions. "Lift your arms. And don't worry, you'll be skating around the rink as you do these moves." Then she adds jazz hands to it and I suddenly feel like I've been recruited into the Ice Capades.

Leo looks over at me and snickers. "Counting isn't your problem. It's the fact you have no rhythm and you're distracted."

Remarkably, he's perfectly in step with Jaz. I had no idea Leo was this coordinated, and it makes me furious. "How'd you get it so fast?"

"What can I say?" He cocks his head. "I'm just talented. I also took dance lessons as a kid." He's like Fred Astaire in skates, and it makes me inwardly writhe in anger.

"At least I'm willing to *try,*" I say through gritted teeth.

He lowers his voice. "Only because she's your girlfriend."

My eyes flit over to Jaz as she spins to the right. "She's *not* my girlfriend."

Not yet, anyway.

As she spins to the left, I notice how her hips sway in time to the music, making every move look good. If I wasn't concentrating so hard on not tripping, I'd enjoy the view more.

Leo notices me staring and gives me a wicked grin. "You've got it bad for her."

"You're just jealous she doesn't look twice at you, Ego," I growl, missing a step and nearly crossing my own feet.

He juts out his chin. "I don't need her to look twice at me. I've got girls lined up in my DMs."

I roll my eyes. If I wasn't trying to help Jaz, I'd take Leo down a couple of notches, or at least his Texas-belt-buckle-sized ego.

I'd like to see a woman come along and crush his tiny heart under her boot heel. It will take just the right one to tame a guy like him.

"If I were you," Leo says, lowering his voice. "I'd test whether she's *really* loyal to you."

I glance at Jaz before looking back at Leo.

"She doesn't need a test," I reply coolly. Leo knows loyalty is my gold standard. I demand it from my teammates. And I'd require it from anyone who wants to earn my heart.

"I just want to see if you can do this," Jaz says, switching to a hip-swiveling Latin move, and I suddenly feel as stiff as a grandma after hip surgery.

Leo follows her cha-cha steps flawlessly. Even his jazz hands are freakishly jazzy. He leans toward me. "Then prove it. See if she'll wear your jersey to one of our games."

"Why would that matter? A jersey isn't proof of loyalty. She can make her own decisions. It's just a shirt," I mutter, remembering Lucian's jersey and the agreement she made with him for the first game. I dropped my hint about her looking better in mine, but she's never asked about it since. After the connection we made zip-lining and the date we had, that stings a little. Why *wouldn't* she wear mine?

"That's what a loyal girlfriend would do," Leo says, as if he can read my thoughts. "Unless she's not all in."

What is that supposed to mean?

Jaz strikes a big final pose and we all stumble to catch up.

"Good job, everyone!" Jaz chirps, turning to face us and clapping her hands. "We'll add the skating tomorrow and go over the moves until we've all nailed it. Does anyone have questions?"

Dawson raises his hand. "Could you teach me that spinning move again?"

"Sure," she says, moving closer to Dawson.

Even though Dawson is built like a monster truck, he's got more rhythm than me. A surge of envy prickles down my spine. I don't like the attention she's giving him, even though he's just asking for help.

Maybe it's because Leo suggested the test with the jersey, and I already know Jaz hasn't mentioned *not* wearing Lucian's to the first game. I'm not a possessive guy, and I want Jaz to make this decision on her own. But I also want her to choose me. Choose *us.*

I raise my hand. "Hey, could you show all of us how to do that move, or is Dawson the only one who gets a private lesson?"

Jaz looks at me. "Anyone else need help?"

Half the team raises their hands. Apparently, I'm not the only uncoordinated one.

Jaz sighs and checks her watch. "We're out of time today. And we haven't even practiced the modeling section. We'll start with that during tomorrow's practice, and if anyone wants to volunteer to go first, I'd appreciate it."

"I'm sure Brax will gladly volunteer," Vale says with a chuckle.

I shoot him a scowl that says, *I'm going to kick your butt on the ice later.*

Jaz notes the look exchanged and gives me an apologetic smile. "Only if he wants to . . ."

"Sure. I mean, how bad could it be?" I say, trying to be a good sport.

"Can't wait to see you strut your stuff," Leo says, smacking my injured shoulder.

"Thanks," I grumble, rubbing my shoulder.

I definitely can't strut, and now I just volunteered to be the first model.

––––––

"Stand still," Jaz instructs as she stretches out a measuring tape across my shoulders.

"So bossy," I tease, trying not to wince as I lift my arms.

"You want the jersey to fit or not? This is all about making you look good." She stretches the measuring tape, her fingertips grazing my skin, sending a sizzle of electricity down my body.

"I didn't know we needed help to look good," I tease.

"*You* don't," she says, playfully smacking me in the abs.

I rub my stomach. "Hey, watch it, Princess. Those are my abs."

"I know," she says. "People love your abs, which is why I'm highlighting all your good assets."

"People as in *you*?" I lift an eyebrow.

"Wouldn't you like to know," she says with a smirk. "Now,

shoulders back, Big Mac." This time, I can't hide the pain from today's practice as I adjust my sore shoulder.

"Are you okay?" she asks, dropping the tape and studying me.

"Yes," I lie, straightening my face. The only thing saving me is her close proximity and the smell of her perfume drifting over me like a drug. If I focus on that, I can ignore the pain.

Jaz grabs my right arm and lifts it too fast, sending pain across my shoulder. I squeeze my eyes shut and say through gritted teeth, "Warn me next time before you do that."

She gasps and drops my arm. "Brax, why didn't you say something? Your shoulder's killing you again?"

"Shhh," I say, glancing out the open door to make sure nobody heard her. Even though we're doing measurements outside the locker room, I don't want anyone to overhear us. "Today's pain is compliments of Leo. Who is *always* a pain."

She frowns. "He seems to have it out for you."

"He has it out for anyone who beats him."

She turns me around, gentler this time. "You don't have to pretend with me, Brax."

If only she knew. I'm always holding back part of myself with her.

She runs the tape down my back, and a line of warmth follows. "Tonight I'm going to make sure you're taking care of your shoulder. I've got Joshua working on some repairs today, so you can have the night off."

I make a mental note to remember to pay Joshua for the repairs later without Jaz knowing. "How are you going to keep me from working? I like helping you."

"Want to test me and see?" she asks, lifting an eyebrow.

I grin. "Can't be worse than facing a defender."

"Wanna bet?" Her gaze dares me to disagree.

I grin, taking in her rose-colored lips. "This time I think you're serious."

"I am." Her mouth curves into a cocky grin as she measures

my chest next. As she steps closer to me, she stretches the tape across my collarbone and her nails graze my T-shirt.

My eyes follow the soft curve of her neck, down to the hollow space of her collarbone peeking from her teal-green blouse that matches the Crushers logo.

She catches me staring and smiles. "Why are you looking at me that way?"

"Because you're in my line of sight and very distracting. Especially this close."

She gives me a playful grin. "I'm pretty sure nothing can distract you on the ice."

My pulse vehemently disagrees.

"I think you underestimate your power, Princess," I murmur as she wraps the tape around my waist, totally oblivious to the fact that her hands are making my heart leap against my ribs. "Careful now. I think you're taking advantage."

"Is that what you call it?" she says, avoiding my eyes as she takes down another measurement. "I'm just trying to make sure your shirt doesn't look like a preschooler made it."

"It would help if your hands were warmer."

"Occupational hazard." She shrugs.

I open my arms. "I'd suggest putting them on me to warm them up."

"Yeah, nice try," she says with a smirk. "But we're keeping this secret, remember? And I've got to measure the next guy."

"All of them?" I grumble.

"Yes, all of them. It's my job, remember?"

Even if it is her job, I don't like the idea of her touching anyone else other than me.

She puts her clipboard and tape down. "Like I said, occupational hazard."

I hesitate for a beat. "Hey, are you coming to the game on Friday?"

She glances up from her clipboard. "Of course. Wouldn't miss it."

I shove my hands into my pockets. "It's expected to wear a jersey, and I know you promised Lucian you'd wear his already. So I wondered if you wanted to wear mine for the second game?"

She bites her lip. She's going to turn me down. I can see it all over her face.

"That's so nice of you to offer, Brax. But I can't. I already promised someone else."

"Who?" I ask in shock.

"Leo asked me yesterday if I needed one."

That little weasel.

I don't answer, I just storm out of the closet and head straight into the locker room where Leo is slipping on his shirt.

I slam the locker next to him. *Loudly.* "You asked her to wear your jersey?" I hiss at him.

The locker room grows suddenly quiet as all heads turn my way.

"You *finally* asked her? Good for you," Leo says.

I fist the collar of his shirt and shove him against the locker. "You set me up. You knew she was already wearing yours. You wanted to humiliate me."

"Get a grip," Leo says, trying to wriggle away, but I press my forearm into his chest harder. "I couldn't believe you hadn't asked her yet. I figured this would get you to actually *do* something."

"I *am* doing something, Leo. I'm going to stuff you in this locker if you don't come clean now." I muscle him into the locker opening, and Leo immediately squirms.

Vale rushes over. "Easy, Brax. Let him talk before you go throwing hands. Coach won't be happy if you hurt him."

I let out a low growl. As much as I hate it, Vale's right. He's one of the best on the team, and he can't stand the fact that I'm scoring more than him in practice games.

I ease up on Leo and back away, but only a step. "Then why do you have it out for me? What did I do to you?"

Leo shakes his head. "That's the problem. You think everything's about *you*."

"First you offer Jaz your jersey, then you slam me into the wall at practice. How could I *not* think it's about me?"

"Sometimes you get a little cocky out there." Leo flicks his thumb toward the rink. "And our competition isn't going to play nice. I'm just preparing you for battle."

"We're supposed to be on the same team, Leo." I shove him just enough to let him know I'm not playing around. Teammates or not.

Vale steps between us as Lucian and Dawson join him.

"You gotta cool down," Vale mutters, pulling me aside. "This isn't the way to teach Leo a lesson or help Jaz." He gives me a look of warning.

The last thing I want is Ego running off to tell the Ice Queen about us dating.

"Fine." I drag a hand through my hair. "What's this about, Leo?"

"I was trying to help you," Leo grumbles. "You're too afraid to take a risk. This was my way of getting you to move."

"By having her wear *your* number?"

Leo steps closer to me. "You wouldn't let an opponent take a shot away from you. Why would you let her get away?"

I narrow my eyes. "So, you were trying to *help* me?" I can't believe I'm saying those words. Why would Leo sacrifice anything for *me*?

"Yes," Leo mutters. "Believe me or don't. But it's true."

I stare at him for a long beat. "Why?"

"Because I'm tired of watching you hold back. Every guy on this team would like to date her, but you're the only one she has eyes for. Why wouldn't you pursue her?" Leo's words hit me like a fist I didn't see coming. Jaz always seems so controlled, like she's trying so hard to help everyone. How is it possible that I missed what was so obviously right in front of me?

"If only it were that simple," I mutter.

"It is," Leo says. "What's holding you back?"

"Alexandra, for one." I glance over my shoulder to check that she's not spying on us in the locker room. Alex wouldn't hesitate for a second to walk in here unannounced. "She doesn't want players and staff dating. Jaz is worried about her job."

Leo balls up a towel and throws it at me. "Forget her. She won't find out. And if she does, she can't fire you for that. You've done nothing wrong."

I glance at Lucian. "What about that girl you dated in the office? I heard she was fired for dating you."

Lucian shakes his head. "We'd already stopped dating by the time she got fired. Truthfully, she was just terrible at her job."

Relief blows through me. I should've asked Lucian before, but I was too afraid he'd guess my secret.

"If you're afraid the team is going to spill your secret, I can assure you they're not." Leo glances around at the guys circling us.

Everyone nods in agreement.

"I can vouch for the entire team," Lucian says. "Coach Thompson values loyalty over everything else. As team captain, I'd call out anyone who isn't backing up a player. If we can't trust each other off the ice, then how are we going to trust each other in a heated game?"

More heads bob in agreement.

I'm normally the guy who's all in. But I was holding back from my teammates, afraid that by telling them how I really feel about Jaz, I'd jeopardize her job and our relationship.

What I didn't understand is that I need these guys' support—on and off the ice. And it starts with trusting them to keep my relationship with Jaz a secret from Alex and the rest of her cronies.

"If I'm taking a leap of faith trusting you . . ." I step back so I'm part of the circle, instead of in the middle. "Then I need to convince Jaz you're all trustworthy."

"She got us to agree to the fashion show, right?" Leo says, grabbing his jacket from the locker. "If that doesn't prove it to her, nothing will. Because we wouldn't do it for anyone else." He heads for the door before I stop him.

"Ego," I call.

He looks over his shoulder.

"Thanks," I say. "I needed to be called out like that."

He nods once and, remarkably, doesn't make a sarcastic comment before heading out the door.

Proof that he does have a heart, after all.

Vale straddles the bench next to me. "That ended better than I thought it would."

I sit next to him. "I wasn't expecting Leo to do something nice."

"Nobody did. You're not the only one who feels like Leo is a wild card." He glances around to make sure no one is left in the locker room before he goes on. "I noticed you left out one piece of important information."

"Felipe?"

He nods. "He won't go away on his own. If the team knows, they can prepare."

I lean my elbows on my knees. "He hasn't contacted me recently. Gives me hope that maybe he's finally grown up. And if not, I've got you on my side."

"You put too much trust in my abilities. If you want to actually win the game, I can't track Felipe and you the entire time."

"Nobody can. That's why the team doesn't have to know. It's my job to take care of Felipe." I take my bag from the locker and slam it shut.

"Brax, you're just being an—"

"Don't even say it," I cut him off. "We share DNA, so whatever you're going to call me, you're essentially calling yourself."

His jaw clenches as he waits a beat. "You're making a mistake by not telling the team."

I shrug. "Maybe. But it's my choice."

Vale frowns. "If Felipe injures you worse, you'll never play again. Hockey is your life. Everything we've worked a lifetime for. You're going to give that up?"

I rub the knot on my shoulder from Leo's hit today. I don't

want to imagine a life without hockey. But lately, I've been thinking about what my future would look like with Jaz, fixing up her house, turning it into her dream home, one renovation at a time.

A place for us *together*.

It's the first time I've ever been able to imagine a life beyond hockey.

"I'm not giving up anything," I tell Vale.

Not even Felipe can stand in my way.

SEVENTEEN

Jaz

Brax sprints down the ice, hustling toward a loose puck with Leo close behind.

Even though it's just a practice, the heated excitement pulsates in my chest. It's a welcome relief from the worry about Sloan's unpaid medical bills, which pile up faster than the players' dirty workout clothes. She feels better every day, *thank goodness*. If that pattern continues, she'll eventually go back to doing what she loves. But money is still an issue until that time comes.

If it wasn't for Joshua and Brax working on the house, I don't know what I'd do. Brax uses all his spare time outside of practice to fix little things, while Joshua slowly makes progress on my bedroom project while painting the kitchen cabinets. When I ask Joshua how much I owe him, he tells me Sloan's chocolate chip cookies cover his fees.

What kind of guy works for cookies?

Brax just winks at me when I try to argue with Joshua about it.

It's a stark contrast from the guy on the ice who is totally focused on his game. He cuts Leo off, forcing him into the wall before Brax slaps the puck toward the goal, where Dawson stands ready. Dawson attempts to block it, but the puck zips by him with practiced ease.

Leo's shoulders slump. Brax skates by me, giving me a smile only I can see.

"Showoff," I mouth to him. It's true, but I love it. Watching him dominate the ice is thrilling, even when it is just a practice.

Vale gives his brother a high five as Coach Thompson calls a break. I watch as Leo mutters something under his breath, shakes his head, and then turns around and skates toward Brax. Then he does something that makes my jaw fall. Leo slaps Brax on the back for a shot well played.

I'm still in shock when Brax skates over to me, stripping off his helmet and running his fingers through his hair. "Are we still on for tonight's private practice?"

I glance up from my laptop, keeping my face in check. Better for everyone to think we're discussing work and not our next moment alone, even if he makes me feel like a tightly wound spring. "This is for charity, you know. Not a date."

He leans on his stick and lifts an eyebrow. "I get you all to myself, and that's the only thing that matters. No guys teasing us. No one else we have to worry about."

I scan the perimeter of the rink and spot Alex watching through a window on the opposite side. "Speaking of people watching, Alex is right behind you."

"For all she knows, we're working on the charity fundraiser together."

"Maybe. But after the team-building event at the zip line, she's watched us like a hawk." So have the rest of the staff. It's like she has her own spy ring. "You should probably go before she gets any ideas."

"I'll be in the gym lifting weights. See you tonight." Brax winks at me with the most adorable grin. He knows Alex can't see his face, but I can and it's unnerving.

My gaze flits over to Alex, who is now openly glaring at me.

I clamp my lips together and try to keep a poker face.

"That was so mean," I mutter to Brax with a smile as he skates off.

———

Alex doesn't hunt me down, thankfully, but that doesn't mean I'm safe. I wait until her light is off and text Brax when I see her car leave the parking lot.

No reason to risk the Ice Queen's wrath about our private practice, which Brax has been begging me to schedule. He's nervous about the opening number and needs help with the choreography, but I also suspect he just wants time alone with me. And finding time for us *alone* has felt like an impossible task, since most days, my house looks, sounds, and smells like a men's college dorm. The TV blares from the living room, smelly hockey gear lines the hall, and it always seems like someone is making food. My kitchen has become as busy as a roadhouse diner.

Which means the only way for us to spend time alone is by sneaking away.

When I arrive at the rink, Brax is waiting at the entrance, leaning against the wall, looking cuter than any hockey player should. His lips curve into a smile when he sees me, and I immediately walk into his arms because I actually can. No one is going to tease us, report us, or call us out for PDA.

"Do you want to practice the opening number first?" I ask, smothered against his chest. I get so few opportunities to hug him like this, I'm going to take full advantage of being wrapped up in his arms like a Brax burrito.

"Let's go for a spin around the rink," he murmurs against my hair.

I tilt my head to look up at him. "That's not on the agenda, and I'm a terrible skater."

"You don't trust me to catch you?" He shakes his head. "I would never let you fall."

"I thought we were here to work," I remind him.

Something sparks in his gaze. "Work can wait. I thought you always wanted a Hallmark movie skating date? That's what you told me before." He arches an eyebrow, waiting for me to remember my confession at Mia's wedding reception.

He snaps his fingers and music comes on. It's Taylor Swift's "This Is Me Trying"—the other thing I admitted to him that night in the closet. While the music soars, the bright florescent lights fade and a slow strobe moves across the ice, suddenly giving the effect of a dance floor with a disco ball.

"How did you do that?" I gasp.

"I have accomplices." He nods toward the sound booth, where Vale and Dawson wave. "If you haven't figured it out, we're not here to practice." He gives me a sly smile.

"We're here for a skating lesson?" I ask.

"A couples' slow skate. I can't give you the snow you asked for, but at least we have the music. You ever skate before?"

"Only in middle school. And just for the record, no one ever asked me to pair up with them or hold hands."

Brax frowns. "That's a shame. They didn't know what they were missing."

"Just for the record, I wasn't exactly a hottie back then. I had frizzy curls that stuck out, shiny braces, and I wore the same T-shirt almost every day until my stepmother finally took me aside and gave me a much-needed girls' trip to the mall. That's the one thing she taught me. How to feel pretty both inside *and* out."

Brax takes the back of his knuckles and brushes them down my cheek, featherlight. "Now it's my job to tell you how beautiful you are, inside *and* out, as much as possible."

Then he holds his hands out to me. "If you'll do me the honor, I'd like to be the first guy to skate with you. If you'll have me?"

I nod, and my chest nearly splits wide open with happiness. After all these years of never being asked, Brax is the perfect partner.

I frown. "But I didn't bring any skates."

"Size seven, right?" Sitting on the bench behind him is a pair of white women's skates and a jersey.

"How did you know?"

"Your sister," he says.

He picks up the skates and nods toward the bench. "Sit, Princess."

I give him a look, and he lifts an eyebrow. I know better than to fight him on this. He kneels in front of me and slips off my shoe.

"This really isn't necessary," I insist. "I can lace my own skates, Brax."

"Not like I can," he says, working his magic, loosening the laces before sliding it on. He does the same with the other foot, then ties each skate, taking care to get it just right.

Then he hands me a jersey. "I know you agreed to wear the other guys' jerseys before I had a chance to ask. But I still want to be the first."

I unfold it, stare at Brax's number sixteen, and smile.

"See how that feels," he says, rising to his feet.

I slide it over my head and give him a thumbs up.

Everything feels fantastic until my blades hit the ice and I wobble like a toddler learning to walk.

Brax leaps forward to grab my arm. "Steady, girl."

I cling to his arm, sure that I'm going to pull us both down even though we're standing still. "Did I mention I'm awful on skates?"

"Your sister warned me." He winks at me, and it makes my heart feel as unsteady as my legs. "It's why I insisted on tying your skates. Wouldn't want you to sprain an ankle. Now, give me your hands." He turns so he's facing me and offers both hands for support. I place my palms in his and wait for the spark of his touch to spread through me. I can't get over how my body lights up whenever he's near. Honestly, I'm not sure I ever *want* to get over it.

"Now, slide forward," he instructs gently.

"But you're in front of me," I say.

"I'll move with you. Don't worry about me," he says with an easy smile. "Skating is like walking for me."

"If only that were true for me." I wobble on the first glide forward, but hanging on to Brax's steady grip gives me confidence.

"Eyes on me," he instructs while skating backwards.

I didn't even realize I was staring at my feet. I tip my face toward his and take in his dark green eyes that look inky black under the dancing lights.

As the ice sparkles around us, his gaze has the same effect on me. *Distracting.* When I finally forget that I'm *actually* skating, my body wobbles, and I pitch backward.

Brax leaps for me, catching me before I bite the dust. All the sparks I felt before are gone, replaced by the sheer rush of adrenaline.

"Good catch," I murmur as he sets me back on my feet like a rag doll. "I didn't know how good you'd be at saving my butt."

"Well, your butt is top priority for me," he says with a smirk.

I burst out laughing. "My tailbone thanks you." Then I glance away from his gaze, sure that my cheeks are blazing.

"Eyes on me, Jazzy," he says, leading me forward on the ice.

"You're distracting to watch," I admit.

"So are you," he comments. "But you're never going to learn to skate if you're watching your feet. I hope I'm more interesting than the ice."

The music switches to Taylor Swift's "Lover" and a lighting effect sends shooting stars around the ice. "Is this a Taylor Swift playlist of my favorite songs? Or are you just exceptional that way?"

"All the above," he answers. "I told the guys to start the playlist and then leave. More like warned them that if they didn't, they'd have to do my dirty laundry for the rest of the week."

"Are you always this bossy?" I tease.

"Only when it comes to you," he assures me.

Even though my ankles are quivering, a warmth rises in my middle as his gaze stays locked on mine. With the music as our backdrop and the lights spinning in dizzying circles, I feel like I stepped into a fantasy world.

I've never been the lucky girl, the one who gets all the breaks.

But I feel like I've just won the lottery. It doesn't seem possible that he would choose *me,* but he did, for reasons I don't understand. He sees something in me I don't even see in myself. Under that tough exterior, he's kind and tender and remarkably funny. *Exceptional in every way.*

"You're getting better," he says, slowing us to a halt.

"Really?" I say in wonder, taking my eyes off him to glance at my feet.

Big mistake. I stumble forward and crash into Brax's chest. But he doesn't even wobble for a moment. Instead, he wraps his hands around my back to steady my body with his.

The impact of our bodies touching is explosive, like someone threw a match on a highly flammable liquid inside me.

I leave my hands on his chest, where I can feel the rise and fall of his breath under my fingers.

With his mouth against my ear, he whispers, "I've got you."

Those three words radiate through me before he adds, "I told you I wouldn't let you fall."

I pull back, just enough to see his expression.

His gaze skates over me, hungry for something that I want too.

"Just one thing more I want," he murmurs. His eyes darken, like black holes pulling me closer.

"What do you want?" My words are a strained whisper.

"I want you to be mine." He rests his forehead against my own, his grip tightening on my back. "I don't know how to make you trust me again. But I'm willing to do whatever it takes. And wait as long as you need me to."

I let him pull me closer so there's no space between us.

Last time this happened, we were on the dance floor at Boots and Buckles and he walked away. But tonight he doesn't move. He's letting me call the shots.

This time, I'm ready.

I cup his face with my hands, the stubble soft and scratchy against my palms, then reach up and bring my mouth to his. It's a slow, tender kiss, and not demanding at all.

Brax is so careful with me, like he's afraid of doing anything that will wreck my heart.

We're not in a hurry. We have all night to do this. The rest of our lives, even.

I let myself savor his closeness, his insatiable hunger for me, and feel the flutter in my stomach just like when I first leapt off the zip-line platform, his words echoing in my ears. *Don't think. Just close your eyes . . . and jump.*

EIGHTEEN

Prax

When the puck drops for our first game against the Texas Stars, I'm hardly aware of the half-empty seats or the tepid applause. I'm only focused on where the puck is and where it needs to be: *in the goal.*

Bodies cram the ice while flailing sticks and elbows fight for space. The smell of sweat fills the air as a body slams into my side.

"Watch it," I mutter as I scramble to reach the puck before my opponent does. Excitement balloons in my chest as I gain control of the puck and pass it to Leo. Without hesitating, he takes a shot that's blocked by their goalie.

As we hustle the other direction, Tate cuts off an opponent, then grabs the puck and passes it to Rourke.

I scramble toward our goal, watching Rourke pivot and flick the puck to Vale, who's in prime position to shoot. Vale slaps it toward the net, and my heart clenches as the puck slips under the goalie's knees.

"Yes!" I mutter under my breath, my gloved fist pumping the air as relief courses through me. I glance around and notice the few people here are cheering enthusiastically.

Apparently, not everyone thinks we're going to have another season as the Carolina Losers.

I crane my neck to see one figure dressed in our team colors of black and teal, leading the cheering section.

Jaz waves her arms and jumps up and down, thrilled that we've just scored. It's only the first period and everything could change, but a surge of pride sweeps through me.

We've worked hard, but it's not just the team that makes me proud. It's Jaz. She's single-handedly going to give this team a fan club.

When I skate off the ice, I slap Vale on the shoulder and glance into the stands, where Jaz gives me a small wave. I wink at her before taking a swig from my water bottle.

The last week has been nothing short of amazing. We're spending more time together—not just as a couple, but as partners in home renovation. While she paints the downstairs in soft grays and pale yellows, I've been chipping away at her massive repair list. A hole in the roof that needed patched. A cracked windowpane. The team even tore out the overgrown landscaping, boosting the house's curb appeal.

She wants to remodel *Rose & Thorn* one room at a time, starting with tearing out the wall between the kitchen and dining room. But she's also trying to take care of her sister. While she takes care of Sloan, I'm taking care of *her*.

"I see you have your own cheering section," Lucian remarks, nodding toward where Jaz now leads a group of enthusiastic Crushers fans in a cheer.

"When she's focused on something, she's a force," I marvel.

"Or when she's focused on you," Leo adds.

"The Ice Queen is here," Vale notes as Alex takes her seat.

"Nice of her to show up," Leo mutters.

When Jaz sees Alex, she abandons her cheering and sinks into her seat.

"We lost our cheerleader," Tate grumbles.

"Let's give them a reason to cheer," I say, thumping my stick on the floor.

Leo taps me on the shoulder. "What happened to Jaz wearing a team jersey?"

I glance at Jaz and notice she's wearing a Crushers sweatshirt.

Maybe this is the reason Alex doesn't like players and staff dating. It creates tension when one player is favored over another. I never asked her to give Lucian's jersey back. But secretly, I was hoping she would.

I wrap my gloved hands around my stick. *Forget playing fair.* I compete at a sport where men throw fists to prove themselves.

I want her to wear my jersey, no matter what Alex thinks about it. That means at some point, we're going to have to deal with Alex's disapproval of our relationship.

"Brax, get ready," Coach Thompson calls.

At that moment, Jaz looks at me, and I point to my jersey, then to her sweatshirt.

Her head discreetly nods toward Alex, who's busy chatting with Tom.

Our boss shouldn't dictate what Jaz wears, but like it or not, she has that kind of power. I'm determined to convince Jaz that we need to show the Ice Queen that she can't control us. That no one can keep us apart, even when they threaten us.

———

By the time we hit the last few minutes of the third period, sweat is dripping down the back of my neck. We're tied three to three with Vale, Leo, and I each having scored once.

My eyes flick toward Alex, who's watching the game with a dissatisfied frown.

Alex isn't my business. Winning is. I'm doing this for the fans and for Jaz. If we win, that will make her fundraising efforts so much easier.

When I search for her sweet face, only an empty seat remains.

I've never relied on having my family or friends in the crowd, but there's something about Jaz that's different.

I need her here. Her enthusiasm is like a shot of adrenaline, the extra pump of energy I crave to push harder on the ice.

Even though I keep things professional when Alex is around, I can't wait to get home and flirt with her until she turns flustered and pink-cheeked in front of the guys.

It's hard to keep my hands off her, and I look for every opportunity, whether it's stealing a touch while cleaning up dishes or rubbing her shoulders when she's tensing them at her desk.

It's even better when those little touches turn into full-on tickling matches where we end up in a cat-and-mouse game of chase, laughing until our bellies hurt.

I glance again at where she should be sitting. *Where is she?*

The sound of skates cutting into the ice pulls my attention back to the game. While I was thinking about Jaz, I lost a chance to gain control of a loose puck. I leap forward to beat my opponent, panic spiraling inside me, and I'm a second too late to reach it in time.

When you lose focus, you lose your shot. It's been drilled into me as long as I can remember.

But I've never had a girlfriend that's so distracting. I have to shut her out of my mind, put my blinders on, and play like a beast.

After the game, I can give my full attention to her.

I hustle down the rink, frustration driving me forward as my opponent shoots toward another player. Adrenaline courses through my veins as I intercept the puck and pass it to Leo, who's swarmed by two opponents. He narrowly keeps control, but they're forcing him back. I skate toward him, hoping that if he can flick the puck to me, I can pass to Vale, who's in position to shoot.

With an angry grunt, an opponent shoves Leo into the wall and steals the puck. I leap forward, and our sticks crack together as I narrowly swipe the puck away.

Rushing forward, I push the puck down the rink at full speed, my skates cutting into the ice as sweat prickles under my helmet. I can't see the clock, but I can feel the buzz of the crowd, the pressure of time slipping away.

I recklessly careen toward the goalie, who's daring me to come at him with a scowl.

Then I slap the puck and watch it narrowly slip in the gap over his right leg, sinking into the net with a precision that's astounding.

The horn blares and the entire Crushers team lifts their sticks into the air, hollering like we won the Stanley Cup.

Vale nearly tackles me on the ice only moments before Leo, Lucian, and Tate swarm me.

But I'm not focused on them or that we won.

My gaze shifts to the only seat in the house that matters. Relief pours through my body when I see her.

Jaz jumps up, lifting both fists with an enormous smile on her face.

That's when I notice why she left in the last period.

She's wearing the team jersey. In front of Alex. In front of everyone.

And it's *mine*.

NINETEEN

Jaz

"What are you doing?" Sloan says to me, eyeing my jersey as we sneak away from Alex to leave the game.

"Finding Brax," I tell her over my shoulder as I grab her arm and yank her along. I zigzag through the halls, attempting to reach Brax before he slips into the locker room.

"I meant wearing that," she warns. "*Number sixteen.* In front of your boss."

I shrug. "I'll give her an excuse if she asks. It's none of her business how I spend my free time. Or with *whom.*"

"Aren't you worried about your job?" Sloan asks, ignoring the crowd and staring at me.

"I'm playing it safe," I assure her. "Brax and I keep things very professional at work."

"Unlike at home, where you're awfully handsy with each other." She raises an eyebrow.

I've confessed to her that I had a massive crush on Brax long before he kissed me, ever since the first time we met at the Maplewood Mistletoe Festival.

Even then, Brax was Mr. Flirty-Pants, and I blamed it on the romantic mood of the festival.

Despite telling myself there was no future for us, I couldn't seem to stop myself, like a car without brakes headed toward the cliff's edge.

When he showed up at the wedding, dressed in a fitted black tux, looking so good he put Chris Hemsworth to shame, his gaze laser-targeted on me, all my weak excuses about why I couldn't fall for Brax crumbled like a cookie in a toddler's hand.

He made it so easy to take a chance on him.

When I danced with him that night, I forgot about every logical reason why I should say no. My world became a tiny point of light focused only on him.

But I don't have that luxury now. I have Sloan to take care of and Alex to please, while raising an army of fans for the Crushers. But that doesn't mean I can't chase down the man I'm crazy about and tell him how proud I am.

"Did you hear me?" Sloan jolts me back into the moment. "I asked whether you're certain Alex left."

I ignore my sister's worried expression. "She split as soon as we won. She asked for me to pass on how proud she was of the team."

"Alex is proud of them?" Sloan's eyebrows fly up. "I thought she only cares about money. Is it possible there's a heart beating under that frozen shell of a woman?"

"Maybe." It gives me hope that if the team keeps winning, Alex will reconsider her plan to shut down the team. Even though the secret is killing me, I can't reveal it to Sloan, or she'd be furious and tell me to quit.

But I know that's not the answer. Not when I have stacks of medical bills and a fixer-upper to keep up.

We finally make it to the hall outside the locker room, where a local TV station is interviewing Brax. His eyes flick to mine, and I give him two thumbs up to let him know what a great job he's doing.

According to Lucian, the local TV station rarely interviews any of the players. This is a good sign that things are changing, and the team is finally getting the attention they deserve.

Brax glances at Lucian and pushes him toward the camera. "This is our team captain. I'm sure he can answer questions you have about the game."

As Lucian takes over, Brax strides toward me.

"Great—"

Before I can finish, Brax picks me up off the floor and spins me around, leaving my stomach fluttery.

With his hands still locked on me, he sets me down, and I murmur, "I was trying to say great job tonight."

"And I was trying to say *I'm happy to see you.*" His smile crinkles his eyes, and my heart gallops harder in my chest.

"Aren't you happy to win?" I ask.

"That, too," he says, not paying attention to the people swarming around us. "Thanks to you."

I frown. "Me? I had nothing to do with it."

"Seeing you cheering was . . ."

"Distracting?" I finish for him.

"I was going to say *very* motivational."

I laugh. "In that case, I plan on cheering for every game. Anything else I can do to motivate you?"

Brax pulls me tighter against him. Even in public, I don't mind him claiming me as his. Only the players are allowed back here now that the reporters have left.

Dawson interrupts us with a wide grin. "I think you deserve something better than a hug for that last shot. It was perfectly timed."

"I agree," Leo says, looking at me. "It's the very least you could do."

The rest of the team immediately starts teasing Brax for not planting a kiss on me.

Brax shakes his head. "I won't force something on her because you clowns think I deserve it."

What kind of guy would honor me over giving in to his friends? Only Brax.

"It's okay," I whisper. "Just do it so they stop teasing."

"No, it's really *not* okay," he says. "I don't care what they think. I'm not caving because of them."

I finally decide *enough is enough*. He doesn't deserve this.

I step toward him and say in my boldest voice, "Then I'm kissing you, Brax MacPherson."

His face snaps to mine as his lips curl into a crooked smirk. "Are you sure about this?"

"Never been more sure in my life." I jump into Brax's arms, wrap my legs around his waist and kiss him with everything I've got.

That'll shut them up.

———

It did shut them up. Mainly because everyone's mouths were hanging open in shock.

Since that moment, there's been no more teasing. And no more kissing in a week. For the record, I've kissed Brax twice, but he hasn't initiated a kiss with me. And now I'm worried.

Why is he holding back? It's not that he's given any hint to make me believe he's questioning it. Every chance he gets, he surprises me with something to make me smile.

After returning from an away game late last night, Brax left me flowers in a vase outside my door with the note: *I want to be the first person every day to make you smile.*

The other night, he snuck up behind me while I was washing dishes and wrapped his arms around my waist. "Has anyone told you that you look beautiful today?" he whispered. "Because you should be told that every day."

The scene caused Tate to yell from the other room, "You're breaking a house rule!"

"What rule?" Brax replied, not letting me go. "Annoying you?"

"Flirting," Tate said, giving him the evil eye.

Brax grunted, then continued to hug me while Tate and Leo hurled insults at us.

The guys can't stop teasing us about the house rules, but Brax refuses to give up his flirty ways, which I can't say I'm sorry about.

He just hasn't tried to kiss me, either. And the longer he waits, the more I want him to show me that I'm someone special. It's like trying *not* to think about chocolate when all you want is chocolate. *Humanly impossible.* After what happened with Brax ghosting me, I want evidence that this isn't a repeat performance.

"Just talk to him," Sloan urges as she stirs a giant pot of spaghetti sauce.

"When am I going to do that?" The house smells like basil and garlic, and Sloan licks a spot of tomato sauce off her wrist. "We're hosting a team dinner tonight. I won't have time for an intimate conversation about Brax's lips."

Sloan props a hand on her hip. She's wearing the *Kiss the Cook* apron to keep sauce from splattering her cute yellow blouse, and her hair is pulled up into a messy bun, highlighting her striking cheekbones. "The longer you wait, the more it's going to bother you. Just pull him aside and tell him. With all the people around, no one will even notice if you're gone."

"And ask what? *Why haven't you kissed me?* Maybe I should wear that apron and see if he gets the hint."

"If it helps . . ." She unties it, willing to stain her adorable blouse just so I'll get kissed. That's *so* Sloan. She'd give me the shirt off her back if I asked for it.

I wave my hands, forbidding her to take it off. "I'm not that desperate. Even if it's driving me crazy."

Sloan tips my chin to hers, like Granny used to do. "I've seen the way he looks at you, Jazzy. Brax isn't playing around. He can't keep his eyes off you."

I smile, feeling that warm glow in my chest, the same one that fills my body every time he's around. "So the guys have reminded me, every time they catch him breaking a house rule."

"You're the one who created the rules," she reminds me with a lifted brow. "Maybe he just wants you to be sure after what happened."

Sloan stops stirring for a second and squeezes her eyes shut.

I freeze, knowing exactly what's happening. Sloan's face grows pale, and I reach up and tilt her face so I can look at her. "I didn't know you weren't feeling well."

"I'm fine," she says, waving it off. "Feeling dizzy and light-headed is an everyday thing since the accident. Probably just a migraine coming on."

"There's no such thing as *just* a migraine," I remind her. "Not since your accident."

Here I am complaining that Brax hasn't kissed me, and she's dealing with an injury that's kept her bedridden for months.

"You should lie down. Sleep it off," I insist, grabbing her arm so she doesn't faint on me. "I'll take over at the stove."

She shakes her head. "I'm not sitting this out. I was looking forward to tonight. The last thing I want is to go to bed."

Sloan hasn't been this happy in ages. Asking her to miss the party is like a slap in the face.

She clenches her jaw. "These guys make me feel like family. Do you know how long it's been since I've felt needed? For once, I want to have some control over my life. Even if it's just tonight."

I can't win this argument. Sloan wants to stay. Who am I to take her joy away?

"I won't send you to bed, sis. Just don't push too hard, okay?"

She rubs her hand over her eyes, forcing back the pain before she turns to me. "I got a call from a specialist at the Cleveland Clinic, the one I've been waiting months to see. He's doing a new medical treatment for patients with brain injuries, and the initial patient response has been incredible."

I step back just enough to see the hope in her eyes. "That's great, Sloan. You should do it." A miracle drug is what Sloan needs at this point. This injury hasn't just altered her life, it's killing her spirit.

"Really?" Her face brightens. "But it's so far from South Carolina. And with our situation . . ."

I grasp her shoulders, leveling my gaze. "I'll make sure you get to Cleveland for this treatment. I'll move the world to take you there myself."

Her smile drops. "But I told them I couldn't."

"What?" I gasp. "Why?"

"Because it's still experimental, insurance doesn't pay for the cost, and it's twenty-five thousand dollars. There's no way I can afford something that might not work."

I shake my head. "I can't let you turn down this opportunity. Call them back. We'll find a way to get the money, even if we have to rob a bank."

Sloan doesn't even blink at my joke. She's still staring at me in shock. "But what about . . ."

"I'm not arguing about it." I take the spoon and stir the sauce, which is now boiling out of control. It splatters my pink silk blouse, leaving a spray of dots across the front, but I don't even care. I just want to see my sister well.

Sloan frowns. "You sure about this? How are you going to get that much money?"

The pot of sauce settles to a simmer, and I bang the wooden spoon on the edge before setting it down. "I'll figure it out. But I'm not letting you miss this chance at finally getting back to normal."

Alex won't like me traipsing off whenever my sister needs to go to Cleveland, but right now, I'm unconcerned what Alex thinks.

Sloan narrows her eyes. "I'm not going to let this affect your life too. It's *my* problem."

"It's *our* problem. Remember our pinky promise?" I wrap my pinky around hers, like we did when we were kids.

Even though we fought like crazy in middle school, we were also attached at the hip. There's nothing like a sister to have your back while you deal with mean girls and boyfriends who break up with you in the middle of third period.

"Here for you always," Sloan and I say together.

Her lips curl into a bright smile that makes her face radiant. Some things never change. Sloan's grin is one of them.

"Right back at you." I tap my sister on the nose with the wooden spoon, which leaves a spot of sauce behind.

"Hey!" She laughs and wipes it away with the back of her hand.

So much is riding on what happens in the next few months. Sloan's health. The team surviving. Keeping my job. This roommate situation which was never supposed to be permanent. But without the guys' rent, I can't afford both this home *and* Sloan's medical bills. And that doesn't even include the expenses for this experimental treatment.

It's like a perfect storm of problems, and I'm drowning in the flood.

The doorbell rings, and before I can reach it, Lucian, Dawson, and Rourke burst into the entry, laughing about something that happened at last night's game. To my disappointment, I'm not allowed to attend away games since Tom told me no one but the top staff travels on the team dime.

Since practices tied up the guys' schedules all day, that means I still haven't seen Brax since he left last night.

"Hey, beautiful," a voice rumbles behind me. I spin around to see a freshly showered Brax striding toward me from the back door.

He picks me up like I'm as light as a daisy and spins me around, the smell of his cologne overwhelming me. I nuzzle my face in the hollow of his neck, breathing in his warm scent, before he sets me on my feet again.

"You're home, *finally*," I murmur with a grin I can't hide. Seeing and touching him is like getting a shot of dopamine. All the happy chemicals whirl around my brain, stirring up so much pleasure. Brax doesn't need to do anything but walk into the room, and my heart is doing inconvenient flips.

"Hi, you." His hands slide to my back and his lips curve as he looks me over. That smile disarms all my defenses. "Sorry I didn't see you last night or this morning," he murmurs against my ear, making a shiver rush down my arm.

Rourke elbows Dawson and nods at us. "Big Mac's got it bad."

Dawson crinkles his nose, like a kid who's been served Brussels sprouts for dinner. "Come on, guys, we're about to eat. You're ruining my appetite."

Brax looks at him, but doesn't let me go. Instead, he grips my back even harder, letting me know we're staying this close no matter what Dawson thinks. "As I recall, Dawson, you were making eyes at that pretty blonde after the game last night."

Dawson grins. "Yeah, well. She said she has a thing for goalies."

Lucian rolls his eyes. "The way you smell after a game? No one is getting near you."

The guys snicker as Dawson ambles toward the table. "You guys are just jealous she wasn't looking at you."

"Jealous?" Leo asks, joining the other guys around the table. "Did she get sick of all your hockey pickup lines?"

"I don't have any hockey pickup lines." Dawson grabs a roll from the table, even though the rest of the food isn't done yet. These guys are like insatiable trash compactors with their food consumption, and Sloan delights in keeping them full.

"Are you kidding me?" Leo's eyes widen before he strikes a typical Dawson pose. "Hey, baby, is this a power play?" Leo says, attempting his best Dawson impression. "Because your beauty gives you an incredible advantage over me."

The guys all groan as Dawson shrugs. "What?"

Unlike Leo, Dawson isn't afraid of looking silly or being vulnerable. He's one of the most genuine guys when you get to know him—a total cinnamon roll beneath that intimidating goalie glare.

"It worked," Dawson says, slapping some butter on his roll. "I got her phone number."

Pots clang in the kitchen as Sloan sticks her head in the dining room. "The spaghetti will be ready in ten minutes."

Vale jumps up from the table. "You need help, Sloan?"

Sloan looks at me, still in Brax's arms. "Sure, since it looks like my sister is otherwise occupied." Then she gives me a quick wink before handing Vale a wooden spoon. I know she's trying to give me a moment with Brax, and my stomach flips nervously.

"Sorry, Vale," I call, but Vale just shrugs.

"I'm not sorry," Brax whispers, pulling me closer so that I'm snuggled into the warmth of his arms. "I missed you last night."

"Me too," I whisper, trying not to sound too sad, since this is what I signed up for. I have to accept him being on the road, even if that means women will flirt with him after games. I'm confident he'll shut them down, but that won't keep them from trying.

"Can I talk to you for a couple of minutes?" The nervousness in my stomach feels like a pot of boiling water ready to bubble over. I'm doing the brave thing I promised Sloan. If this is going to work, I have to put our trust issues behind us.

"Sure." Brax frowns. "Is something wrong?"

"Not wrong, exactly." I glance around and notice that everyone is busy. The perfect time to sneak away. With his hand in mine, I lead him into the back hallway.

"This must be serious if you're taking me here. Unless we're planning on doing other things?" He lifts a suggestive eyebrow that makes me want to forget talking and take up his invitation.

I wait a beat, and he just grins, but still doesn't kiss me. If only he would make a move, then we wouldn't be having this conversation.

A few pots clang in the kitchen, and then the clatter of metal hitting the floor. Vale yells, "Oops! That wasn't supposed to happen."

"Everything okay in there?" I call down the hall.

"It will be!" Sloan replies.

I'm torn between helping my sister and having this conversation with Brax.

"You were saying . . ." He tilts his head, studying me, like I'm the only one here, even though more players are shuffling in.

Sharing a house with hockey players is like living in Grand Central Station. It's never quiet, and people are forever coming and going.

Since Sloan invited the entire team, I won't get another opportunity to have Brax to myself for the rest of the evening.

"Can I ask you a question?" I swallow down the lump in my throat.

"You can ask me anything you want. You know that, Jaz. I'm an open book."

"I know, it's just that . . . everything's been so great between us. I almost feel guilty."

His smile fades. "Wait, are you breaking up with me?"

"No!" I insist. "Why would you think that?"

"You look concerned." He smooths my wrinkled brow with his thumb.

"Nothing's wrong." My stomach clenches at my own twisted truth.

"The look on your face doesn't agree."

He can see right through me, which makes me feel flattered and a little terrified. *Am I that easy to read?*

A face peeks around the corner. "What are you guys doing back here?" Tate asks.

Brax shoots him a look that says *not now*. "Trying to have a conversation. Get out of here."

"I was going to wash my hands before dinner." He nods at the bathroom in the hall.

"Go upstairs," Brax demands.

Tate sighs and turns to leave.

"We need more privacy," I say.

"Story of my life," Brax mutters.

Every time Brax and I are alone, we get interrupted. It makes life challenging, and our alone time nearly impossible.

"Come in here." I pull him into the same pantry closet where I had a private conversation with Sloan when I discovered Brax was our new roommate.

I flip on a single bulb in the cramped space. Brax's body is almost pushed up against mine, sending spirals of heat through me.

His lips curve into a smirk. "I never knew about this closet."

"I use it all the time with Sloan."

"But not me?" He looks around at the shelves stuffed with mac and cheese and cans of soup. "This could be a seriously good make-out spot."

"Funny you bring that up," I say with a nervous laugh.

Brax shoots me a puzzled glance.

"You want me to be honest with you, right? Because that's what got us into trouble before," I say, twisting Granny's ring. The butterflies in my stomach are bumping around, but it's not the same panic I felt on the zip-line platform. Brax is my safe space, and I know he won't laugh at me, no matter how foolish I feel. "I'm trying to do the right thing this time, instead of feeling like I messed things up between us."

He tips my chin toward his face. "Whatever it is, you didn't mess it up. I want your honesty, because that's what's going to make this work between us. But right now, the suspense is killing me."

Roger that. Get to the point. "Remember what happened the other week? After the game?"

"Outside the locker room?" he guesses.

I nod.

Then he says slowly, "You're having second thoughts about kissing me?"

I shake my head. "No, I thought *you* were."

"Me?" A laugh of disbelief escapes his lips. "Believe me, I have *not* had second thoughts about that. Unless you're counting the hundreds of times I've replayed it in my head." He gives me a mischievous grin as my cheeks heat.

"Then why haven't you . . ." My voice drops, afraid of saying what's really on my mind.

"Kissed you?" he finishes for me.

My eyes drop to the floor, where our toes almost touch. I'm still afraid that I'm not enough for him. That all my baggage somehow makes me unlovable.

He cups my face with his hands and slides his thumb over the hollows of my cheeks. "When you kissed me last week in front of the guys, I didn't know if you felt pressure from them. I want you to trust me one hundred percent. That's why I'm waiting to kiss you, so you know it's not *just* physical attraction. I lost your trust before, and I'm working twice as hard at earning it back. Until you trust me with your heart, I'll be here waiting for you."

He says the words softly, and I feel like a tub of ice cream left out of the freezer too long. "My sister was right," I say, shaking my head in disbelief. "She told me to ask you. I was scared you'd changed your mind."

His other hand cups the back of my neck as he pulls me toward him. "When it comes to you, I could never change my mind."

He leans toward me, his lips only a breath away. My pulse leaps, and I know I'm finally going to get my wish.

Footsteps patter down the hall. "Jaz?" It's Dawson, and he's outside the pantry closet.

As the door swings open, I pull away from the kiss and spin toward the shelf of cereal, studying it intently.

"We need some cereal, don't we, Brax?" I smack Brax on his arm, trying to get him to play along.

Dawson glances between us. "Yeah, like *that's* believable." A grin props a corner of his mouth.

"You're interrupting us," Brax growls in a tone that is anything but friendly.

"I see that, but Sloan needs you."

That's when I notice how quiet the kitchen is. Something isn't right.

As I hurry down the hall, Vale's voice rises above the clatter, "Are you sure you shouldn't lie down?"

I round the corner. Sloan is hunched over the counter, her head flush with the edge.

"I'll be fine," she groans. "Just give me a minute." Her eyes are squeezed shut, her body clenched.

"Sloan, what's wrong?"

My sister lifts her face and that's when I panic. Her face is grayish white and her forehead glistens with sweat.

"I'm not . . ." Her eyes roll back, and my stomach clenches with fear.

"Sloan!" I scream, running toward her, but I'm too late.

She collapses before I can reach her.

TWENTY

Prax

"Call 911!" Jaz calls, the terror in her voice slicing through the chatter from the dining room. I'm on it before she can even reach Sloan's side. Jaz kneels next to her sister, pulling her onto her lap and talking to her gently, patting her face.

"Sloan, you've got to wake up," Jaz pleads. "We're calling an ambulance, sis. Stay with me." Jaz strokes her sister's face gently, but her words are urgent, desperate.

Sloan's eyelids flutter open, and we give a collective sigh of relief. But we know she's not out of the woods yet.

Jaz is adamant that Sloan go to the ER, just to be sure nothing is wrong. When we arrive, they put her through a battery of tests while Jaz and I wait for answers that aren't quick to come.

When the doctor arrives, he insists that Sloan's fainting episode was likely because of her injury, and there's nothing else they can do. The news isn't entirely surprising, but I can see the lines of worry on Jaz's face. She wonders what will happen if her sister doesn't get better. And I wonder what will happen to Jaz if she's always carrying the weight of everyone's problems on her shoulders.

I assign more chores around the house, and even convince the guys to put in new landscaping around the front porch. Anything looks better than the empty patch of dirt left over after we pulled out the overgrown bushes.

I also ask the team to give up more of their free time for our volunteer initiatives, including a retirement home visit, more elementary school visits, and even a local meet-and-greet, which turns out to be a big hit and gives us lots of free publicity on social media. We advertise the upcoming *Fashion on Ice* fundraiser, and the newspaper catches wind of it and does a feature story on the event.

When the local TV stations hear about our volunteering, they schedule an interview with Jaz that later gets picked up by some national news outlets.

Even our attendance is up. Instead of barely filling a quarter of the seats, we're now selling fifty percent of the Ice House's capacity.

Alex has taken notice, but she doesn't exactly seem pleased, which is odd since she's invested in our success.

Jaz shakes her head as she scans over a dozen emails from media outlets. They're all interested in our team's random acts of kindness, which draws more media attention than our wins.

"Another news channel wants to interview you and Vale about your recent visit to the nursing home," she says.

"I don't know why." I'm eating a peanut butter and jelly sandwich at her desk over lunch since this might be my only shot to see her today. Between her schedule and mine, we've barely had time for each other.

She picks at the salad in front of her while staring at the screen. "They heard about your impromptu waltz with that ninety-year-old woman and how your brother cut in very sweetly."

I set my sandwich down and wipe my hands. "First, *that* was not a waltz. I just followed Betty's moves and tried not to step on her toes. It was Vale's idea to cut in. He's a hopeless romantic and loves the attention." Then I lean toward her, cupping her cheek. "Personally, I'm not interested in talking with anyone except you.

Right now, you're all mine." I brush a kiss across her nose, then her lips.

Jaz tilts her head. "Brax MacPherson, are you flirting with me on the job?"

"I will flirt with you any chance I get," I promise, pulling her onto my lap and nuzzling her ear.

"We need to be careful." She lifts her eyebrows in a mock warning, but from the curve of her lips, she likes it just as much as I do.

I carefully brush my finger across her lips. "I'm being *so* careful." Then I kick my foot out so it slams the door shut. "I have five minutes before I need to head back to practice before Coach notices I'm missing."

"Five minutes to work on the fundraiser?" she teases.

I shake my head. "That's not what I was thinking. I want five minutes of your undivided attention."

She wraps her arms around my neck. "If all I get is five minutes of you today, I'm going to enjoy it."

I cup the back of her neck and tug her closer, just as someone knocks at the door.

"Seriously?" I groan, dragging my hand through my hair.

She hops off my lap, smoothing her hair. "I should make sure it's not Tom with my new budget for the fundraiser."

I frown. "Pretend you're not here." My hands slide to her waist, keeping her from moving.

The knock rattles the door, louder this time.

Whoever it is, they're not going away.

She gives me an apologetic look. "I'll make it up to you later," she whispers before kissing my forehead.

When she opens the door, Alex stands on the other side.

Her eyes slide from Jaz to me as a look of disapproval crosses her tightened lips.

"Sorry for the interruption, but I have bad news," Alex says, not looking sorry at all. "Tom advised me that the *Fashion on Ice* event is costing too much. Even though attendance is up, he said we shouldn't take any financial risks, especially on a glorified fashion show."

"Risks?" Jaz frowns at Alex. "We'll get all the money back, and it goes to a good cause. It's not a *glorified* fashion show. It's a chance for the community to see our team in a new way. To build loyalty. That's priceless. Surely, you can see that?"

Alex plants her feet in the doorway, arms crossed. "There's too much at stake. We're a hockey team. Not a bunch of do-gooders."

I stand. "Don't we want to make this team something the community is proud of?" I join Jaz by her side, a united front. "We're giving back to the people in this town. Doing something worthwhile to benefit a charity."

She waves me off. Helping kids like Ethan is the least of her worries. "Tom understands the financial risks of such a venture," she says. "And we need to be the ones benefitting from the team."

Like Queen Alex hasn't already benefitted the most.

"But we've sold hundreds of tickets," Jaz pleads. "We'd need to return all the money if we cancel now, and we'd lose the deposit from all the vendors we've contracted."

Alex looks away, like she's displeased by this news. Apparently Tightwad Tom didn't ask about all these details that Jaz already knew.

Alex lets out an exasperated sigh. "I'll talk to Tom about it again. But remember, this isn't part of our long-term plans."

Long-term plans? I thought building community support was an overarching goal?

Jaz gives a weary nod. "I understand."

Her gaze flicks to me before landing on Jaz. "When I get back from my business trip, I need to talk to you about some changes." Then she whirls around and stalks down the hall.

"That woman is as cold as ice," I mutter when she's out of earshot.

Jaz sighs. "She's being her usual queen-bee self. I'm trying to walk a tightrope between her demands and the potential I see in this team. But it's hard when the owner and general manager are against you."

"What do you think she wants to talk about?"

Jaz blinks. "I'm not sure. But whatever it was, it didn't sound positive. Did you notice?"

"Same." I pick up my bag, trying not to think about whether Coach has noticed my long absence. Vale and Lucian will cover for me with an excuse. Unlike Alex, Coach Thompson has an understanding way about him.

A flicker of worry flits across Jaz's face before she turns to me. "At least you guys are winning now. But the next two weeks are critical. Both for the fundraiser and when you face off with the Wolf Pack."

I immediately stiffen at hearing her mention Felipe's team. "Why do you say that?"

"I just heard Felipe's team is good. They play rough. I don't want anything to happen to you." She wraps her arms around my waist and looks up at me with concern.

"Nothing will happen to me," I say. "Trust me."

"I do trust you. It's your enemy I don't trust."

Jaz and I continue to orbit around each other, never quite stopping long enough to spend much time together, grabbing brief moments here and there. A hug before work. Her hand lingering on my back as she makes dinner. A quick kiss on the cheek before she collapses into bed. Not only is she swamped with the *Fashion on Ice* event, but she's also traveling with Sloan to Cleveland Clinic.

I give her a long hug before she leaves, so she knows how much I'll miss her.

"How am I supposed to leave after that?" she murmurs against my ear.

"I wouldn't want you to fall for any handsome doctors."

She shakes her head. "No chance of that happening." She spiders her fingers up my back. "Not when I have *this* to come home to."

I pull her close to me so that our foreheads touch, but we're interrupted by Sloan, clearing her throat behind us.

"I don't want to miss our plane because you two lovebirds couldn't stop making eyes at each other." Her disapproving tone can't hide her grin. "Also, Grant's waiting at the airport."

"Who?" I ask.

"You met him at Mia's wedding, remember?" Jaz says. "Ella's husband is a pilot. He agreed to fly Sloan and me to her appointments."

I kiss Jaz's forehead one more time, trying not to feel the emptiness that follows me like a cloud whenever she's gone.

"It's only two days." She touches my lips with her finger. "But that kiss makes me never want to leave."

"I'll leave you alone so you can make out without me standing here awkwardly, pretending not to watch," Sloan jokes as she rolls her suitcase outside.

Jaz shakes her head. "She's just jealous." Then she gives me an intense kiss on the lips before flying out the door. "Don't miss me too much!"

I already do.

After watching her and Sloan leave for the airport, I head into Jaz's bedroom and survey the work Joshua's done so far. I want to surprise Jaz with a finished bedroom and the downstairs painted before she gets back, but only if I can convince the team to help me. If we make good progress, I'd even like to knock out the wall between the kitchen and dining room.

The doorbell rings and I assume it's Joshua, here to work for the day.

"Come on in, Joshua," I call out the bedroom door, but the ringing persists.

When I glance out the front window, a man with tanned skin

and enviously thick black hair waits with a leather backpack. I get the vague feeling I've met him before.

"Can I help you?" I ask, looking him over with arms folded across my chest.

"Brax," he says, holding out his hand with no explanation. "Jaz here?" His arm is covered in tattoos, and he wears a camouflage T-shirt under his jean jacket. He looks like some sort of ex-Marine alpha type. What does he want with Jaz? I don't like strange men showing up at her door, asking for her.

I glance at his hand and reluctantly take it. "Do we know each other?"

"I'm Brendan. We met at the wedding. I'm good friends with Jaz."

I tighten my grip on his hand as a surge of jealousy snakes through me. "Friend, huh?"

Brendan blinks, like he's feeling the pressure, but he doesn't let go. Instead, he returns a fierce grip. It's now a competition to see who will let go first.

"Just friends, man," he says firmly. "We go way back."

I narrow my eyes, still not backing down. "Did you ever date her? Are you that kind of friend?"

"We never went out. Ask her if you need proof," he urges, finally releasing my hand. I notice he rubs his palm a bit and eyes me carefully. He looks like the type who cares a lot about his appearance, from his immaculate leather boots to his defined shoulders and sculpted body. His hair is neatly trimmed and styled with enough pomade to keep it in place through a hurricane. No wonder he and Jaz hit it off. He's like the male version of her with his eye-catching style.

He clears his throat. "I didn't mean to imply anything. Jaz and I have never gone out."

"Even *once*?" I ask, testing him.

He shakes his head adamantly. "We don't see each other like *that*. I'm more like her overprotective brother, the one who'd rather talk about what *not* to wear than matters of the heart. She always begged to join my blended Puerto Rican family. My mom would've been thrilled if I had dated her. But we just never had feelings for each other. She's not into ex-military types." He looks me over. "But hockey players? That's no surprise."

My shoulders ease a bit. As long as he's not her ex, anyone who welcomes Jaz into their family is a friend of mine.

"You know Jaz just left?" I ask, looking over his shoulder and seeing his Harley in the driveway.

"I wondered if she was gone yet," he says, setting down his bag. "She didn't tell you I was coming?"

"Apparently not." I scratch the back of my head. I guess she's been so busy she forgot to mention Brendan was visiting.

"I travel a lot, and she offered Sloan's room while I'm here. She thought I'd enjoy hanging out with the team while I help with the fundraiser."

"You're staying with us?"

Brendan nods. "Is that okay?"

"If Jaz says so." I've been bugging her to ask for help, but I didn't know she'd take me seriously or invite Brendan for a sleep-over. "What are you going to do for Jaz?"

Brendan pulls out a business card. "I used to work for my uncle's minor league baseball team as a strength and conditioning coach, as well as doing odd jobs for the team, like community outreach. My uncle collects teams like some people collect cars. I know baseball isn't the same as hockey—but certain parts of the management aren't that different. When I heard about Sloan, I offered to help. Jaz isn't good at trusting people to take over her responsibilities. But I promised to keep up with her fundraiser, and that seemed to take a load off her mind. I owe Jaz a favor—something she did for me a long time ago." He shoves his hands in his pockets, looking a little embarrassed. "You're a lucky man, because she's got a heart of gold. And I say that like a brother."

I nod. *Heart of gold is right.* She'd lay down her life for any of us, whether or not we deserved it.

Brendan glances around and walks through the living room,

eyeing the fireplace and crown molding. "Good bones in this place. I can see why Jaz wanted to buy it. She was going to send me instructions later today. Do you have anything I could help with?"

"Maybe." I look him over, unsure if a guy like him has any experience getting his hands dirty. "Are you good with power tools?"

He grins. "Are you kidding me? Give me a drill, and you won't see me for hours."

Like that, I know that we're going to be friends.

———

Over the next few days, I'm too busy finishing Jaz's bedroom with Joshua and Brendan to spend time thinking about how much I miss her. Maybe it's a coping mechanism, but I'd much prefer to whack a nail into a board or crush someone on the ice than discuss my emotions.

With Joshua's guidance, we finish the built-in desk and bookshelves as well as a spectacular window seat that's remarkably like the picture Jaz had on her phone.

Gorgeous floor-to-ceiling bookshelves painted in a rich navy blue flank a matching desk that looks out on Granny's rose garden. I even installed a small gold pendant light over the desk to match the shiny gold handles on her drawers. On the other wall, a new window seat offers the perfect view of the magnolia tree and bird feeder.

I'm a *go big or go home* kind of guy, and decided the bedroom wasn't enough. Vale and I tackled the demolition of the wall between the dining room and kitchen, too. With the help of the hockey team, we remodeled the space into one giant room and painted the entire downstairs with the colors Jaz had picked out.

Despite my initial skepticism about Brendan, he's turned out to be an invaluable help. Not only is he wildly talented with a power drill and paintbrush, he's also a management genius. He's checked with every vendor for the upcoming fundraiser, secured two more sponsors, and even made sure our fashion show had all the right touches with Jaz's approval, including custom hats, socks, and one-of-a-kind Crushers boxers. Even though we will not model them for the event, he claims women will beg to order them for their significant others afterward.

Based on how women flock to Brendan's magnetic smile, the man could probably sell Crushers' ice and make a killing.

He even agrees to rehearse with the team for the fundraiser's opening number. Because the man has no end to his talents, I quickly discover that he dances like a Latin pop star.

After watching the routine twice, he picks up the moves with a flair that's enviable. His hips definitely don't lie.

"I thought this guy was here to help Jaz with administrative stuff?" Lucian whispers as we run through the synchronized skating moves for our opening number.

I shrug. "That's what he told me. I didn't know he could dance."

"Maybe he should perform with us," Leo says. "So he can take the attention off you."

"Thanks for the support." I bump his shoulder.

Dawson's mouth falls open as Brendan adds an extra turn to the choreography. "If I could dance like that, we'd raise a million dollars."

"We're hockey players, not dance stars," I mutter as we form a crooked line.

"No, we're embarrassing," Tate says as we all move at different times. "We can't even do a straight line."

"Speak for yourself," Leo says, jutting out his chin. He's annoyed by how easily Brendan picked up the moves even though he refuses to admit it.

We hit the final pose with big jazz hands, and Brendan scratches his head as we hold our pose. He bites his cheek and frowns. "You're not staying together with the choreography, but I don't think it's your fault. What this routine needs is not more moves, but *less*."

"We feel stupid," Rourke huffs. "No offense to Jaz. But we're not dancers. We're athletes."

Brendan nods. "I agree. We need to simplify the routine and play to your strengths. Emphasize the skating more and dancing less. But there's one missing ingredient—your style."

Leo raises a hand. "What about people who have no style? Like Rourke, here?"

Rourke gives Leo a shove, and he quickly retaliates by pushing back. Brendan's jaw clenches as the men quickly descend into a juvenile shoving match.

He storms over to them, and in true military fashion, places a hand on their chests and gives them a look that says *cool it*. "We're not fighting about it. When I said style, that's something *anyone* can have. It's like personality. It's bringing that unique aspect that only *you* possess. You might think you're a macho hockey player, but I want you to check your pride at the door and think of the kids who will benefit from your presentation. This is for a charity —for kids who can't do everyday tasks without help, some in wheelchairs. And you're worried about looking bad?"

Every guy looks at the ice.

Brendan shakes his head. "That's why I'm going to simplify the routine and cut the middle section. Instead, you'll come up with your own dance break."

"What?" Vale and I say in unison. That sounds scarier than doing a choreographed routine.

Brendan holds up his hand. "You each get about five seconds to do whatever you want. The robot. The moonwalk. The Macarena. You're in skates, so keep that in mind. But the crowd will love it, because it's *you*. The idea isn't to look good; it's making these kids smile. Can you do that?"

He glances around at the team. Lucian raises his eyebrows. Leo mutters to himself. Tate is already googling dance moves. Even Dawson, our eternal optimist, is noticeably silent.

Vale steps forward. "I'll do it." Then he glances at me and flicks his thumb for me to follow.

I reluctantly take a step to the front. "Me too."

Dawson follows. Then a few more guys. Finally, Rourke joins us. "Guess if Big Mac thinks he can dance, then I can too."

After simplifying the routine and adding individual dance breaks, it somehow comes together even better than before.

We might not be the most coordinated, but what we do have is personality. That's the magic ingredient we've been missing for this event. A chance to show our community that we're good sports, even if it means looking like dancing fools.

After running through the opening number a few more times, we call it quits and head for home.

Before I leave the Ice House, I get a message from Jaz asking me to pick up a hard drive in her office for Brendan to use.

As I head up the dark staircase to her office, a strip of light escapes from under Alex's office door. The low rumble of a man's voice comes from the other side. *Why would Alex have a meeting this late?* I lean in closer, knowing if I get caught, I'll have some explaining to do.

A strange voice asks, "Why not sell the team?"

I freeze, while every bone in my body goes cold.

"If I got a good enough offer, I'd consider it," Alex answers. "But I'm not sure I can wait that long. We need to move forward with this sports complex."

"And the fundraiser?" another man asks. "Are you actually going through with it?"

"For now," Alex says, hesitating slightly.

Tom's voice rumbles, "We need to make this as hard as possible for Jaz. If she succeeds with this fundraiser, then it makes us look bad when we shut down the team and build a new sports complex. Those guys are becoming heroes in the community. Have you seen the attendance numbers?"

Alex pauses. "It's never that simple, Tom. It's a fundraiser for charity. We're splitting the proceeds. I can hardly see how sabotaging a charitable event works to our advantage. She's already got the sympathy vote."

Tom speaks up, "I can make sure that the money raised disappears . . . and we fire her for the mistake."

Alex hesitates. "You'll throw Jaz under the bus?"

"Would you rather be the one?" Tom asks.

Alex is noticeably silent, and my fists curl in rage. I want to bust down this door, grab Tom by the collar, and shove him against the wall hard enough to knock some sense into the man.

But anger and fighting have never solved my problems. Just look at Felipe.

If I take my anger out on Tom now, it'll only leave a black smear on my reputation. He might be a slimy weasel, but I have to outsmart him and Alex with something better than fists.

I take a deep breath and back away from the door. *If only I knew how to protect Jaz.*

TWENTY-ONE

Jaz

I grab Sloan's hand and squeeze it as she gets hooked up to another IV. "You feel anything yet?" I ask hopefully, looking at the liquid drug that I'm hoping is her miracle cure.

"Doc said to be patient. It's not an instant fix," she reminds me. "It could take a week before the headaches ease and I feel better."

"I'm not patient," I say. "I want healthy Sloan back now."

"Me and you both," she says with a sigh. "All the Crushers agree."

She holds up her phone filled with text messages from the players wishing her luck with the new treatment.

Vale: Sloan, we miss you terribly. But don't worry, I'm cooking in your place, and Brax hasn't died yet! Fingers crossed I don't spread any food poisoning.

Tate: I read all about the studies for this treatment. A 95% success rate?! May the odds be ever in your favor.

Brax: How's my Sloan girl? Take good care of yourself and give Jaz a hug for me. You know she'd give anything to take your place.

Leo: I'm not a happy thoughts kind of guy. But this house is not the same without you. Vale is getting on my nerves. And you're way prettier to look at.

Rourke: I miss your pasta nights. Get better because Vale is not nearly as good of a cook as he thinks he is.

Dawson: When you come home, I'm throwing a party and bringing cheese balls!

The last two make us laugh, which is just the pick-me-up we need. If there's any good that's come out of this situation, it's that this team has become like family—a cheese-ball-loving, pasta-consuming family who sometimes punches each other for fun. Not much different than your average family, really.

My phone buzzes in my pocket, and I glance at the screen and frown.

"Brendan never calls unless something's wrong."

Sloan gives me a look before flipping another page of her magazine. "You don't know that. Maybe he has good news."

"Hey, Bren, what's up?"

"Not much, other than a teeny tiny problem."

"What kind of problem?" I sit up straighter in my chair, and a dozen bad scenarios flash through my mind. *Brax is hurt. My house burned down. Alex is firing me.*

Brendan answers, "Somebody canceled the order for the jerseys and the custom merchandise we're auctioning at the fundraiser."

"*Canceled?* I ordered the jerseys weeks ago. And I personally approved the custom designs."

"I knew something wasn't right when I got an email about it. When I called the company, they said the credit card had been shut down."

"But I put that order on the company credit card." I run my

palm over my pant leg nervously. This cannot be happening. Without the custom jerseys, there is no fashion show.

"I figured that. But I don't have access to the account to see what's going on," Brendan answers.

There's only one person who has access to the cards, and that's Tom. But why would Tom close my account unless there was a problem?

"I'll take care of this, Brendan. Thanks for letting me know."

"Are you sure there's not something more I can do?" he asks, concerned. "Brax offered to punch whoever's fault this is."

"His offer is sweet, but it won't really solve the problem."

Brendan sighs. "Call me if you need *anything*."

"Thanks, Brendan. You're a good friend," I say, reminded why I've always gotten along with this guy who has a bad-boy image but is actually so much more.

"I know," he says, which makes me smile. "In case you weren't sure, Brax misses you terribly."

"Thanks, Bren. I feel the same," I murmur, wishing I could set up Brendan with someone in town so he'd finally settle down in Sully's Beach. Just need to find him the right woman who'll make him want to give up his bachelor status for good.

"What's going on?" Sloan flips another page of her magazine as I end the call.

"We have no clothes for the fundraiser, which is kind of a problem since it's a fashion show. I'm hoping it's a mistake." I scroll through my phone, looking for a number to call.

"Maybe we should just walk out of here and forget the new treatment."

My head jerks up. "No! We're not leaving until you finish this treatment. Everyone from the team is counting on it."

She rests her head against the chair. "Listen, I'm glad you're here. I really am. But I want this fundraiser to be a success for you and the guys." She turns her gaze to mine. "Go home . . . for *me*."

I stare at her for a beat. "I'm not leaving you in a strange hospital by yourself."

"You're not leaving me. Ella offered to come if I need some-one. Grant can fly you back and bring her here. All I have to do is ask."

"No, I won't leave you," I insist.

Sloan gives me a stubborn look. "Jaz, I'm not asking. I'm telling you to leave."

My mouth flies open. "I can't believe you'd kick me out."

She flips another page. "You'd make me do the same thing if I were in your shoes. And I know you're missing Brax like crazy. You said so yourself. I've never seen you this head over heels for a guy before."

I bite my lip. She's not wrong. "I always thought I was a strong, independent woman who didn't need a man, but now I can't stop thinking about him. Does this mean I'm hopeless?"

Her lips curve up on one side. "No, it means you're in love. And you're still a strong, independent woman. Loving someone doesn't change that. Have you told him yet?"

"That I love him?" I shake my head. "I'm not sure I can. Trusting him is the hardest thing I've ever done."

She smiles, like she's proud of the progress I've made. "You're braver than you think. And you will tell him when the time is right." She takes my hand and squeezes it, the same way I did for her before. "Now, listen to me. I want you to go to Sully's Beach and plan a kick-butt event that raises an obscene amount of money for those kids. Got it?"

———

I don't even stop at home when I get to the airport. I head straight into work because of an urgent text message I received from Alex.

Alex: I need to see you as soon as you return.

The woman has never been warm and fuzzy, but this is bordering on ridiculous.

At least I'm feeling slightly better about the custom merchandise order. When I called the supplier, they said somebody from the office had canceled it but couldn't tell me why. Since the jerseys were already done and sitting in the warehouse, all I needed was a way to pay.

In desperation, I looked up the one other credit card I've used before. Alex let me use her company card when I first started, and I figured I could explain the reason when I got back. She approved this event, so it's not like I'm spending this money unknowingly.

When I step inside her office, a scowl forms on her lips, and she motions for me to sit.

Then she circles her desk, wearing an immaculate black suit and shiny pumps that have the Crushers logo on the toes.

I don't know why, but it feels wrong that she's wearing the logo on her shoes. Like she's trying to make sure everyone *knows* she's a fan when I know she's considering canning the team.

She folds her arms across her chest and glares at me. "What's this about using my company credit card for an order?"

Shoot. This wasn't how I wanted Alex to find out.

"I can explain," I say. "My company card was canceled, and we needed the jerseys shipped as soon—"

"Stop." She cuts me off with a raised hand. "I did not allow you to pay with *my* company card."

"But you approved the fundraiser's expenses. This was an emergency. Otherwise, we wouldn't get the jerseys in time."

"That card is mine, and you didn't ask." Alex slams her fist on the desk so hard I jerk.

"But you let me use it before," I stammer. "You gave me approval for budget expenses. I'm sorry I didn't ask, but that's what I was planning on doing today."

"It doesn't matter," she argues. "You violated my trust. What kind of person hides something like this?"

I straighten my spine, the frustration rising in my chest. "It's not as bad as someone who secretly plans to shut down an incredible team."

Her jaw flexes as she glares at me. "You do not know what I've sacrificed for this team. Do you know how hard it is to represent a hockey team as a single woman? To be looked down on in an industry full of men?"

For once, her tough exterior cracks, and I see her insecurities peek through. She doesn't want to lose either. Not just the team, but her reputation. Her success. This is her way of saving herself.

"Then give us a chance," I beg, trying to make her understand that we're a team. "Be a woman who shows the men we're tougher than they believe."

She sighs. "My hands are tied. The developers want to move on this before . . ." Her voice abruptly halts.

"Before the team becomes too popular?" I arch an eyebrow.

From the look on her face, I know I'm right.

She goes back to her plush leather chair and sinks into it, defeated. "This is the last year for the Crushers."

After all the school visits, nursing home trips, autograph signings, and the hours spent practicing for the fundraiser, she's giving up.

"But what about the fundraiser?" I ask slowly. "Don't give up on this team, Alex."

She looks me over for a beat. "Tom wants me to cancel it, but I'll reconsider." She taps her perfectly manicured red nails on her desk. "That doesn't mean you won't be punished for the credit card. Tom says it's a perfectly acceptable reason to fire you. Just don't be ridiculous and think that this fundraiser will change my mind."

I study her for a beat. "Why did you approve the fundraiser, then?"

She jerks her eyes to mine, then back to her desk. That's when I realize it. It was her way of making it *look* like she'd tried everything. She was using it to prop up her reputation.

"I won't announce it to the team until after the fundraiser."

Like this should make me feel better.

"Until then, you can't say *anything* about it," she says. "Not even to that boyfriend of yours." She arches an eyebrow.

"How did you . . ."

She shakes her head. "How could anyone *not* know? The way he looks at you like a lovesick puppy."

"Are you going to fire me for dating him?" I blurt out before thinking.

"I thought about it, but no," she says, rifling through her papers, like this is the extent of her mercy. "But I *will* fire you if you tell him about shutting down the team. And I'll use the credit card purchases as my reason."

I grit my teeth. This is blackmail. I always thought that kind of devious arm-twisting happened to people in the movies. Not *real* people. And especially not me.

All this time, I've been working tirelessly for the team, going above what was asked, only to make one thoughtless mistake for her team.

"Am I clear?" she asks, looking over her glasses at me.

I nod once, but refuse to show any emotion.

"You can go," she instructs in a clipped tone, like she hasn't just crushed me. I feel like an ant under the heel of her shoe.

She doesn't even bother looking at me as she dismisses me with a wave. "Just remember, it's our little secret."

If there's one thing I hate—*no, two things*—it's Alex's stupid shoes and her dirty little secret.

"The room looks amazing." Brendan surveys the new built-in bookshelves, desk, and window seat in Jaz's transformed room.

Even Joshua stopped in to see the finished work. He runs a crooked finger over the desktop, the one he designed and built. "Looks mighty pretty."

"Couldn't have done it without you," I say, handing him a check for his time. "Now I'm excited to start on the next phase of the house."

He pockets the check without even looking at it before he heads to the door.

"You're going to make that girl awfully happy," Joshua says, turning to me with his crinkled eyes that always are laughing.

"It's my goal," I say. "Even if I can't say it in words."

Joshua loops his thumbs in his overalls and studies me for a beat. "I don't know much about love, but I can see it written all over your face."

I look at him in surprise. "You can?"

He nods once. "Let me give you a piece of advice, son. Something I learned the hard way. Don't keep your feelings from her.

Even if it's the hardest thing you'll ever do." He pats my shoulder once before he leaves. I know it won't be the last time I see him.

If Joshua had said that a month ago, it would have scared me away. But now I can see myself being with Jaz for a lifetime.

This place, with its worn wood floors and immense windows framing the morning light, represents so much more to me than a sprawling fixer-upper. It's the place where we were forced to work through the ugly parts of ourselves and fix the parts that needed work. Just like *Rose & Thorn*, our relationship needed a remodel.

While Brendan and Vale line up Jaz's books on the shelves, I set out all of Jaz's favorite things. Granny's jewelry box. Her pink journal collection filled with fashion drawings. Pictures of her with Sloan. Another with Granny. Jaz with her parents.

Then I add two more to the collection: a picture of Jaz with the Crushers hockey team on the night we won our first game and a picture of us at Mia's wedding. I've got my arm around her waist and we're both wearing smiles a mile wide. I don't want to forget that night or how beautiful she looked in her pink silk gown with her shoulders shimmering in the light. She's even wearing the tiara we found in the closet, the one that made me call her *princess*.

When I look at it, I see how much has changed, how I'm owning my mistakes now, and becoming the man she needs me to be. If that means risking everything for her, then I'll do it. Her future happiness is everything to me.

"Brax? Hello? Anyone home?" Jaz's voice calls from the front door.

We rush to meet her before she spoils her surprise.

"Hey, Jaz," Vale says, stopping abruptly so that Brendan almost runs into him from behind.

"Welcome back," Brendan exclaims, wrapping Jaz in a hug before she sees me and rushes over. She nearly falls into my arms, and my pulse immediately skyrockets.

"I missed you," I murmur into her ear before she whispers back, "Missed you more."

Brendan and Vale line up behind her, looking guilty and excited.

Jaz looks us over, a curious grin hitching up the corner of her mouth. "What's going on?"

"A surprise for you," Brendan says.

"What surprise?" She glances around and gasps when she spies the new colors in the kitchen, dining and living room. The dappled sunlight makes the pale grays and soft buttery yellows look magnificent against the hardwood floors. "Did you paint while I was gone?" Before I can answer, she takes a few steps toward the dining room and freezes when she discovers the wall between the two rooms has disappeared.

"You took out the wall?" she exclaims.

"Team effort," I reply, taking her hand and leading her to the bedroom next. "I couldn't have finished this remodel without everyone's help. Especially Brendan and Joshua." I push open her door and wait for her to take in the transformation of her bedroom.

Her mouth drops. "You. Did. This?" She spins around to face me, her eyes wide.

"Joshua was a tremendous help. Brendan and I finished it off."

"Wait, Joshua was here? I promised to pay him." She rushes toward the front door.

"Already taken care of," I tell her.

She wheels around. "I'll pay you back."

"I can't let you do that." I shake my head. "Even if you try, I won't accept."

"No, Brax, this isn't your responsibility." She crosses her arms.

"I know that, but I wanted to do this for you." I stride toward her, hoping that I can break through the stubborn look in her eyes. "You have Sloan to take care of, remember?"

"But this is *my* house," she insists.

"And this is *my* gift to you." I move close to her, wrapping one arm around her back while I brush the back of my hand across her cheek. "You said you'd always dreamed of having a window seat along with a wall of bookshelves and a desk overlooking the rose garden. It's not fair you have that ridiculously small office at the Ice House. You deserve better. And I want to give it to you."

She blinks as she looks up at me, and I can see the conflicting emotion in her eyes. "But no one has ever given me something like this. I'm used to doing things myself. I can't accept things I don't deserve."

I shake my head. "That's just it. You deserve every good thing. You've never had anyone show you that kind of love. The kind that says I'll take care of you. You do so much for everyone else, making sure they're happy. Now it's time for you to get that same treatment. You might as well get used to me spoiling you. Because I'm not planning on stopping."

Her eyes swirl before she steps toward me and falls into my arms, like I'm her support, the one keeping her afloat. Then she whispers, "Thank you," as she wraps her arms around my neck.

I take in her dizzying scent, the soft silk of her hair against my cheek, the way my hands fit around her body, like they were made to hold her.

"You have no idea how much I've needed this," she says, her voice catching with emotion. Maybe she's just missed me, but the way she clings to me is different, like she's finally willing to let me help her carry the load.

Vale and Brendan peek around the corner.

"Are you going to take all day, or do you want us to show you all the amazing things we did to your house while you were gone?" Brendan asks with a mischievous grin.

"Are you in a hurry?" Jaz asks, pulling away from me.

"Date tonight with an old friend," Brendan admits.

"Date?" Jaz squeals. "Oh, do tell." She lifts her eyebrows at Brendan before hurrying back to her bedroom for all the gossip.

The doorbell rings, and I start down the hall, yelling over my shoulder, "Don't forget to show her the custom desk drawers and the new pictures." I swing the door open, and a man with a slicked-back ponytail in a sharp black suit wheels around. As soon as his eyes meet mine, my stomach drops.

"Felipe," I mutter.

"Well, well, if it isn't the Crushers' star himself," he snarls. He's got an East Coast accent that makes me feel like I'm in a bad mafia movie, and he's dressed to kill. If I had to guess who, it's most likely me.

I step onto the porch and shut the door behind us so Jaz won't overhear. "What are you doing here, Felipe?"

"Was in the neighborhood and thought I'd stop by, Braxy." He gives me a wicked smile, using the nickname he knows I hate.

"We both know you don't live here."

He takes a pair of sunglasses out of his suit pocket and polishes them with a silk cloth from his pocket. "We have unfinished business." He glances at me with a bored expression. You'd never guess he was a threat.

"As far as I'm concerned, our business is finished. Anything else can be settled on the ice."

He slides on the sunglasses, so I can't see his eyes. If he's trying to intimidate me, it's not working. "Nothing is ever done, Brax. That's why I'm here."

I roll my eyes. "So what if we dated the same girl? We weren't even compatible. I'm a different guy than I was a year ago. I'm not interested in grudges."

His face doesn't change. He keeps that same bored expression.

I step closer to him. "Didn't we settle the score when I got hurt?"

"Not at all," he says, leaning against the porch railing like he has all the time in the world.

"Well, I'm saying it is." I turn my back, ready to slam the door in his face.

He glances at a newly planted rose bush. "Do you remember when you were sixteen, playing for that junior league in Vermont?"

I frown. "What?"

"The Vermont Lumberjacks?"

I slowly turn around. *How does he know this?*

"Yeah, why?"

"My junior league played yours. And I went up against you. Do you remember?"

I cross my arms. "I thought we didn't meet until we were both playing for the AHL?"

He shakes his head. "No, we met when you were sixteen and I was eighteen. You played center and were the Lumberjacks' big star."

I narrow my eyes. Felipe would never compliment me willingly. "It was junior league, dude. Big fish in a *very* small pond."

"Not to me, it wasn't. I had dreams of making it to the NHL. But then I went up against your team and we lost." He holds up a finger. "Correction. *I* lost."

I shake my head, not understanding. "One loss won't keep you out of the NHL. It's your talent and potential that matters."

"Which I had until that game derailed me. That injury was your fault."

I blink, my mind scrolling through faded memories of junior league. "What injury?"

His jaw clenches before he answers. "You hit me from behind so hard, it fractured my skull." His mouth twists. "I had to take a break from hockey for six months. It was almost career-ending."

A foggy memory emerges. The sound of our bodies crashing and the chilling thud when his helmet hit the ice. His face is a blur because I didn't know who he was back then.

"That hit wasn't intentional," I argue. "There were three of us going for that puck, and I crashed into you. They told me it was a concussion."

"You never bothered to check what damage you'd done. You went on to play college hockey and worked your way up."

I look around incredulously. "This is the reason you hate my guts? Because of an accident in the junior leagues?"

"Don't you understand what it cost me?" he shouts, his face flaring. "I could have bypassed the lower leagues and gone pro. That was my plan. But you changed everything."

Sweat pricks the back of my neck. "That's why you threaten me and the people I love. All because of an injury I didn't even know about?"

He studies me for a second before shaking his head. "You've always known, Braxy."

I let out an exasperated sigh. I can't convince him of the truth. "If it makes you feel better, that shoulder injury you gave me hasn't healed."

"Good," he says with a smarmy grin.

At least we've gotten to a point where he's finally being honest.

His eyes flick over my shoulder once, then back to me. "How's the new girlfriend?"

I take a step toward him. "Leave her out of it. She's no business of yours."

"I always knew you had a weakness." His mouth quirks into a menacing smile. "Turns out it's her."

He wheels around and starts down the porch steps.

"Felipe," I call, running after him. "Can we talk about this?"

He keeps walking and ignores my pleas.

I catch up to him. "Fine. I'll talk. You listen. Sorry I ruined your chance of getting into the NHL early. But I want to bury the hatchet now. End this rivalry, once and for all."

I stop when we reach his car, hoping to get through to him.

He opens the door to his black Mercedes. "See you at the game, Braxy."

———

It's just another game. That's what I tell myself when I put on my pads in the locker room.

But even my teammates seem tense about playing the Hartford Wolf Pack.

Maybe it's because I finally confessed my entire history with Felipe last night after Vale told me I had to. As painful as that was, the guys said they'd have my back, no matter what.

But now that we're about to face off with them, everyone is quiet. Finally, Dawson brings up what's on everyone's mind. "I'll take Felipe out for you," he says, sliding on his jersey.

"You're the goalie. You need to guard the net," Tate reminds him, stretching his calf muscles.

"That doesn't mean that goalies don't get into fights," he says. "I'm the person he least expects."

"Not if I get to him first." Leo gives Dawson a look. "One wrong move, and he's mine." Considering that Leo hated me not so long ago, this is progress.

"I like to stir up trouble." Rourke sits on a bench. "I don't even need a reason."

The guys chuckle.

I shake my head. "Why am I not surprised?"

Rourke is always getting into fights, even though he never actually seems mad. He just likes the way it riles up the crowd, and the fans love him for it.

"We won't pick fights intentionally with this jerk," Lucian instructs. "We don't want that kind of reputation as a team."

"I agree with Lucian," I say. "Like Coach Thompson told us last practice, 'If you let your anger control you, you'll lose.'"

Leo arches an eyebrow at me. "Says the guy with a short fuse."

"What if he's out for blood?" Tate asks as he threads new laces on his skate. "If it comes to that, I'd break the rules."

Dawson gasps. "Sheriff might break a rule? No way." He ruffles Tate's hair as Tate swats his hand away.

"If we're playing a good game, he won't target me. But that's up to us." I give my teammates an easy smile. I'm trying not to act worried, even though there's a niggling feeling inside me. Tonight, *everything* could change.

Remarkably, the first two periods of the game go smoothly. Other than a few body checks and some rough scrambles for the puck, Felipe only scowls at me once.

With the help of my teammates, I keep my distance from Felipe and try to lie low, letting the other guys dominate.

When the horn blasts at the end of the second period, I notice Vale smiling at Sloan in the stands.

I lean toward him. "I thought I was the only one who was distracted by a certain fan."

I lift my glove to acknowledge Jaz, who's wearing my number sixteen jersey again. I'm still inwardly gleeful that she never wore Lucian's or Leo's jerseys and promptly returned them after I gave her mine. A big grin spreads across her face, making everything in my body feel lighter, even my worry about Felipe.

Vale plays with his stick. "I'm just making sure Sloan feels okay. You know, with her headaches and this new treatment."

"Yeah, yeah. Headaches." I elbow him in the ribs as we head toward the locker room. "Give me another excuse."

"What's that supposed to mean? You think I like her?" Vale looks at me incredulously.

"All I know is that after you scored that goal, you looked at *her* before you looked at me."

One side of his mouth curves up. "Are you jealous?"

I shake my head. "For twenty years, you've always looked at me after you score. You didn't think I'd notice?"

He points at me with his glove. "You're the one who started it. Searching Jaz out in the crowd. Which was a lot easier when this place wasn't so packed."

I stop at the door to the locker room as Vale heads inside.

Between keeping my mind on the game and watching Felipe, I hadn't even noticed the full crowd. Things are finally going right for once, and I breathe a sigh of relief.

Suddenly Alex rounds the corner, a scowl lining her features.

"Dawson, I can't believe you let that shot get through," she barks.

I turn around and see Dawson stopping in the hall, his face heated. "Sorry, ma'am," he mutters, his shoulders slumping.

"Anyone could have blocked that final shot," she grumbles. "Maybe you're not cut out for the Crushers after all."

I frown. He couldn't have blocked that last shot. Nobody could. How dare she say that when she's thinking of shutting down the team?

Anger rises in my chest. "Dawson's blocked eighteen of their shots. Did you notice? The guy's been on fire tonight."

She glares at me, like she's annoyed I'm standing up for Dawson. "But he let two slip through. That's all that matters. Hartford is known for their third-period goals, which means you need to step up your playing tonight. I noticed you haven't scored once."

Apparently she didn't notice my two assists that led to successful goals. Maybe she doesn't care since she's thinking of closing the team anyway.

I step closer to her. "I thought you wanted us to lose so you could have an excuse to shut the team down and build your sports complex."

Her face drains as she stares at me, dumbfounded.

"What sports complex?" Dawson asks, looking from her to me.

I'm sorry Dawson had to find out this way. But I won't let her tear him down when he's the one keeping us from losing.

"Why would you shut down our team?" Dawson asks, still processing this news. "We're finally winning."

Alex doesn't respond. She doesn't even ask how I found out.

I step closer to her, not wanting anyone else to overhear. "Everyone deserves to know, Alex. It's not fair to the team."

"It's not like the players won't find other teams," she says, defensively. "We're waiting to announce it until the end of the season, for obvious reasons."

"I'm telling them sooner." I shake my head, refusing to meet her demands. If she wants to wait to announce it to the press, that's fine, but I refuse to keep this from Jaz or my teammates any longer.

Alex locks eyes with me. "If you tell, Jaz will lose her job. Do you really want to risk her future?"

My grip tightens around my stick. "You can't fire her for no reason."

She narrows her eyes, daring me to challenge her. "She used my credit card to purchase merchandise, even though I didn't approve it."

"You'd given her permission to buy those things." I can't believe she's doing this after everything Jaz has done for the team.

She folds her arms across her chest. "It's still a legitimate reason to fire someone."

I clench my teeth. "She deserves to know."

Alex tilts her head, and a flicker of understanding crosses her face. "She already knows. She's known before the season even began."

I hesitate, trying to figure out if she's bluffing. "Why would she put everything into this fundraiser?"

"If you don't believe me . . ." Her eyes flick over my shoulder. "Then why don't you ask her yourself?"

I wheel around and see Jaz in the hallway, her brown eyes wide, her mouth open like she wants to say something but can't.

"Tell me you don't know," I say slowly. "Right? You. Don't. Know."

She takes a step, holding out her hand. "I can explain . . ."

My stomach drops. "You knew?"

"I wanted to tell you," she pleads, still reaching for me.

I immediately recoil, devastated she didn't tell me. I've worked tirelessly to gain her trust back, only to have her keep this secret from me.

The last few weeks have been the best of my life. All this time she was hiding something that could destroy the team and my future?

I narrow my eyes. "I don't want to know why you kept this from me."

I turn to leave as Alex watches this moment unfold, a smile playing on the corners of her lips. This is exactly what the Ice Queen wanted. She's the chess master in this game, playing us against each other.

Jaz grabs for my sleeve, trying not to let me walk away. "At least give me a chance to explain."

I rip my arm away so fast, she looks shocked. "I don't want your explanation. I don't want anything from you."

Then I turn my back to her, heading toward the rink. "I need to finish my game."

TWENTY-THREE

Jaz

As soon as the door slams shut after Brax leaves, I turn to Dawson with my heart in my throat. The poor guy looks devastated. How am I going to face the rest of the team?

"I'm sorry about this," I mumble as I force back tears, keeping my back to Alex. I won't let Alex see me crumble, but Dawson is different. I'm invested in every guy on this team and would do anything for them.

Dawson puts a big, gloved hand on my shoulder and squeezes it gently, like he's already forgiven me.

"He'll get over it. He can't stay mad at you." He doesn't bother looking back before he lumbers to the locker room.

I lock eyes with Alex and cross my arms. "You got your way. You wanted to drive a wedge between Brax and me."

She lets out an annoyed sigh. "Look, he's the one who confronted me. I naturally assumed you had told him." She says it like *she's* the victim here and not me. "It wasn't until you walked in that I realized he didn't know."

I drop my arms and approach her. "I kept your secret because you let me believe I had a chance to turn this around."

She looks at me like I'm a naïve child. "You really believed that? I thought you were smarter than that."

I narrow my eyes and pin my fists to my sides so I don't accidentally punch her. Maybe these hockey guys are rubbing off on me. "I worked hard to get more fans here to see this amazing team. And you're going to tear it all down."

"And build something better," she finishes. "I won't fire you if you agree to my terms."

"What kind of terms?" I ask, hoping she doesn't see how desperate I am.

"If we hold a big press conference at the end of the season to make the announcement, you can stay on staff and help me orchestrate this transition. You'll need to convince Brax and Dawson to stay quiet. As long as our fans don't find out before then, things should go smoothly."

Is this her offer? For me to stay quiet and help her sneak out the back door when the time comes?

This whole thing feels so gross.

I've already disappointed Brax and the team by keeping secrets from them. But I refuse to be her puppet any more.

I jut out my chin. "You won't need to fire me, because I quit."

Her mouth falls as the locker room door bursts open. The team pours out, ready for the final period as I slip down the hall.

I hurry back to my seat, where Sloan waits alone with a hot pretzel in one hand and melted cheese in the other.

"Where were you?" she asks, dipping her pretzel in the cheese.

I grab her arm. "I can't explain now, but we need to leave."

If Alex returns to the game, she'll see me in the staff section and ask security to remove me, which will be beyond humiliating after everything that's happened.

Sloan looks at me, puzzled. "Why do we need to . . ."

"I quit," I blurt out.

Sloan gapes at me for a beat. "Quit what?"

Didn't she hear me? "My job."

Her face blanches as she stops chewing. "You did *what?*"

"Don't ask." I grab her hand and pull her down the aisle until we reach the exit that leads to the concession area. "Alex told me she was shutting down the team, and Brax found out that I knew."

"She's doing WHAT?" Sloan nearly screams through a mouthful of pretzel.

"Since I'm no longer employed by the Crushers, we technically don't have tickets for this game."

Sloan stops and rips her arm away from my grip. "I'm not leaving. Not in the third period when we're tied."

"But we can't," I explain, trying to reach for her arm. "No tickets, no seats."

"I don't care." She backs away from me. "I'm not going with you. They need us. Brax needs *you.*"

My chest tightens at the thought of him going up against Felipe alone. "I don't think Brax wants to see me right now. He was so angry at me, Sloan. I don't know if he can get over this."

She tosses the rest of her pretzel in the trash, like she's suddenly lost her appetite. "He'll get over it. He loves you."

"I don't know if he does anymore," I say, my voice faltering. He hasn't exactly told me so, and after what happened, I'm not sure he ever could. I thought I could save the team by keeping Alex's secret. But I was horribly mistaken for thinking I could pull this off without hurting Brax.

A lump rises in my throat. Now I've lost everyone, except Sloan. If I can't afford to pay for her medical treatments, I'll lose her too.

I cover my face, trying to keep from falling apart. "I'm so sorry, Sloan. I messed up everything, and I don't know how to fix it." The emotions are ballooning inside my chest, feeling like they're about to burst.

She pulls me into a hug instantly, the same way Granny used to do when we were hurt. Sloan takes my face in her hands and forces me to look at her, tilting my chin so her gaze meets mine. "You didn't mess up anything. You're the strongest person I know. You've taken care of me through every horrible day, every hospital visit, every time I've broken down. Now it's my turn to take care of you, Jazzy. We're going to fix this, I promise. But first we need to finish the game. Brax needs you out there." Then she slides her hands to my arms, holding me so I don't crumple to the ground like a rag doll.

"No, Sloan." I shake my head. "I'm afraid Brax doesn't want me around anymore. Not when he can't trust me."

She levels her gaze at me. "I'm your sister and your friend. Brax will forgive you for whatever happened. But he needs to know you'll stand by his side and won't leave when it gets tough." Her eyes drill into mine, like she's trying to give me the strength I don't have.

"I don't know where to go that Alex won't find us," I say, glancing around, hoping she doesn't jump out from any dark corners.

"There needs to be a place where we can watch the game and Alex won't find out. Think, Jazzy. Where can we sit and finish the game?"

"I remember a few seats they keep open for last-minute guests of staff and players," I say. "Last I heard, no one was using them."

I take Sloan's hand as the horn sounds for the third period. Let's hope my luck has finally turned.

When we arrive on the other side of the rink, I'm relieved to see empty seats. We hurry to settle in and hope Alex doesn't spot us since we're mixed in with the fans.

When the puck drops, my gaze flicks to number sixteen. He frowns in concentration and hustles across the ice, never glancing away from the puck for a second. After what just happened, I don't know if I can repair the broken trust between us. My stomach churns with the slow realization of what I've potentially lost.

If Sloan's right and Brax loves me, then maybe I have a fighting chance.

But first, we've got a game to win against Felipe.

Tension rises as blades scrape ice and sticks collide. Leo and an opponent are using their sticks like swordplay, trying to stop the other one from gaining control of the puck. The referee calls them on it before play resumes, and Vale takes control of the puck. He hustles toward the goal before passing it to Brax, who shows off his expert stick handling. As he effortlessly maneuvers around two defenders and heads toward the goal, he's nearly sideswiped by another player.

Felipe knocks Brax off-balance and slams him against the wall, but he quickly recovers as Felipe steals the puck and skates away.

Judging by Brax's scowl, he's not about to let Felipe get away with this. He hustles after his enemy before Vale cuts him off and gives his brother a warning look.

"What was that about?" Sloan asks, perched on the edge of her seat, her eyes glued to the tense action.

"Vale was reminding his brother to back off. The last thing they need is a penalty."

Tate quickly pursues Felipe and catches him, their sticks crashing together, causing the black disk to skitter away just in time for Leo to grab it.

Brax remains focused, navigating the rink with practiced ease while Felipe glides past and yells something at him. I'm too far away to make out the words, but from the way Brax's jaw clenches, Felipe is taunting him.

I grip the seat, tension rising in my chest.

"Yeah, I definitely think someone should punch him," Sloan mutters under her breath.

The two men lock eyes, and an electric current of mutual disdain crackles between them.

Vale takes a shot that's blocked by the goalie, and Brax leaps into action, going for the loose puck as Felipe chases him down. Every nerve ending in my body prickles with energy as I watch Felipe tear after Brax like an animal on the hunt.

But Brax outsmarts him, taking control of the puck and quickly pivoting the opposite direction, leading him around the back of the net until he reaches the other side. He only needs a short, precise shot on goal with a quick flick of his stick, a shot he's probably practiced a million times in his sleep.

Felipe barrels toward him and holds Brax's stick, which causes the puck to spiral out of control. Brax's face flares as fans leap to their feet in anger and the referee blows his whistle. Felipe mutters something as he's sent to the penalty box for holding. I drop my tense shoulders, relieved that Brax will get a short break from his enemy.

Sloan turns to me. "I can hardly stand seeing Felipe chase down Brax like that."

"Felipe's right where he should be. In time out," I mutter as play resumes.

The Crushers use the power play to their advantage, passing the puck around, anticipating their opponents' moves. Without the threat of Felipe, watching them in this synchronized dance reminds me how far they've come this season.

At the beginning of the season, their quick tempers kept them from playing like a real team. But seeing them play now fills me with pride. If they only had more time, they could be the best team in the league.

But time is what they don't have.

Anger burns in the back of my throat. Alex can't shut this team down. Not when they're finally playing like a dream team.

As Leo grabs control of the puck, he circles behind the goal and looks for who's open. Then he sends the puck flying with a perfectly timed pass toward Vale.

"Shoot!" someone behind me yells.

But instead of going for the goal, Vale quickly pivots, flicking the puck toward Brax, who's in position near the goal. Brax doesn't even hesitate. With a precise shot, the puck flies into the net.

The crowd jumps to their feet with a roar that's deafening. Sloan and I scream even though our voices are drowned out by the roar.

Sloan leans toward me. "Did you see Vale and Brax use their twin power? That was amazing!"

"They're unstoppable when Felipe's not there."

That's when I see him rise to his feet. Felipe's time in the penalty box is up.

From the look on his face, he's about to get even.

TWENTY-FOUR

With the crowd erupting in cheers and adrenaline surging through my body, I do it without thinking—look up to where Jaz normally sits, expecting to see her smiling face and that brief connection between us.

But this time, there is no moment. Her seat is empty. My stomach clenches as the anger comes roaring back.

She knew Alex's secret and didn't tell me. *Why?*

I barely have time to think before Felipe is out of the penalty box and on the hunt for me. His eyes burn into me from across the rink.

That man is nothing if not persistent.

Coach Thompson calls us out for a line change. When I reach the bench, I wipe the sweat off my neck with a towel.

"What happened to Sloan and Jaz?" Vale asks when he sits next to me. "Jaz would never miss a game."

Now's not the time to tell him what happened. I doubt even Coach Thompson knows about Alex's plans.

"Don't know," I growl, keeping my eyes on the game.

"Do you think Sloan's okay?" he asks, his forehead wrinkled in concern. "Why else would they leave before the end?"

Vale can't let it go, and I don't want him to worry needlessly.

"Sloan's fine. I had a fight with Jaz. She probably left for that reason. Can we stop with the questions now?"

Vale stares at me like he refuses to believe it. "No way would she leave a game. Even if you had a disagreement, she would *stay*. Sloan wouldn't let her walk away."

I won't meet his eyes. "It was more than a disagreement. She kept something from me."

"You'll get over it," he says, trying to reassure me.

"I trusted her," I say, refusing to look at him. "If she can't be honest with me, what future is there for us?"

Vale turns away from me, stunned.

At least he's respecting my wishes by not asking more questions.

"Now isn't the time to make a rash decision," he mutters.

"Then we both agree on something."

The crowd groans as bodies clash and sticks fight for the puck. Rourke and Felipe battle against the boards, followed by the shrill blast of whistles. Rourke flashes Felipe an angry look before pushing him hard in the chest.

"Not good," I mutter as Rourke gets sent to the penalty box.

If the team can't stay under control, we're going to lose this lead.

"Rourke's itching to fight," Vale notes, taking one last swig of his water bottle. "At least he didn't throw a punch at Felipe. He saw the way you were being treated and couldn't wait to get his hands on the guy. Can't say I blame him."

We're down a player, and it will be tough keeping Felipe from using that to his advantage.

We head back on the ice, and when the puck drops, I'm ready to end this game with Felipe.

My shoulder gives a familiar throb as I weave between opponents, while trying to keep my anger in check. I glance over at Felipe, who's locked on me with a sickly glare, like he's waiting for an opportunity to take me out.

The cold, crisp smell of the ice fills my nostrils as the puck hurtles across the rink toward my opponents. We're outnumbered until Rourke can return, which means we're going to need to play better than we ever have before.

Fear and adrenaline spiral through my chest as Felipe watches my every move. I keep my distance so I can stay two steps ahead while my mind churns through a whirlwind of strategy. How will I outmaneuver the man who knows his playbook almost as well as I do?

I push away that seed of doubt, lunging forward to gain speed.

As soon as Leo gets the puck and passes it to Vale, Felipe switches direction and skates toward me with a hunger in his eyes. I instinctively hustle away from him, my skates carving the ice with precision. He's chasing my heels, trying to bear down on me, waiting for the right time to attack me.

My pulse hammers in my ears, trying to keep one step ahead of Felipe, while simultaneously watching the puck.

If there ever was a time I needed twin telepathy with my brother, it's now. Because if Vale passes to me while Felipe nips at my heels, he'll use the move to take me out. That's how hungry for revenge this jerk is.

As my heart races, I cross in front of Felipe, and he body-checks me hard enough that I lose my balance for a second and crash against the boards, my shoulder throbbing in pain.

I recover quickly only to see that Felipe is locked on Vale now, barreling toward him like a freight train, while Vale's back is turned.

Vale rotates just in time to see Felipe charging toward him recklessly. There's a second of hesitation in his eyes, that critical moment of decision. With a deft flick of his stick, the puck hurtles toward me, but is slightly off-mark, landing just beyond me. Felipe pivots quickly, circling back like a lion headed for the kill. There's no way I can make a shot from this angle while avoiding Felipe, but maybe I can end this now.

With my heart hammering, I race toward the puck while my

opponent charges toward me. It's inevitable now, but I refuse to cower in fear or back off from a fight.

This ends tonight.

Felipe has played his cards well, anticipating that I wouldn't give up chasing the puck. He knows I've got a hunger to win. We both do. But only one of us can win this game.

Without even looking, I feel him closing in, like a missile locked onto its target.

I slap the puck away as Felipe's body collides with mine, his chest slamming into my shoulder with a sickening crack.

I hear somebody scream "No!" as my world tilts and I fly backward, my helmet smacking the ice with an awful thud.

The lights of the stadium blur, and the roar of the audience turns into a muted, distant buzz. Pain erupts across my head and neck, radiating through my body like a bolt of lightning. The only thing I'm tethered to are the voices around me, but even those are fading, like I'm slipping under the ice.

"Brax, stay with me." Vale's face is blurry as he hunches over me, and I'm suddenly surrounded by dark shapes that I can't make out.

Struggling against the darkness, one last voice slices through my mind.

"Brax!"

Her voice is the last thing I reach for before my world turns to black.

TWENTY-FIVE

Brax

Beep, *beep, beep.* The annoying high-pitched chirp next to my head makes me want to punch something.

"Where am I?" I mumble, but it comes out sounding like an unintelligible string of grunts. My tongue feels thick and heavy, like I've just taken an enormous bite of peanut butter.

I move my arm and pain shoots up my shoulder. I groan like an angry bear who's been poked by a stick.

"Is he in pain?" someone asks.

"He's going to feel like he got run over by a truck for a couple days." I immediately recognize the voice as my brother's. "But he'll get better. And when he does, I'm going to kick his butt for trying to protect me."

I groan again, trying to let Vale know I will *gladly* do the same to him even though I'm injured.

"If you want to say something, Brax," Vale argues. "At least have the decency to open your eyes and say it to my face."

Even when I'm hurt, my brother doesn't take it easy on me. I wrench my eyes open and see Vale's stupid grin first.

"Thought that might work," he says, looking pleased that he coerced me into waking up.

"Your face is not the first thing I want to see," I mutter.

Vale chuckles. "I see the concussion didn't take away your sense of humor."

I slowly lift my head and attempt to sit up, but there are wires everywhere, and my body aches with every movement.

Vale puts a hand on my shoulder. "Not so fast. You're going to give yourself a splitting headache."

I settle back on my elbows, squeezing my eyes shut. "I already have a splitting headache." I dig a palm into my eye as the pain slowly throbs against my eyeballs. "This is worse than getting slammed into the boards."

Lucian joins Vale next to my bed, and when my vision clears, Leo and Tate come into focus.

"What, am I dying or something?" I ask.

Vale shakes his head. "Felipe couldn't get that lucky."

"At least tell me the jerk got a penalty," I say.

Tate smiles. "Even better. He got kicked out of the game."

"And we won," Lucian adds. "Thanks to you."

I lie back on my pillow, relieved.

Tate sits on the edge of my bed. "The league is going to review the hit and will take disciplinary action against him. I think they'll suspend him for the rest of the season."

Tate knows the rules of the game better than almost anyone. If he believes the league can suspend Felipe, then there's a good chance he'll get kicked out.

"His plan backfired," Vale says. "Which means he won't bother you anymore. At least, not if he wants to play again."

Which means I don't have to worry about Felipe threatening me or Jaz.

"What did the doc say? Can I leave right now?" I swing my legs over the bed and suddenly get dizzy.

Vale puts a hand on my chest. "Easy, partner. Doc said you'll make a full recovery, and that you might return to practice as soon as next week. Not that we'll be doing much hockey since next week is the fundraiser."

"Have you talked to Jaz?" I ask, suddenly wishing I could see her beautiful face and hold her in my arms. Then I remember what happened. The secret she kept from me. The way Alex threw it in my face.

Vale looks at Leo and Tate. "She stopped by to see you."

"She was here?" I sit up a little straighter.

Vale rubs the back of his neck. "Stayed until the nurses kicked her out last night."

At least she doesn't hate me so much she wouldn't visit. I was irate about Alex's secret, and I took it out on Jaz. Regret twists inside my chest.

"Has she been back?" I ask.

"She didn't know if you would want to see her," Vale says, looking uncomfortable. "She was pretty broken up last night. She knows how you feel about girls crying."

As much as I hate to see anyone cry, with Jaz, it's different.

Leo turns his phone around for me to see. It's footage a fan caught when Felipe crashed into me. "That hit you took was one of the worst I've seen. He drilled you head-on."

I cringe to watch my body crumple on the ice.

"Guys," Lucian warns. "He might not be ready for that."

I shake my head, ignoring the pain in my head. "It's okay. I'd do it again for the team."

Lucian points at me. "Not while I'm captain. We need you on this team, Brax." Then he turns to Leo. "Don't we?"

If there's anyone on this team I've butted heads with, it's Leo. He might be full of himself, but he's also a brilliant player.

Leo swipes his hand across his jaw. "Okay. Fine. You make us all better players." Then he mumbles, "Even me."

Tate's eyebrows fly up. "Someone get this on video. Leo is humble-bragging."

Leo frowns. "I'm not bragging. I'm being nice."

Vale chuckles. "We're not used to you being nice."

Leo rolls his eyes.

I turn to my teammate. "Leo, as hard as it is to admit, you make me a better player, too."

Tate's phone buzzes. "Dawson asked if the team can sneak up here."

"Only four allowed at a time," Tate announces, like it's the law.

Lucian slaps Tate on the shoulder. "Like that will stop Dawson."

I look around the tiny room. "They won't fit in here."

"Too late," Vale says as the door bursts open.

The entire team pours inside my hospital room with shouting and laughter. Rourke comes in last, carrying foil balloons. One says "It's a boy!" in the shape of a huge diaper, next to a balloon that says "You're expecting!" in the shape of a pink stork.

"Sorry. The gift shop selection was a little limited." Rourke shrugs.

"Thanks?" I say, taking the balloons from him.

"You survived!" Dawson howls with relief, falling into me with a bear hug.

"I was never dead," I mutter into Dawson's chest. He squeezes me so hard, I let out a strangled, "But I might be after this hug."

Lucian pulls Dawson off me, while Vale smirks. "Somebody missed you."

Dawson holds up a small wireless speaker. "It's our practice day for the fundraiser, and we're not letting you miss it."

I point at my pale green hospital gown. "Pretty sure Doc won't allow me to do choreography yet."

"Not you," Dawson says as he starts the opening number on his phone and all the guys squeeze together in front of my bed. "Us."

To my surprise, the guys begin the choreography, except there's not enough space to practice the moves. Before long, they're bumping into each other, throwing off the whole routine, while I double over with laughter.

When it's time for the individual dance breaks, it turns into something reminiscent of sugar-high preschoolers in a bounce house. Leo attempts to breakdance and spins into Rourke, who can only do the same robot move stuck on repeat. Tate moonwalks into Dawson, who's attempting to leap across the floor like a dancing bear. If they hadn't woken up the entire floor before, they have now.

My head might still be sore, but I feel ten times better than before. Despite our differences, this is the best team I've ever played for. They're my brothers, and there's part of me that aches when I think about leaving them.

The party lasts all of fifteen minutes before the head nurse shuts it down and points the team out the door.

The guys moan as they're forced out. Lucian hangs back a second and flicks a business card out of his pocket.

"I know you have a lot on your mind right now. But two apartments just opened up near the Ice House. They'll go fast, so if you want it, I wouldn't wait."

As Lucian leaves, I stare at the card.

It feels like an awful weight in my gut, forcing me to deal with the fallout between Jaz and me. Maybe this would give us the space we need until we can work things out. After what happened, I need to sort through my feelings, to see if she's willing to fight for me and to figure out if we can both trust each other enough to get over the hurts we've caused. Because seeing her every day—but not being with her—would be torture.

I hand the card to Vale. "See how soon they can get us in for a tour."

He frowns. "You don't want to think about it first?"

I shake my head. "Thinking will only make it worse."

TWENTY-SIX

Jaz

As I watch Brax slowly climb out of Vale's car, flinching in pain, I have to resist the urge to run out and help him. It's strange to accept that this powerhouse player can break if he's hit hard enough. I thought this man was unbreakable, that what we had was incapable of being destroyed. But with enough force, anything can be broken.

A dull ache squeezes in my chest. I don't know if he's still mad at me, if we're on a break, or what we are now. And I can't stand *not* knowing. But I'm also terrified that I'm the one that caused this pain. *It's my fault.*

Sloan puts one hand on her hip. "Are you going to stare out the window creepily, or get over here by the door and greet Brax like a normal human?"

I bite a nail. "Are you sure this is a good idea?"

"Get over here." She points at the floor next to her. "You will face Brax."

I glower at her. I haven't seen Brax since the night of the accident, when I held his hand at the hospital and stayed by his side until the nurses forced me to leave. I figured he couldn't be mad at me while he was sleeping, and he looked so peaceful, like I'd turned back time to when we were happy together.

But now, he seems to have a permanent frown on his face, and I feel like I'm the reason.

"Are you coming?" Sloan asks, gripping the door handle.

I twist Granny's ring nervously around my finger. "Do you think he hates me?" I've already told her everything that happened with Alex and Brax and the fallout afterwards.

Sloan gives me a look. "He could never hate you, Jaz. Even if he tried, he could never stop loving you."

Even if that were true, it doesn't mean Brax will want me back in his life. You can love someone without being with them.

I slide next to Sloan as she swings open the door.

"Welcome home, Big Mac!" Sloan exclaims, opening her arms to him.

Brax drapes one arm around her, like she's the breakable object and not him. "You're making a big deal out of nothing. I don't need you to hold the door for me."

"It won't happen again." She gives him a playful smile. "You should enjoy me being nice to you, for once."

Brax tries to hide a grin. "Only once?"

She releases him and turns to Vale, who grins at her. I don't have time to ask what is going on between those two, because Brax shifts to me next, and I suddenly forget everything. With one look, something spirals inside my chest like a small pinwheel.

I only hope he can't see the effect he's having on me.

I reach out to hug him as his face closes off and he steps backward slightly. There's a distance in his eyes that feels horribly wrong. Disappointment settles in my gut when I realize he doesn't want to touch me.

I drop my hands as my face burns. "Welcome home, Brax," I murmur and resume twisting Granny's ring.

Even if I could pretend he's not affecting me, the disappointment is all over my face. I'm not good at hiding my heart. Especially with him.

He nods as he takes in my outfit. I'm wearing a Crushers sweatshirt and a pair of ripped jeans he always said were his favorite. He frowns and looks away, and I wonder if he disapproves of me wearing something connected to him. He might not understand it now, but I'm still their biggest fan. What I did for the team was my attempt at saving it, even if Brax will never understand why I hid it from him.

"I didn't think you'd be here," he finally says. "Aren't you supposed to work today?"

I run my fingers over my messy bun, suddenly wishing I'd taken more time with looking presentable. I've been a hot mess of tears since Brax's injury, wallowing in misery.

Sloan stares at me. "You didn't tell him?"

"I wanted to tell him in person," I say, looking nervously from Sloan to Brax.

Brax frowns. "Tell me what?"

I fold my arms across my chest. "I quit working for the team. Alex was going to fire me anyway, and I didn't want to give her the satisfaction." I lift a shoulder, pretending it doesn't matter, even though I'm crushed by it.

As much as I can't stand Alex, I loved my job. I love the team. And this man in front of me? *I'll always love him.*

But my life is a train wreck of loss upon loss. The grief feels like it's going to crush me.

He stares at me for a long beat, his eyes wide. "Why would you do that?" he asks in a tone that verges on angry. "What about Sloan's medical care? All the work we've put into the fundraiser?"

I give him a half-hearted smile. "I thought you'd be *relieved* not to perform."

He looks taken aback at my statement. "I'm not. I *want* to do it."

I shake my head as a wave of melancholy sweeps over me. "You don't have to pretend for me, Brax. I know how you really feel about it."

He blinks. "If you think I wasn't all in, I was," he says adamantly, like he needs me to believe him.

"There's no point if Alex has other plans."

Brax frowns like he wants to argue with me but then thinks better of it. "We could still do the fundraiser. It doesn't matter what Alex says."

I rub my palm across my forehead. "Do we have to talk about this now? Can't we just get you settled in first?"

Brax glances at his brother, and a look passes between them. "That's the other thing," Brax says, rubbing his neck. "We aren't staying. Vale and I need to head out. The Bayside Apartments had two places just open up."

The news catches me off guard, and my face snaps to his. "You're moving?"

Brax looks at the floor, his face unreadable. "We haven't decided yet."

My stomach clenches and I suddenly feel lightheaded. I brace the wall for support.

If we lose our renters, I won't make my house payments. There will only be two options, then—find more renters or sell the house. It's unlikely that I'll find a group like this one. They've become like the brothers I never had.

Nausea hits me again, this time harder.

"If we decide on it, you'll find other renters," Brax says. "It's for the best."

For the best? Meaning, being together is *not* what's best?

The bile rises in my throat. "If that's what you want."

It's not what I would choose. I want Brax here, so I can prove to him I'm not the person he thinks I am.

I wait for his reaction to show that he's willing to fight for *us*. But his silence is like another blow.

A wave of panic rises inside my chest, making it hard for me to breathe.

Oh, please. Not now.

My body cannot betray me in front of Brax. The last thing I want him to remember is me falling apart.

I back up a step, searching for an escape, and nearly trip over a pair of shoes left by the door.

Brax catches my arm. "You okay?" he asks, frowning, his eyes studying my face intently.

"I'm fine," I say, tearing my arm free, because his touch is going to break me if I don't. "I'm no longer your problem."

If I'm going to fall apart, I won't do it in front of him. He doesn't need to see how weak and pathetic I am.

I wheel around and rush to my room, locking the door behind me before I crumple to the floor, dragging breath into my burning lungs. The last time this happened, Brax held my hand and wouldn't let me go. But now the only way through it is to ride out these waves alone.

I curl into a ball and let everything—the regret, the fear of losing Brax, all the mistakes I've made with my heart—wash over me.

I know this will be over soon. I know I'm strong enough to survive. I've always been a fighter.

But the one thing I don't know? How I'll ever get over my feelings for him.

———

By the time the panic attack is gone, so is Brax. Sloan told me he looked sick with worry after I ran off, like he was torn between tearing after me and busting down the door or leaving me alone.

"He chose not to stay," I comment dryly while chopping apples for the muffin mix.

Sloan cooks when she's happy, and I bake when I'm sad, and the fact that there's no one to do either for makes me even sadder.

"Does it help to know he looked heartbroken?"

"It doesn't," I snap, chopping another apple, the dull thud of the knife strangely cathartic.

"I've never seen the man show emotion like this, but he looked devastated. Vale thought you'd beg Brax to stay, that this was a surefire way to force you to work things out. He was shocked you didn't fight for him."

"Wait. You knew about this?" I turn to look at my sister, and her cheeks flame. I point my knife at her. "You planned this and didn't tell me?"

"Stop pointing the knife at me." She pushes my wrist down. "It wasn't a plan, exactly."

I frown. "Then what was it, *exactly?*" I lean against the countertop and wait for an answer.

Sloan steals the knife and resumes chopping. "Brax thinks you want him out. I thought you'd argue with him and make him stay. I never expected you to just let him go."

"I didn't let him go. He made his own decision. For the record, he didn't fight for me either." I study her for a beat. "How long have you known about the apartments?"

Her eyes drop to the ground. "Vale texted me while Brax was in the hospital. He didn't want me to be blindsided."

"Unlike me." I lift an eyebrow and steal the knife back. Vale and Sloan have become so close since the guys moved in. A twinge of jealousy reminds me that they still have a close friendship, while Brax and I are in unknown territory.

"Vale wants to stay," Sloan explains. "Brax said no. Told his brother he needs space to think about the future. Vale believes you're the only one who can change Brax's mind."

I focus on chopping and refuse to look at my sister. "I can't make that man do anything. Especially now that I . . ."

Sloan grabs my arm, sending the knife clattering onto the cutting board. "Don't you even say it. You did *not* betray him."

"That's not how Brax sees it." I grab the knife and slice through another apple. "He's spent months earning my trust back after hurting me. What did I do to him? Hid crucial information that affects his career. Brax loves hockey. This team means everything to him."

"It wouldn't have made a difference!" Sloan argues.

I turn to face her. "It might have. Brax knows people. He could have found someone to buy the team . . . or, I don't know, he'd save the team himself."

"You did what you thought was right."

I stop chopping and pinch the bridge of my nose. "That's just it. I protected myself and not Brax."

She levels her gaze at me. "No. You protected *me*."

I halt mid-cut and look at Sloan. Her beautiful dark lashes. The cupid's bow of her mouth. After her car accident, I was terrified of losing her, and I couldn't take another loss. Watching the people I love disappear from my life, whether by choice, was suffocating me. I had already lost a piece of my past when Mom and Granny died. But when my stepmom and Dad walked away, that left me feeling abandoned in a different way. I couldn't lose Sloan too. Even now, I'd do anything for her. *Anything.* Even if it meant hiding the truth from Brax.

Sloan's face softens. "I know you kept the secret because you were afraid." She brushes a curl from my face. "You carry the whole world on your shoulders. Who's going to carry you?"

I don't answer. I wish Granny or Mom were here, but they're not. Without them or Brax, there is no one to carry me.

I had to make a choice between keeping a secret or losing my job, and I chose Sloan. *Family comes first.* Now I need to find my own way and see if I can handle the fallout.

She slides her hands to my shoulders and looks me straight in the eyes. "He needs time. But he'll be back. He looked sick over losing you, Jazlyn."

"And if he doesn't come back?" I ask, scared of the answer.

"He will," she murmurs.

"But the team won't." I shake my head. "This is it, Sloan. Their last season together."

For once, she doesn't have an answer.

TWENTY-SEVEN

Brax

Strike number one. Everything about this new apartment feels cold and sterile, like a beige box with none of the character of Jaz's house.

The tiny galley kitchen is appallingly small, and the bland living room can barely hold a couch, which means we won't be able to have the team over.

The only redeeming feature is the view that overlooks the bay, which also triples the cost. *Strike number two.* Considering this apartment is ridiculously expensive, I'm not really thrilled about living here. We won't have dinners together. Or team parties. Or movie nights with the girls.

"At least you won't have to play handyman here," Leo remarks. "Since we're two floors away, you won't have to see me anymore. That's an advantage." Leo socks my arm. I get the feeling he's trying to lighten my mood, which has been surly ever since I left Jaz's house. The fact that Leo feels sorry for me puts me in an even worse mood.

Make that three strikes against this place. Leo and Tate are far enough away that we won't hang out as much anymore, no matter how much Leo annoys me. What's more, I liked playing handyman for Jaz. It took my mind off hockey, and I loved surprising her with another task marked off her to-do list.

Tate flips through a binder of rules we were given on the way in and scowls.

"As much as I like rules, she gave us an entire booklet of ridiculous ones, like no leaving personal items in the hall. Where are we going to put our hockey gear? This apartment isn't big enough."

"I'm shocked you don't like the rulebook, Sheriff." Leo pretends to gasp while Tate rolls his eyes.

"I'm not sure I can live with him." Tate points to Leo.

"Believe me, I feel the same," Leo shoots back.

I lean against the counter. "You've been making it work since we met. What's the difference?"

"I'm not *alone* with him," Tate says. "I have that entire house to hide in, and Granny's chair next to the fireplace is a primo spot for reading."

Leo closes his eyes and shakes his head. "You want a freaking grandma chair? Then buy one, you big baby."

Tate storms over to Leo and points in his face. "This is why I can't live with you. You're egotistical. *Rude.* And you only care about yourself."

"What's wrong with that?" Leo asks, shrugging him off.

Tate's hands curl into fists, and for a second I think he's going to slug him.

I wedge myself between the two men and put a hand on Tate's chest.

"Calm down. Are you going to room together or not? We need to decide."

I look between them. Neither says a word.

Tate crosses his arms. "Not if he's going to be my roommate."

"Fine." Leo throws up his hands. "I'll find a different roommate. But don't come crying to me when you can't find a place to live."

Tate juts out his chin. "I won't have to. I'm living with Jaz and Sloan again."

I shake my head. "Not an option."

Tate frowns and holds up his phone. "That's not what Sloan said. She texted me a few minutes ago and said I could stay as long as I wanted."

I glance at my phone, which is blank. "I didn't get a text."

"Maybe she doesn't like you now that you and Jaz are fighting," Leo says.

I knew I shouldn't have told the guys on the way over, but I felt like they had a right to know.

"Leo, don't be a jerk," Vale warns.

Tate looks at me. "Maybe we should rent a house in their neighborhood. Or even better, buy one."

Leo frowns. "We're not married, stupid."

"I don't mean us. I meant Vale and Brax." Tate points at us. "You could buy a house, and we could rent from you."

"Not going to happen," I say, still looking at my phone, wishing that Jaz would send me a text. "We're not staying long enough to buy a house." The words slip out before I realize it. Vale is the only one I've told about Alex's secret, and I was waiting for the right time to share it with the rest of the team.

Tate's face snaps to mine. "What do you mean you're not staying? Are you leaving the team?"

I glance at Vale, trying to figure out how to backpedal. "No."

Leo approaches me with a frown. "Do you know something we don't?"

I let out an inaudible sigh. "Alex is planning on shutting the team down and turning the Ice House into a multi-sports complex. It's a done deal." I slump against the wall. This isn't how I wanted them to find out.

Leo's jaw clenches. "Says who?"

"Says Alex. Who do you think?"

Leo folds his arms across his chest and stares at me. "Don't tell me you've given up."

"I haven't given up. I just don't know what to do about it. If I could buy the team, I would."

"That's just it." Leo circles the room slowly. "We can't buy the team. But what if someone else could?"

"Like who?" Tate asks. "You got a rich uncle?"

"No." He narrows his eyes, deep in thought. "But Brendan does. Didn't you hear Brax mention it? He said Brendan's uncle likes collecting teams."

"That was a minor league baseball team," Tate corrects. "Not hockey."

"Who says he wouldn't be interested in hockey?" Leo shrugs.

I shake my head. "It's a long shot at best."

"What about the fundraiser?" Tate asks.

"It's off now that Jaz is gone," I answer.

"Why couldn't we do it anyway?" Vale suggests. "Not make it an official team event under Alex's control, but one that's strictly player-organized?"

I push off from the wall. "Are you suggesting we raise the funds to save the team?"

"Yeah, why not?" Vale answers. "Maybe we could convince Alex to keep the team rolling for another season."

I shake my head. "I don't know if Alex would buy it, and I would feel bad not sharing the funds with a charity. That's how it's been promoted."

"Vale's right, though." Leo goes over to the kitchen island and sits on it, facing us. "What if we tell everyone what Alex is proposing and we get our fans riled up about it? Then we use the fundraiser to gain support. If it works, our fans will have our back, and we'll still donate some to charity. In the end, we make Alex look like the bad guy."

I frown. "Scare tactics?"

"More like . . . *revolution.*" The word rolls off Leo's tongue.

"I don't know if we can pull this off without Jaz." I cross my arms. "The fundraiser was supposed to happen next week. It would be impossible to do this without her."

Vale looks at me. "Then we invite her and bring Brendan back. He said he wants to see the cute girl named Scarlett at the coffee shop again. Let's give him a reason to return."

Tate furrows his brow. "How do we stop the cancellation announcement that's going out tomorrow?"

Leo lifts his hand. "I'll talk to Aurora in the office. She's got a crush on me and, conveniently, can't stand Alex. She'd love to be part of our scheming."

Vale fist-bumps Leo. "Never thought your flirting would come in handy."

"Keeping this from Alex won't be hard," Tate says. "I overheard her say that she's leaving for a trip. By the time she comes back, it will be too late for her to stop it."

"Perfect," Vale says.

"I'll call Brendan." I glance at my phone, pulling up his number. "Maybe I could get my sister's husband to perform for the event. Jace Knight is a huge country star."

"That would be incredible. But what about Jaz?" Tate asks. "Don't you think she should know?"

I glance around and realize all eyes are on me. "Don't look at me." I shake my head. "Things between us are rocky."

"Let me talk to Sloan," Vale says. "But you need to think about what you're going to say to Jaz when she finds out."

I'm not looking forward to that conversation. "I'll tell the rest of the team tonight. Sound like a plan?"

Vale smiles. "No, sounds like a *revolution*."

TWENTY-EIGHT

Jaz

The rest of the week is strangely quiet. Maybe it's because I no longer have a job and I'm stuck at home all day while the guys return late, exhausted and quiet. Even Brax goes straight to his room, avoiding any conversation, while the others are strangely tight-lipped.

The only person who seems to care is Sloan. Her awful headaches are gone, and for once, she has more energy than me. She credits the new treatment, and my heart is holding on to this tiny bright spot, because it's the last scrap of hope I have these days, especially with the thought of Brax leaving. They haven't told me when they're moving, and I feel left out. In some ways, not knowing is worse than having a departure date.

That's why I put a *For Rent* ad in a local online newspaper a few days ago—just to make sure I have a backup plan in case the guys bail. Almost immediately, someone wanted to check out the rooms.

"If they decide to take the apartments, it's not like they're leaving right away," Sloan reminds me as she hands me a bag of Brussels sprouts to put in the fridge after her grocery run. "Vale told me they're still deciding. Have you seen their rooms? They're not packed."

I hold a green pepper in my hand and peel off the sticker. "That's not exactly helpful. Guys can pack in like five minutes."

"So you'll have five minutes' notice." She shrugs. "If you're so worried about it, why don't you ask Brax?"

As much as he's gone, it's like he's *trying* to avoid me. "Brax barely says two words to me all day. He won't even look at me."

She turns to face me. "I catch him looking at you all the time. You just don't notice."

A rush of warmth runs through me. *He still looks at me?*

I don't want to hold on to false hope. It'll hurt too much when Brax moves and the fairy-tale ending gets ripped off like an old bandage.

"All I want to know is when they're moving," I mutter, plucking a cucumber from the bag. "If they're too afraid to confess, then I'm going to force the issue. I have a potential renter coming over today."

Sloan stares at me. "Why didn't you tell me?"

"Because you don't like the idea of somebody new living here. But I can't sit around and wait for our savings to dry up. We need renters."

She hesitates for a beat. "Could you tell the guys when they get home? I'm heading out for a few hours, so I won't be here to meet the new renter."

I spin on my heel and head to the basement, digging out the *For Rent* sign and hanging it on the front door. If that doesn't communicate that I'm moving on, then I don't know what will. Maybe it will finally force Brax to talk to me about his plans—and whether I'm included in them.

Then I slip into a form-fitting pink dress that Brax once told me is his favorite. If he really is looking at me, then I might as well make it so he *can't* look away.

When Brax arrives home after practice, he stares at the *For Rent* sign before slamming the door. Then his gaze swings to me, and his eyes nearly pop out of his head as he takes in my dress.

He blinks once before tearing his eyes away, and the annoyed expression returns to his face. "What's this about?" He points to the sign.

"Some of us have a mortgage to pay," I reply, daring him to challenge me. I wipe my hands on the dish towel I'm holding. "I can't be abandoned at the last minute."

His eyes meet mine for the first time in days. "You think I'd leave you like that?"

It's not a question. It's an accusation. But I refuse to back down, even though he still makes me feel things I'd rather not. "I think you'd avoid me and then leave without saying goodbye."

I wheel around and head back into the kitchen, letting my words sink in.

He follows. "Jaz, I would never do that to you."

I toss the dish towel on the counter and cross my arms. "Really? Because based on how much you've tried to avoid me this week, it seems like you might."

Then I walk to the sink and plunge my hands in soapy dishwater. It's easier than facing him. If he looks into my eyes, he'll know that I still love him and want him to stay, even if I'm furious right now.

His footsteps stop behind me, and his gaze burns a hole into my back.

With my head down and eyes averted, I scrub a dirty plate.

"There are things I can't tell you about yet," he says in a low voice. "I thought you, of all people, would understand this."

I swivel around to face him. "I may have been wrong to keep Alex's secret from you, but I didn't really have another choice."

His gaze pierces mine. "There's *always* another choice, Jaz."

Doesn't he know that I've already beat myself up a thousand times since everything fell apart? What does he even mean by *another choice?* If I'd had another choice, I'd be with him right now, instead of watching him distance himself from me.

A knock on the door interrupts our conversation, and Brax frowns at the intrusion. I wipe my hands and brush by him as he growls, "We'll finish this later."

When I open the door, a middle-aged man in crooked glasses stands on the front porch.

"I'm Chad. I saw the ad online and wondered if you've rented the rooms yet?"

I blink at the realization that he could be my next renter, even though it makes me sick.

"Yes. Come in. I'm Jaz."

As he enters, Brax steps into the hall and stares at the guy like he'd like to dismember him.

I give Brax a look that says *stop it* before turning back to the guest. "Let me show you a room upstairs."

I don't know why, but this man makes me feel uneasy. The only renters I've had are the hockey players, and none of them made me feel this way. Not even Leo, with his relentless flirting. They wouldn't dare touch me or look at me the wrong way. If they did, Brax would tear them apart with his bare hands.

As I lead Chad upstairs, we pass Brax on the way. With his arms crossed and eyes narrowed, he looks as friendly as a serial killer.

Seriously? I don't need him glaring at my potential renters like that. I toss Brax a quick look on the way up. *Be nice.* Then I add, "I'm going to show him your room."

I don't ask. I demand. Based on his expression, I think he'd prefer getting mauled by a tiger than letting this guy in his room.

"Then I'm heading out," Brax growls as he strides toward the front door. I'm halfway up the stairs when I hear it slam shut.

When I open Brax's bedroom, the heady smell of cologne hits me like a gut punch. It's all I can do to push away the image of Brax next to me, pulling me close as I settle in his arms.

I wander toward Brax's dresser, where a framed photo sits. It's from the night he taught me to skate. He's gripping my waist, pulling me into a hug, eyes fixed on me. Vale must have taken it from the sound booth. My stomach clenches at the memory and the incredible kiss we shared.

Brax has always kept his dresser completely bare, like every other surface in the room. This is a new and puzzling addition, one that makes me wonder if he still cares about me.

"Looks like a nice place," Chad says.

"It is," I answer. I'm so distracted by the picture I don't notice Chad behind me.

When I turn around, he's moved closer to me. *Too close.*

"What are you doing?" I ask, stepping away from him.

"Nothing," he says, but he doesn't stop moving toward me.

There's something about this guy that feels *off.*

Stepping back, I bump into the dresser and freeze, my body buckled down by a paralyzing panic I'm all too familiar with.

There's no place to go.

The door of the room suddenly flies open, and Brax storms in with a look of murder on his face. He grabs Chad by the collar and slams him so hard against the wall that the man's glasses fall off.

"If you ever threaten her again, you will regret it. Do you understand me?" he says in a voice that gives me chills.

Chad nods as he gasps for air, and Brax loosens his grip just enough so he can breathe.

The man sputters and coughs, then asks, "What's she to you?"

Brax shoves his forearm against Chad's chest, pinning him to the wall again.

He narrows his eyes. "She's *mine,*" he growls.

Then he grabs the back of his collar and throws him out the door.

As Chad races down the stairs, Brax yells, "*Never* come back."

When I finally hear the door slam, I let out a shaky breath, the vise around my chest finally releasing.

I slump against Brax's dresser, weak with shock and relief. Brax wheels around, his eyes darting to me. His expression shifts from anger to something different—frantic worry.

He crosses the room in a few strides and sweeps me into his

arms. He knows I can't stand on my own right now, and because I'm so weak, I can't fight him. I don't even want to.

I let him cradle me in his arms and nuzzle my face into his chest as his hands find my back and stroke gently. I'm still breathing hard, even though the panic is gone.

Brax feels like everything I need right now. *My safe place.*

He rests his cheek against my head and whispers, "Are you okay? Tell me he didn't hurt you."

I shake my head, staying in his arms. "I'm okay. Just shaken." I try to fight the emotions churning inside me, the fear from what happened and the worry that Brax will leave me alone. Now that his arms wrap around me, this is the only place I want to be. Right here, in the safety of his arms.

"Why did you come back?" I ask, looking into his eyes.

"I forgot something. When I walked inside, I heard you ask him what he was doing. That's when I knew something wasn't right." He shifts back to look me over, sliding his hands to my arms. "I need to make sure he didn't hurt you." Then he searches my face, and I see the concern in his eyes.

"He didn't hurt me," I assure him.

"I saw the way he looked at you," he says. "I should have punched him in the face."

He's jealous? How is that possible?

I swallow and look Brax in the eyes. "When I showed him your room, I was reminded of the last time I was here with you. Then I found this picture."

I hand him the picture of us on the night we skated together, and something sparks in his eyes.

There's a lump in my throat, but I ask anyway. "Why do you still have this when you won't even talk to me? When you're planning on leaving?" The words catch in my throat, and I cover my face so he won't see me like this, completely gutted.

He puts the picture down and gently pulls my hands away even though I resist. "Don't hide from me. I want to see you. There's nothing you can't ask me, Jaz."

"Then tell me why you said it," I ask.

"I don't understand," he says. "Said what?"

"You called me *yours*."

He hesitates for a beat. "You don't know why?"

I shake my head, but I still refuse to meet his gaze.

He drags his knuckles lightly down my cheek. "*Jazlyn*, look at me."

He hasn't called me Jazlyn since I asked him not to. He tips my chin toward him and grasps my hand to his chest, placing it over his racing heart.

"I said it because it's true," he murmurs. "You'll *always* be mine. Even if you refuse to see me or push me away, I will never stop loving you."

I pull away just slightly so I can search his gaze. What I see there isn't anger or distrust, just love.

"But I thought . . ." I begin, hardly believing it. "You said you couldn't trust me. I thought you were mad at me and wanted to move out."

"Trust is something I'm working on," he admits slowly. "I used to think hockey was everything until we met. When I saw you at the wedding again, I knew I had to be with you. But Felipe was sending me threats, and I was afraid he would target you out of hatred for me. That's why I didn't contact you afterwards. To protect *you* over everything. And you did the same for Sloan when you kept Alex's secret from me. I understand that now." He searches my face. "But then I fell for you all over again when I came here. This time, I wanted you too badly to care if I lost my career." His fingers tighten around my waist as he tugs me closer. "Because you are *everything* to me."

He cups the back of my neck and pulls me to him, his mouth covering mine with an intensity that makes my knees weak. His hand splays across my back, holding me steady against him as he kisses my mouth, my cheek, the curve of my neck, before he leaves the last kiss right above my brow.

He reluctantly pulls away, his breathing ragged as he studies me. "I love you, Jazlyn. I will never let another man hurt you like that again. I will always be there for you." Then he pulls me into his chest, locking his arms around me and burying his face in my hair. "I thought I was going to lose you. I was so scared."

The same guy who regularly body-checks men twice Chad's size was afraid of losing me?

"Seeing him look at you that way made me go crazy," he says in a low voice. "I've never lost control of my anger like that. Not even with Felipe."

I stroke my hand across his cheek. "Brax. You don't have to worry about me. I've always been yours."

He leans toward me and kisses me again. Unlike the intense kiss he just gave me, this one is gentle, soft, warm.

He cups my face, stroking his thumbs across my cheeks before a slow smile curves his lips. "That's good. Because seeing you date anyone else would make me a violent man."

I chuckle. "Save it for your games, Mac. Even if Alex is shutting down the team."

His face brightens. "That's the reason I've been so quiet all week. The fight to save the team isn't over."

TWENTY-NINE

To say I'm nervous is an understatement. I'm used to being on skates in front of hundreds of people. I can handle the pressure of competition, the fights on the ice, even a bully like Felipe.

But to perform in front of a crowd feels like I'm skating naked. Actually, skating naked sounds easier.

I'm not the only one who's nervous and distracted. Leo is drowning out his nerves with music. Tate is reading. When Vale's nervous, he spends even *more* time on his hair.

We're on edge because Brendan's bringing his uncle and we're still waiting on the custom jersey delivery. If it doesn't show up in the next hour, we really will skate naked.

Jaz has been secretly posting videos on social media, thanks to Aurora who handed over the passwords. Turns out, Leo's flirtatious ways have come in handy by giving us an ally in the front office. She even secretly dropped hints to some of our fan accounts, and now they're spreading viral messages urging fans to show up tonight.

Our super-fans have become our squeaky wheel on the internet, the best free advertising for igniting a hockey revolution.

Vale glances up from his phone, his face in shock. "Brax, you didn't tell me you made a video."

"Brax made a video?" Dawson jumps the bench to watch it over Vale's shoulder, along with Lucian, Tate, and Leo.

"Wait, is that the kid from the elementary school we visited?" Lucian asks.

"Yep, that's Ethan," I say. "I told him the team needed his help to promote this cool thing we were doing to raise funds for charity. He even decorated his wheelchair."

"Over two million views," Vale marvels. "This kid stole the show."

"That was all Jaz's doing," I say. "She got him to talk about his love for the Carolina Crushers. She even gave him a ticket for tonight."

"But will people give money just because they saw a cute kid?" Leo asks.

Everyone looks at me for an answer. "It's the best shot we have."

"Guys, we got the delivery!" Sloan yells as she bursts into the locker room with an enormous box. Jaz follows behind her.

"Wow, Sloan," Vale says, lifting an eyebrow. "You could at least knock before you barge into the men's locker room."

She gives him a wry smile. "What? And miss you without your shirt on?"

Vale is conveniently shirtless and only seems too happy to have Sloan acknowledge it. "Well, we could have had our pants down."

"That still wouldn't have stopped me," she says with a grin.

Vale's eyebrows shoot up as the others snicker.

"Somebody's feeling better," Vale notes with a smirk. "You even dressed up."

She's dressed in a short black dress with a swingy skirt, leopard-print heels, and a leather jacket. Her hair hangs loose around her shoulders.

"You look . . . *wow*," he says.

Sloan blushes at the compliment. "I feel good. I've hardly had any headaches or dizziness lately. I'm not out of the woods, but the doctor says it's a good sign that the treatment is working."

I glance over at Jaz, who is blinking back happy tears. She would never cry in front of the guys, but seeing her sister well again means more to her than anything.

As Sloan passes out jerseys, there's a flurry of noise outside. When Jaz opens the door, my sister, Mia, stands in the hallway.

"Surprise!" she yells, lifting her arms in the air.

Jaz practically knocks her over with a ferocious hug full of laughter and happy shouts.

Jaz turns to her with a bewildered look. "I thought you weren't coming."

"I didn't want to ruin the surprise!" Mia beams as she loops her arm through Jaz's. "When Brax invited me, I told Jace there was only one choice: to be here to support you."

"Hey, what about us?" Vale asks. "Don't I get a hug?" He opens his arms to his sister.

"Only if it's gentle," she warns.

Vale gives me an evil look. "Time for a MacPherson sandwich?"

I give Vale the signal, and we sandwich Mia in a hug from two sides.

She squeaks between our chests. "I prefer to breathe!"

When we finally let go, she steps back and crosses her arms, pinning me with a look. "Were you going to tell me you were dating my best friend? Or just let me hear about it on the internet?"

I glance at Jaz for help.

She shrugs.

Mia pokes me in the shoulder. "It's good to see you turn red. But at least contact me before you propose, okay?"

I frown. "I thought you didn't want us to date?"

She tilts her head. "Jaz is my best friend, and I was scared if you hurt her, it would ruin our relationship. There was also the question about whether you'd ever settle down. You've always been married to hockey."

"You didn't think I'd change my mind?" I ask.

"A MacPherson brother can *change*?" She lifts an eyebrow. "Only the right woman could do that."

"The right woman was always in front of me," I admit, my gaze swinging over to Jazlyn, who's beaming now. "I just had to discover her for myself."

Coach Thompson bursts through the door, and everyone snaps to attention. His eyes flick around the room as he looks over our new jerseys. "You guys clean up well."

"Thank you, Coach," Rourke says, looking proud of the fact he's not sporting any recent purple bruises from fights.

We settle on the bench as Coach stands in the middle of the locker room. "I'm really proud of this team. The work you've done has paid off, and you finally play like a team. So no matter what happens tonight, this team *will* go on."

"Let's do it!" Dawson roars as he pounds the air with his fist. We all rush toward Coach for a team huddle on the count of three. The electricity in the air feels like we're ready to head into a championship. But this isn't a game, and we may not even be a team anymore.

What we're about to do is the craziest, most insane thing ever.

As I head out the door, Jaz grabs my arm to pull me aside.

"Break a leg, Mac," she murmurs. Then she spins around and shows that she's wearing my jersey again.

"You look good in my name," I murmur.

When she turns back, she grabs my shirt and pulls my body toward her, kissing me so hard, it takes my breath away.

After a sendoff like that, I'm finally ready.

———

We're waiting in the tunnel just outside the rink when the lights dim and the crowd roars in response.

"Remember, we get into a semicircle position first," Tate whispers. Like we'd forget the choreography after Jaz and Brendan drilled it into us hundreds of times.

"Shut up, Tate!" Leo whisper-yells. "We know what we're supposed to do."

Skating onto the ice is the part I'm actually comfortable with.

"Oh, great. The Ice Queen is here," Lucian growls in a low voice.

"In the audience?" Dawson asks, craning his neck to see.

"No, behind us." Lucian points at his target.

We all turn at the same time and watch as Alex stops in the tunnel.

"If it isn't the ridiculous dancing monkeys," she says in a mocking voice.

"Not ridiculous to our fans," Dawson argues. "They love us."

"Are you sure they're not laughing *at* you?" she suggests.

She's trying to shake our confidence so we'll fail.

"Your little plan to pull this off without me failed miserably," she says. "But good news, I get to see you fail firsthand!"

I cross my arms. "After this, we'll see who the joke's on."

She gives us a tight smile before wheeling around and striding away.

"Forget her," I say to the guys. "She is *not* one of our fans. Those people are." I point to the roar on the other side of the tunnel. I think of Jaz, Sloan, and all the fans who showed up when our season opened and the arena was mostly empty. I think of Ethan in his decorated wheelchair and Ms. Bennett's kindergarten class, who are cheering us on alongside the elementary school.

As soon as the strobe lights flash, the crowd erupts. The roar is deafening.

Vale is the first one out of the tunnel. Since I'm toward the back, I have time to scan the audience, but what I see catches me off guard. The place is packed.

"You're after me." Tate elbows me to make sure I'm paying attention before he races out onto the ice to find his place. I lock eyes with Jaz from her front-row seat. She's cheering wildly and blows me a kiss.

As I take my place, I see Brendan behind Jaz, sitting with a man who I guess is his uncle.

The audience hushes as the music begins, and the energy in the place feels electric. It's enough to make us perform better than we ever have. I don't miss a single move, and when it's time for our individual dance breaks, no one holds back. Just like Brendan predicted, the crowd goes wild for everyone's solo moves. They don't care if we can actually dance. They like that we're willing to put on a show that's unlike anything else.

As we reach the final pose, the crowd leaps to their feet. Every single guy is soaking up the attention.

Vale gives me a nod and whispers, "You're not a bad dancer after all."

I mutter, "It's the last time you'll ever see me dance in public."

As we line up for the next event, I spot Ethan in the crowd. He's waving to me while Coach Thompson steps up to the microphone to deliver a rousing speech.

I only have a minute, but I skate over to Ethan, who beams at me as I pull up to the plexiglass. Janie Bennett is a few rows behind Ethan, and everyone from her Little Monsters' class waves at me like I'm a superhero.

"You were amazing out there!" Ethan claps, and I can't help but smile. I know he'd say that even if I'd fallen on my face.

"Thanks. I was pretty nervous."

"YOU get nervous?" he asks, his eyes growing wide.

"Yep. Even hockey players feel afraid sometimes. Especially around pretty girls."

I sneak a glance at Jaz, who gives me a puzzled frown across the arena.

Ethan catches who I'm staring at and asks, "Are you going to marry her?"

I laugh. "It's a little too soon for that."

"Well, do you love her?" he asks, like it's just that simple.

I look at Jaz's smile that lights up her face, and I know I could never be happier.

"Yeah, I do," I say slowly, not taking my eyes off her.

"Then you should tell her, because she's really cute."

I laugh again. "You have good taste . . . for a kindergartner."

"I know." He shrugs, like this is common sense.

Tate waves me to return for the next segment, and I skate back in line. This is the happiest I've ever been, and it's not because my life is perfect. I haven't made it to the NHL. I don't even know what will happen to the team next year.

But I have Jazlyn. We'll make it through whatever life throws at us, because she's my endgame now.

The rest of the *Fashion on Ice* fundraiser goes flawlessly. We model our jerseys, let fans bid on the silent auction and Jace even performs a song at the end as a special surprise for the fans. After the show ends, we spend the next hour signing autographs. It's only when I look toward the back of the arena that I see Alex with her arms crossed, her face resolute.

Jaz meets me at the door in the wall and glances at Alex. "She looks positively livid tonight." Then she gives me a smile, because no matter what happens now, we pulled off something amazing.

"I think Alex needs one more reason to hate us," I suggest, arching an eyebrow.

"Oh, really? What's that?" Jaz asks with a grin.

"Kiss me," I say in a low, urgent voice.

Instantly, Jaz jumps into my arms, kissing me hard on the lips as I spin her around on the ice.

If Alex hated seeing us together before, she's *really* going to hate this.

I tangle my fingers in her hair as she sweeps her arms around my neck, tugging me closer. My lips consume hers, hungrily, eagerly, without any embarrassment.

Whatever happens after tonight, I know one thing: We've already won.

Epilogue

THREE MONTHS LATER

Jaz

As I place another picture frame into the packing box, I glance around my closet office. No more cramped, dark troll cave.

But I'm also going to miss the sweet memories, like the time Brax brought me dinner for our first date. Or the many times he bumped into me and reminded me there are advantages to small spaces.

Brax peeks his head through the door. "How's the packing going?"

I wave my hands around the mostly empty office. "Good, but strange. It just feels really empty and lonely."

"The empty part I can't fix." A slow smile curves across his lips as he slides his hands to my waist, and skirts them across my lower back, tugging me toward him. "But the lonely part? I can most definitely help with that."

Then he presses kisses in a trail along my cheek, all the way to my weak spot next to my earlobe.

"Keep doing that," I murmur. "And I'm never going to finish packing."

He steals the stack of papers from my hands and growls, "You didn't need these anyway." And then tosses them over his shoulder so they float to the floor.

"Brax," I weakly protest, "we're supposed to be cleaning up. Not making me a hot mess."

"But I'm so good at making you a hot mess," he murmurs between kisses.

He finds that spot by my earlobe again, and my eyes flutter closed. "Yes, *too* good."

Thanks to Brax, I wouldn't notice if a jumbo jet landed in my office right now.

He pulls away gently, sweeping a hand across my cheek. "We have a new office to make memories in."

I link my hands behind his neck. "Brendan's uncle is officially my favorite person now that he bought the team. Moving into Tom's office is going to feel like such sweet revenge."

"Tom got what he deserved," Brax mutters. "Rafael Marco doesn't want a tightwad who's going to control the purse strings. It's not that he doesn't want to make money. But he's more interested in building something *great*."

When Brendan's Uncle Rafael saw the team's infectious spirit at the fundraiser, his interest was piqued. Then he watched the Crushers win a few games, and he was sold on the idea of adding the team to his collection.

"It didn't hurt that our fans threatened a massive boycott of Alex's proposed plan," I add, feeling a little smug that we toppled the Ice Queen off her throne.

Thanks to our fans, city officials backed off their support of the project. When Alex's developers started dropping like flies, she was forced to abandon her plans and leave town.

Since the Crushers are no longer in financial trouble, the money raised from the fundraiser was split evenly between the charity and paying off Sloan's medical expenses, something the whole team kept secret until they threw us a surprise party and presented us with a massive check.

"Did you notice how excited Brendan was about coming on as the new conditioning coach?" I ask Brax. "It surprised me he wanted to work for the Crushers. Some of the team didn't really like being bossed around by a guy who's never played hockey."

"After we experienced him whipping us into shape for the fundraiser, he'll do just fine. Plus, he has motivation to stay now."

"Besides the job?" I ask.

"He's been hanging out with Scarlett at the coffee shop," Brax says with a smirk. "Turns out, he and Scarlett are old friends. He mentioned some agreement they made a long time ago. If you ask me, sounds like they're going to be more than friends soon." Brax gives me a wink before kneeling to pick up the papers he tossed earlier.

I frown. "Sounds like a contract. What kind of agreement was it?"

He shrugs. "Brendan likes being a mystery."

"Well, he's also a man of honor. Whatever it was, he wouldn't go back on his word."

Brax pauses. "Or maybe he doesn't want to. Maybe he's invested in her." He returns to picking up papers before I realize I'm taking advantage of his kindness.

"You don't have to do that." I kneel beside him, reaching for a paper.

He grabs my hand and arches a brow. "Stop helping. I want to." Then he kisses the back of my hand, my body warming in response.

"Well, okay, you win." I willingly give in, putting my feet up on my desk and lacing my fingers behind my neck.

Actually, I'm pretty sure I'm the one winning here. I have a man I love. A job I adore. And a house of my dreams, even with four rambunctious hockey players living upstairs. A few months ago, it became painfully obvious, once they toured the Bayside Apartments, that it wouldn't be the same as living with us. And we didn't have to twist their arms to convince them to stay. *Rose & Thorn* is their home now.

Somehow, the living arrangement feels more like a family than just housemates. We sometimes get on one other's nerves, but mostly we're glad to have each other and not be alone. To my surprise, I've been searching for a place to belong, and I found it in the place I least expected: with this team.

"You have time for a quick break?" Brax asks as he picks up the last paper. "I have a little surprise for you."

"What kind of surprise?" I say, sitting up straighter.

"No questions, Princess. That would spoil the fun." He takes my hand and leads me to his car.

When we arrive at the house, he winks at me and says, "Stay here."

Then he runs around to my door, opens it and sweeps me off my feet.

"What are you doing?" I protest as he carries me into the house. "I'm perfectly capable of walking."

He laughs at the suggestion. "And I'm perfectly capable of carrying you."

He kicks the door shut behind us and doesn't stop carrying me until we reach his bedroom. The bed is still neatly made, dappled light spilling across it.

He sets me on his bed gently before he takes a step back, studying me.

"What's wrong?" I ask, my stomach dropping. "Is someone hurt? Is Sloan okay?"

"No, Sloan's fine," he insists, but I can tell there's something he's dying to say. "My agent called yesterday. He said I might be called up to Tampa Bay next season."

I blink, realizing what this means. "The NHL? Oh, Brax, that's wonderful!" I reach up and smother him in a hug. This is everything he's wanted. "I'm so proud of you. The NHL is your dream."

"Was my dream," he corrects, shaking his head and pulling back from me. "You're all I want now. I could quit hockey tomorrow, and if I still had you, it wouldn't matter."

I press my finger into his chest. "It would still matter to you."

"Not the way you do," he insists, leveling his gaze. "I turned them down."

"But the NHL, Brax!" I nearly yell. I'm not sure if I should feel flattered that he chose me or push him to reconsider. I can't be Brax's reason for settling. "I don't want to hold you back."

He shakes his head. "You could never hold me back," he urges. "I want to build a life with you. And you're here, which means I'm not moving."

"Are you sure about this?" I ask, my chest constricting. I don't want Brax to let go of his dreams for me.

"Never been more sure, Jazlyn." He pulls out a black box from his pocket. A small velvet one. "I want this to be our home. And for you to be my wife. If you'll have me." Then he kneels in front of me and opens the box, revealing a solitaire diamond.

My heart stutters in my chest. "Wait. You're asking me to marry you?"

"Told you I'm not leaving," he says with a grin. "I don't deserve you, Jazlyn. Every day when I wake up and hear your laughter downstairs, I feel like the luckiest man alive. You're the most beautiful woman I've ever laid eyes on. You make people feel at home, like they belong here, which is really special. And you're crazy stubborn when you want something, which is why you didn't give up on me. You know how to take broken things and fix them up. You fixed *me* in a lot of ways I didn't know I was broken. And I realized if you found out I'd turned down the NHL, you'd be ticked at me. But I couldn't ask you to leave *Rose & Thorn*. I love this place too much to let it go."

"But I would for *you*," I protest.

He presses my lips gently with his finger. "I know, and that's why I'm saying no. Because when I'm sure of what I want, I go for it. And I want you." He punctuates his words with kisses across my face. "What do you say, Jazlyn? Do you want to make a life with me?"

"More than anything," I say, laughing and crying at the same time. He pulls me against his very solid, very warm chest and kisses me hard, nearly taking my breath away.

Even though I don't want to stop, I still have one more question. "Brax, I don't understand. Why would you choose me?"

"I love you so much, Jazlyn. I want to make this *our* home. And you, *my* wife."

He cups the back of my neck and tugs me to his lips again in a kiss so tender, it's the only answer I need.

"I love you so much, Brax MacPherson," I whisper against his lips.

He leans his forehead against mine. "You were always the one for me. Which is why I don't want to wait long to marry you," he says in a voice low and urgent. "For now, let's celebrate with the team."

"I think we're doing a good job celebrating right here," I say, kissing him on the nose.

A little growl comes from his throat. "Wish I could." He sighs. "But the team is coming any moment to surprise you with an engagement party, because I knew I might not stop kissing you otherwise."

"Someday, you won't have to," I say, making him a promise I plan to keep.

Suddenly, there's the sound of a door slamming below and a rush of feet stomping through the house.

Sloan's voice comes up the steps. "She better have said yes, or I bought all this food for nothing."

"Don't worry, she agreed to be my wife," Brax yells back, and all the guys erupt into cheers so loud it nearly shakes the house.

Brax grins and turns back to me. "One more thing. Whatever you want to plan for the wedding is fine, as long as you marry me soon. I don't want to go any longer than I have to sleeping in this bed alone. And I only have two requests for the wedding."

"Only two?" I ask, suddenly curious what Brax would demand.

He hands me a small cardboard box from his end table. When

I open it, I see the most decadent red velvet cupcake with cream cheese frosting.

"You want red velvet cake?" I ask.

"No, you do." He grins, like he knows how much this pleases me. "But the second thing is *my* request."

He reaches over to a small drawer and pulls out a tiara, the same one he found the night he first kissed me. I had no idea he'd kept it. He places it on my head, just like the night of the wedding.

"I want you to wear this, *Princess*."

———

Get ready for the next sizzling book in the hockey spin-off series!
Vale and Sloan's book: Perfectly Wedded
Best friends, accidental spouses.
What could possibly go wrong?
Find out in *Perfectly Wedded*—their unforgettable love story!
GET IT ON AMAZON!

Want more books from this series?
Three more romcoms for you to devour!
All are standalone novels that you can read in any order.

The Neighbor Renovation
grumpy/sunshine romcom

The Second Chance Fixer Upper
single mom, second chance romance

The Mistletoe Makeover
rockstar romance at Christmas.

You're going to love the whole Renovation Romance Series.
Available in Kindle Unlimited and Amazon.

Bonus Epilogue
Join Jaz and Brax on their wedding day
with all the hockey players!
You don't want to miss this incredible bonus scene to The
Roommate Remodel!
Available at graceworthington.com

The Next Book: Perfectly Wedded

Book One in a Hockey Spinoff Series about the Carolina Crushers

Who gets married out of convenience? Apparently, I do.

I got married last night...and I don't remember it.

A recent car accident left me with temporary memory issues, and my insurance won't cover the medication I need.

But shouldn't I remember marrying my best friend, who's also a handsome hockey star?

He was only supposed to be my fake date to a high-stakes Vegas event. But when my ex showed up with another woman on his arm, my friend suggested the ultimate payback: pretending we were engaged.

When I accidentally mention my insurance issues, he proposes taking our charade to the next level—a temporary marriage until I get better.

I nearly spit out my drink.

Yeah, right. Like that won't completely ruin our friendship.

But we can't go back now. Our charade worked so well that everyone bought it—even the journalist who leaked our Vegas wedding all over the internet.

Now we have to go through with this farce...at least until I'm better and the media storm dies down for my hockey star husband.

That means we have to sell this to our friends and family by fake kissing and sharing a bedroom, all while sticking to our friend zone rules behind closed doors.

But there's just one tiny secret he doesn't know:

I've been in love with my best friend since I met him.

When he pulls me close and says, "my wife," I know I won't ever forget that.

I might have married my best friend out of convenience, but love is anything but convenient.

Perfectly Wedded is a closed door hockey romcom that includes tropes like marriage of convenience, second chance romance and friends to lovers. This is the first book in a clean, closed door hockey spin off series!

Get it on Amazon!

Acknowledgments

I can't tell you how truly humbled and grateful I am for your support. Writing has been my dream for so long, and I never take it lightly when someone reads one of my books or tells me how much they enjoyed a story of mine. Your encouragement inspires me to keep writing!

Enormous thanks to my husband for his ongoing support and for bringing me a steady supply of caffeine/chocolate/sanity when I need it. Thanks for being my first reader, my best friend, and my number one cheerleader. I'm glad we have the best love story of all.

Thanks to my kids, who continually inspire me to be a better mom.

Thanks to Heidi and Joy—you make these stories shine and you keep me on track with all the details. Plus, you're adorable in real life too. Thanks for being the best readers a girl could ask for.

Thanks to my publishing team, including my editor, Emily Poole, my incredible team of cover designers at Alt 19 Creative, and my proofreader, Judy Zweifel.

Also, a huge thanks to the bookstagrammers, ARC team readers and my faithful readers who share my books with your friends. This means the world to me and so many of you have become friends!

Anne, Janna, and Elysia, thanks for your ongoing support.

Whether you're a new reader or a reader who's been with me since my first book—thank you!

You make it possible for me to support my little family while giving you these fun romcoms that I adore.

I hope they bring you as much joy as they bring me.

———

Let's keep in touch!

I'd love to meet you at a reader event or on Instagram, but the best way to keep in touch and find out about my next release is to sign up for my email of awesomeness at graceworthington.com.